P9-DLZ-727

"Moore's cockeyed view of the world is amusing on its own, but add to that his ability to capture the speech patterns of his disparate characters—from a bum suffering illusions of grandiosity to a creepy goth-girl enamored with death—and his writing becomes hilarious."

—St. Louis Post-Dispatch

"A raunchy slapstick comedy of young vampires in love. . . . Moore is in top form, and this reviewer laughed all the way through this page-turner. Enthusiastically recommended."   *—Library Journal*

"[Moore] glides comfortably through the book's loony little corner of San Francisco and through drastic changes of mood. . . . As with his best work, there's a fundamental sweetness beneath the antics."

—New York Times

"Moore handles [the] goofier-than-thou plot adroitly. . . . Think of a collaboration among Anne Rice, S. J. Perelman, and Pedro Almodóvar. In other words, Moore in the usual vein (jugular, that is)."   *—Kirkus Reviews*

"Moore makes fun of just about everything, especially the cobwebby genre of vampire fiction. He creates a bizarre alternate world with enough anchors in reality that crazy things seem normal. Which is why I try not to think about it too hard, but just go with it. Moore is the insane conductor, and I'm just along for the ride. And I really enjoy the ride."

—Palm Beach Post

"Few things get the blood moving like a Christopher Moore tale about vampires. . . . As he does in earlier work, Moore is telling us about the frailties of the human condition. Take away the fangs and the nighttime binges and Moore describes young love. The joys, the awkwardness, the fears, the lust. . . . Tommy's journey through first love is one we all take. Moore makes this trip a joy, filled with absurd characters who allow people in the dark to laugh and see the light."   *—Cleveland Plain Dealer*

© Charlee Rodgers

About the Author

CHRISTOPHER MOORE is the author of *A Dirty Job, The Stupid-est Angel, Fluke, Lamb, The Lust Lizard of Melancholy Cove, Island of the Sequined Love Nun, Bloodsucking Fiends, Coyote Blue,* and *Practical Demonkeeping.* He invites readers to e-mail him at BSFiends@aol.com.

Also by Christopher Moore

YOU SUCK

A LOVE STORY

CHRISTOPHER MOORE

HARPER

NEW YORK • LONDON • TORONTO • SYDNEY

HARPER

This book is a work of fiction. The characters, incidents, and dialogue are drawn from the author's imagination and are not to be construed as real. Any resemblance to actual events or persons, living or dead, is entirely coincidental.

A signed limited hardcover edition has been privately printed by Charnel House. www.charnelhouse.com

A hardcover edition of this book was published in 2007 by William Morrow, an imprint of HarperCollins Publishers.

HarperCollins books may be purchased for educational, business, or sales promotional use. For information please write: Special Markets Department, HarperCollins Publishers, 10 East 53rd Street, New York, NY 10022.

FIRST HARPER PAPERBACK PUBLISHED 2008.

Designed by Betty Lew

The Library of Congress has catalogued the hardcover edition as follows:

Moore, Christopher.
    You suck: a love story / Christopher Moore. —1st ed.
        p.cm.
ISBN: 978-0-06-059029-1
ISBN-10: 0-06-059029-7
1. Vampires—Fiction. I. Title.

PS3563.O594Y682007
813'.54—dc22   2006047083

ISBN: 978-0-06-059030-7 (pbk.)

08 09 10 11 12 WBC/RRD 10 9 8 7 6 5 4 3 2

For my readers,
by request

ACKNOWLEDGMENTS

Thanks, again, to the usual suspects: my agent, Nick Ellison, and Sarah Dickman, Arija Weddle, and Marissa Matteo at Nicholas Ellison, Inc.; Jennifer Brehl, Kate Nintzel, Lisa Gallagher, Michael Morrison, Mike Spradlin, Jack Womack, Debbie Stier, Lynn Grady, and all my friends at William Morrow; and, of course, to Charlee Rodgers, for putting up with the frozen turkey bowling.

Get Over It, a Lot of People Are Dead

"You bitch, you killed me! You suck!"

Tommy had just awakened for the first time as a vampire. He was nineteen, thin, and had spent his entire life between states of amazement and confusion.

"I wanted us to be together." Jody: pale, pretty, long red hair hanging in her face, cute swoop of a nose in search of a lost spray of freckles, a big lipstick-smeared grin. She'd only been undead herself for a couple of months, and was still learning to be spooky.

"Yeah, that's why you spent the night with *him*." Tommy pointed across the loft to the life-sized bronze statue of a man in a tattered suit. Inside the bronze shell was the ancient vampire who had turned Jody. Another bronze of Jody stood next to him. When the two of them had gone out at sunrise, into the sleep of the dead, Tommy had taken them to the sculptors who lived on the ground floor of his building and had the vampires bronzed. He'd thought it would give him time to think of what to do, and keep Jody from running off with the old vampire. Tommy's mistake had been drilling ear holes in Jody's sculpture so she could hear him. Somehow, during the night, before the bronzing, the old vampire had taught her to turn to mist, and she'd streamed out of the ear holes into the room, and—well—here they were: dead, in love, and angry.

"I needed to know about what I am, Tommy. Who else was going to tell me if not him?"

"Yeah, but you should have asked me before you did *this,*" Tommy said. "You shouldn't just kill a guy without asking. It's inconsiderate." Tommy was from Indiana, and his mother had raised him to have good manners and to be considerate of other people's feelings.

"You had sex with me while I was unconscious," Jody said.

"That's not the same," Tommy said. "I was just being friendly, like when you put a quarter in someone else's parking meter when they aren't there—you know they appreciate it later, even if they don't thank you personally."

"Yeah, wait until you go out in your jammies and wake up all sticky in a cheerleader outfit and see how grateful you are. You know, Tommy, when I'm out, technically, I'm dead. Guess what that makes you?"

"Well—uh—yeah, but you're not even human. You're just some foul dead thing." Tommy immediately regretted saying it. It was hurtful and mean, and although Jody was, indeed, dead, he didn't find her foul at all—in fact, he was pretty sure he was in love with her, he was just a little embarrassed about the whole necrophilia/cheerleader thing. Back in the Midwest people didn't mention that sort of thing unless a dog dug up a pom-pom in some guy's back yard and the police eventually discovered the whole human pyramid buried under the swing set.

Jody sniffled, completely for effect. Actually she was relieved that Tommy was now on the defensive. "Well, welcome to the Foul, Dead Thing Club, Mr. Flood."

"Yeah, you drank my blood," Tommy said. "A lot."

Damn, she should have pretended to cry. "You let me."

"Again, being considerate," Tommy said. He stood up and shrugged.

"You just let me because of the sex."

"That's not true, it was because you needed me." He was lying, it was because of the sex.

"Yes, I did," Jody said. "I still do." She held her arms out to him. "I really do."

He walked into her arms and held her. She felt amazing to him, even more amazing than she had before. It was as if his nerves had been dialed up to eleven. "Okay, it was because of the sex."

Great, she thought, *in control once again.* She kissed his neck. "How do you feel about it now?"

"Maybe in a minute, I'm starving." He let go of her and

stormed across the loft to the kitchen, where he pulled a burrito out of the freezer, threw it into the microwave, and hit the button, all in one smooth motion.

"You don't want to eat that," Jody said.

"Nonsense, it smells great. It's like every little bean and pork piece is sending out its own delicious miasma of flavor vapor." Tommy used words like "miasma" because he wanted to be a writer. That's why he'd come to San Francisco in the first place—to take life in big bites and write about it. Oh, and to find a girlfriend.

"Put the burrito down, and back away, Tommy," Jody said. "I don't want you to get hurt."

"Ha, that's cute." He took a big bite and grinned at her as he chewed.

Five minutes later, because she felt responsible, Jody was helping him clean bits of masticated burrito off the kitchen wall and the front of the refrigerator. "It's like every bean was storming the gates of repressive digestion to escape."

"Yeah, well, being refried will do that to you," Jody said, stroking his hair. "You okay?"

"I'm starving. I need to eat."

"Not so much eat," Jody said.

"Oh my God! It's the hunger. I feel like my insides are caving in on themselves. You should have told me about this."

She knew how he felt—actually, she had felt worse

when it happened to her. At least he knew what was happening to him. "Yeah, sweetie, we're going to have to make a few adjustments."

"Well, what do I do? What did you do?"

"I mostly fed off of you, remember?"

"You should have thought this through before you killed me. I'm fucked."

"*We're* fucked. Together. Like Romeo and Juliet, only we get to be in a sequel. Very literary, Tommy."

"Oh, that's a comfort. I can't believe you just killed me like that."

"And turned you into a superbeing, thank you very much."

"Oh, crap, there's burrito spooge all over my new sneakers."

"You can see in the dark, now," Jody said cheerfully. "Wanna try it? I'll get naked. You can look at me in the dark. Naked. You'll like it."

"Jody, I'm starving over here."

She couldn't believe that he didn't respond to the naked persuasion. What kind of monster had she created? "Okay, I'll find you a bug or something."

"A bug?! A bug!? I'm not eating a bug."

"I said there'd have to be some adjustments."

Tommy had been dealing with more than a few adjustments since he'd come west from his hometown of Incontinence, Indiana—not the least of which had been finding a girlfriend, who, while smart, sexy, and quick-witted, drank his blood and tended to fall unconscious at the exact moment of sunrise. He'd always suspected that she might have just picked him because he worked nights and could walk around during the day, especially since she'd once said, "I need someone who works nights and can walk around during the day," but now that he was a vampire, he could close the door on that insecurity and open another onto a whole new world of insecurities he'd never even considered before. The appropriate age for a vampire is four hundred years old—he should be a world-weary and sophisticated creature, his human anxieties long since overcome or evolved into macabre perversions. The problem with a nineteen-year-old vampire is that he drags all of his adolescent insecurities into the dark with him.

"I'm really pale," Tommy said, staring at himself in the bathroom mirror. They'd figured out early on that vampires do, indeed, cast a reflection in a mirror, just like they could tolerate proximity to crucifixes and garlic. (Tommy had run experiments on Jody while she slept, including many involving cheerleader outfits and personal lubricants.) "And not just winter in Indiana pale. I'm, like, pale like you."

"Yeah," said Jody, "I thought you liked the pale."

"Sure, it looks good on you, but I look ill."

"Keep looking," Jody said. She was leaning against the door frame, dressed in tight black jeans and a half shirt, her hair tied back and streaming down her back like a flaccid red comet tail. She was trying not to appear too amused.

"Something's missing," Tommy said. "Something besides color."

"Uh-huh." Jody grinned.

"My skin cleared up! I don't have a single zit."

"Ding, ding, ding," Jody onomatopeed, signaling that Tommy had hit on the correct answer.

"If I had known my skin would clear up, I'd have asked you to change me a long time ago."

"I didn't know how to a long time ago," Jody said. "That's not all, take off your shoes."

"I don't understand, I—"

"Just take off your shoes. "

Tommy sat on the edge of the tub and took off his sneakers and socks.

"What?"

"Look at your toes."

"They're straight. My little toe isn't bent anymore. It's like I've never worn shoes."

"You're perfect," Jody said. She remembered finding out this condition of vampirism and being both delighted and horrified because now she felt that she'd always need to lose five pounds—five pounds that were preserved for eternity.

Tommy pulled up the leg of his jeans and studied his shin. "The scar where I hit myself with a hatchet, it's gone."

"And it always will be," Jody said. "You'll always be perfect, just like you are now. My split ends even went away."

"I'll always be the same?"

"Yes."

"Just like I am now."

"As far as I know," Jody said.

"But I was going to start working out. I was going to be buff. I was going to have abs of steel."

"No, you weren't."

"I was. I was going to be an awesome hunk of muscular man-meat."

"No, you weren't. You wanted to be a writer. You were going to have little stick arms and get winded when you hit the back-space key more than three times consecutively. You're in great shape from working in the grocery store. Wait until you see how you can run."

"You really think I'm in great shape?"

"Yes, I thought I made that clear."

Tommy flexed his chest in the mirror, which showed not at all through his flannel shirt. He unbuttoned his shirt and tried it again, with little effect, then shrugged. "What about the writer thing? Will my brain always be like this? I mean, will I get any smarter, or is that stuck in time, too?"

"Well, yeah, but that's because you're a man, not because you're a vampire."

"You spiteful harpy."

"I think I've made my point," Jody said.

Jody had put on a red leather jacket, even though she could no longer feel discomfort from the cold fog coming in off the Bay. She liked the way it looked with her black jeans and a low-cut black lace camisole she'd rescued from a Nordstrom Rack Store before some slut got hold of it. "Come on, Tommy, we need to go find something for you to eat before we run out of night."

"I know, but I have something I have to do. Give me a minute." He was in the bathroom again, this time with the door shut.

Jody heard the zipper of his jeans go down, then a slightly breathless man-scream. The bathroom door flew open and Tommy, his pants and underwear around his ankles, bunny-hopped in two great leaps across the bedroom.

"Look at this. What's happening to me. Look at this!" He was pointing furiously to his penis. "It's like I'm some radioactive mutant freak."

Jody went to him and grabbed his hands—held him steady, looked him in the eyes. "Tommy, calm down. It's just your foreskin."

"I don't have a foreskin. I'm circumcised."

"Not anymore," Jody said. "Evidently, when you turned, it grew back, just like your toes straightened and your scars all went away."

"Oh. You don't find it creepy, then?"

"No. It's fine."

"You want to touch it?"

"Thanks. Maybe later."

"Oh, sorry, I freaked. Didn't realize. I—uh—I still feel like I have to finish what I was going to do."

"That's fine," Jody said. "You're fine. You go finish up. I'll wait."

"You're sure you don't want to give it a quick fondle?"

"If I do, can we get out of here?"

"Probably not."

"Well then, back in the bathroom you go." She spun him around and gave him a gentle shove. He bunny-hopped his newly recovered foreskin back into the bathroom and closed the door.

Jody shuddered at the sound of the door closing. She hadn't thought about whether or not Tommy would retain his incessant horniness after he turned, she had just wanted a companion who could understand what she was, what she felt, what the world looked like through vampire eyes. If it turned out that he was going to be nineteen forever, she might end up having to kill him for real.

The Last Poop

So that was it?"

"Yep."

"Never again?"

"Nope."

"Not ever?"

"Nope."

"I feel like I should save them or something."

"Would you just flush and come out of there."

I Am Poor and My Cat Is Huge

Jody walked a step or two behind Tommy, just watching him, as they made their way up Third Street toward Market. She was watching his reaction to his new senses, giving him some room to look around, whispering hints about what he was experiencing. She'd gone through this herself only a couple of months ago, and she'd done it without a guide.

"I can see the heat coming off the streetlamps," Tommy said, looking up and spinning as he walked. "Every window in every building is a different color."

"Try to just look at one thing at a time, Tommy. Don't let it overwhelm you." Jody was waiting for him to comment on the aura that each person was giving off. Not a heat aura, more of a life force. So far they'd only seen healthy red and pink ones—not what she was looking for.

"What's that noise, like running water?" Tommy asked.

"That's the sewers running under the street. All that stuff will fade after a while—you'll still hear it, but you won't notice it unless you focus."

"It's like a thousand people are talking in my head." He looked around at the few pedestrians who were out on the street.

"Televisions and radios, too," Jody said. "Try to focus on one thing, let the rest fall back."

Tommy stopped, looked up at an apartment window four floors up. "There's a guy up there having phone sex."

"Figures you'd zero in on that," Jody said. She focused on the window. Yes, she could hear the guy panting and giving instructions to someone on the phone. Evidently he felt the caller was a dirty little slut and therefore needed to apply varieties of hot salsa to her body. Jody tried to hear the voice on the other end of the phone, but it was too faint—the guy must have been wearing a headset.

"What a freak," Tommy said.

"Shhhh," Jody said. "Tommy, close your eyes and listen. Forget the salsa guy. Don't look."

Tommy closed his eyes and stood in the middle of the sidewalk. "What?"

Jody leaned against a "No Parking" sign and smiled. "What's just to the right of you?"

"How do I know? I was looking up."

"I know. Focus. Listen. Two feet from your right hand, what is it?"

"This is dumb."

"Just listen. Listen to the shape of the sound coming from your right."

"Okay." Tommy squinted, showing he was concentrating.

A couple of androgynous students dressed in black with severe hair, probably from the Academy of Art on the next block, walked by and barely gave them a look until Tommy said, "I can hear a box. A rectangle."

"Acid noob," said one of the students, who sounded like it might be a guy.

"I remember my first trip," said the other, who was probably a girl. "I wandered into the men's room at the Metreon and thought I was in a Marcel Duchamp installation."

Jody waited for them to pass then asked, "Yes, a rectangle, solid, hollow, what?" She was a little giddy now, bouncing on the balls of her feet. This was better than buying shoes.

"It's hollow." Tommy tilted his head. "It's a newspaper machine." He opened his eyes, looked at the newspaper box, then at Jody, his face lit up like a toddler who has just discovered chocolate for the first time.

She ran into his arms and kissed him. "I have so much to show you."

"Why didn't you tell me?" Tommy asked.

"How could I? Do you have words for what you're hearing? For what you're seeing?"

Tommy let her go and looked around, took a deep breath through his nose, as if checking the bouquet of a wine. "No. I don't know how to say these things."

"See, that's why I had to share this with you."

Tommy nodded, but looked a little forlorn. "This part is good. But the other part . . ."

"What other part?"

"The foul, dead, blood-drinking part. I'm still starving."

"Don't whine, Tommy. Nobody likes a whiner."

"Hungry," he said.

She knew how he felt, she was feeling some of it herself, but she didn't know how to solve the feeding problem. Tommy had always been her go-to blood guy; now they were going to have to hunt. She could do it, she had done it, but she didn't want to do it. "Come on, we'll figure this out. Don't pout. Let's go watch people on Market Street. You'll like it." She took his hand and dragged him up the street toward Market, where rivers of tourists, shoppers, and freaks were flowing up and down the streets and sidewalks. Rivers of blood.

Everyone smells like whiz and feet," Tommy said, standing on the sidewalk in front of a Walgreens drugstore. It was still early in the evening and the convention crowd from the hotels was flowing down the sidewalks like a great migrating herd, looking for dinner or a watering hole. Out on the edges, hustlers, homeless, and hangers-on worked their angles, playing the secret path of eye contact to the pocket, while the herd defended itself by paying rapt attention to their companions, their cell phones, or a spot on the sidewalk twelve feet ahead.

"Feet and pee," Tommy continued.

"You get used to it," Jody said.

"Is there a clean pair of underwear anywhere on this street?" Tommy shouted. "You people are disgusting!"

"Would you settle down," Jody said. "People are looking. They think you're crazy."

"Which makes me different, how?"

She looked up the street—for the three blocks she could see there were about three people per block shouting at passersby, wild-eyed and angry, and obviously bat shit. She nodded. He had a point, but then she snatched his shirt collar and pulled his ear down to lip level. "The difference is that you aren't living anymore and it's not a good idea to attract attention to yourself."

"Which is why you chose to wear that delightful ensemble from the skank-wear collection at Hoes-N-Thangs?"

"You said you liked it." Jody had become a little more provocative in her dress since becoming a vampire—but she saw it more as an expression of confidence, not a means to attract attention. Was it a predator thing? A power thing?

"I did—do like it, but every guy who passes is staring at your cleavage. I can hear their heartbeats go up. Did you have to turn to mist to get into those jeans? You did, didn't you?"

A tap on Tommy's shoulder. A young man in a white, short-sleeved dress shirt and a black tie had sidled up to him, holding out a pamphlet. "You sound troubled, brother.

Maybe this will help." The pamphlet proclaimed REJOICE! on the cover in big green letters.

Jody covered her mouth and turned away so the guy wouldn't see her giggling.

"What?!" Tommy said, turning on the guy. "What? What? What? Can't you see I'm trying to discuss my girlfriend's— uh—well, those." Tommy gestured to Jody's shoulder, which was now where those had just been. "Show him, Jody," Tommy said.

Jody shook her head and started to walk away, her shoulders shaking with laughter.

"There's a message here," said the tie guy. "It can bring you comfort—and joy."

"Yeah, well, I was trying to show you some examples of that, but there she goes with them."

"But this is a joy that goes beyond physical—"

"Yeah, like you'd know," Tommy said, cupping his nose and mouth as if covering a sneeze. "Listen, I'd love to discuss this with you, buddy, but right now you have to GO HOME AND WASH YOUR ASS! You smell like you're smuggling a stockyard back there!"

Tommy turned and strode after Jody, leaving the tie guy blushing and crumpling his pamphlet.

"It's not funny," Tommy said.

Jody was trying so hard not to laugh, she snorted. "Yes, it is."

"Can't they see we're damned? You'd think they could tell. At least you. We are damned, aren't we? "

"No idea," Jody said. She hadn't really thought about it.

"Didn't cover that in your advanced vampire course with the old guy?"

"Forgot to ask."

"No problem," Tommy said, with no effort at all to suppress sarcasm. "Minor detail. Anything else you might have forgotten to ask?"

"I thought I'd have more time, for follow-up," Jody said. "I didn't realize that the man I love was going to bronze us that first night."

"Yeah—well—okay. Sorry."

"Where's the trust?" Jody said.

"You killed me," Tommy said.

"Oh, there you go again."

"Please, folks. I need a dollar," said a voice from the left. Jody looked down to see a guy sitting against the granite wall of a closed bank. He was dirty beyond age or race, sort of grimy to the point of shine, and on his lap was an enormous long-haired cat. There was a cup on the sidewalk in front of him and beside it a hand-printed sign that read I AM POOR AND MY CAT IS HUGE.

Tommy, who was still fairly new to the city and hadn't learned to look past this sort of thing, stopped and started digging in his pocket. "That is sure a huge cat."

"Yeah, he eats a lot. It's all I can do to keep him fed."

Jody nudged Tommy, trying to get him back into the pedestrian flow. She liked that he was a nice guy, but it could really be irritating sometimes. Especially when she

was trying to teach him the profundities of being a creature of the night.

"Mostly fur, though, right?" Tommy asked.

"Mister, this cat weighs thirty-five pounds."

Tommy whistled and handed the guy a dollar. "Can I
touch him?"

"Sure," the guy said. "He doesn't care."

Tommy knelt down and poked the cat gently, then
looked up at Jody. "This is a huge cat."

She smiled. "Huge. Let's go."

"Touch him," Tommy said.

"No thanks."

"So," Tommy said to the cat guy, "why don't you give
him to a shelter or something?"

"Then how am I supposed to make a living?"

"You could print up a sign that says 'I'm poor and I lost
my huge cat'? That would work on me."

"You may not be the best sample," said the cat guy.

"Look," Tommy said, standing now and digging into his
pocket. "I'll buy the cat. I'll give you, uh, forty—"

The cat guy shook his head.

"Sixty—"

Furious head shaking . . .

Tommy untangled bills from a wad he'd pulled out of
his pocket, "One hundred—"

"No."

"And thirty . . . two—"

"No."

"And thirty-seven cents."

"No."

"And a paper clip."

"No."

"That's a great offer," Tommy insisted. "That's like four bucks a pound!"

"No."

"Well screw you, then," Tommy said. "I don't feel sorry for you and your huge cat."

"You can't have your dollar back."

"Fine!" Tommy said.

"Fine!" said the cat guy.

Tommy took Jody by the arm and started to walk away. "That's a huge cat," he said.

"Why were you trying to buy it? We're not supposed to have pets in the loft."

"Duh," Tommy said. "Dinner."

"Yuck."

"It's a stopgap," Tommy said. "You know that the Masai of Kenya drink the blood of their cattle with no apparent ill effect to the cow."

"Well, I'm sure it violates our lease if we get a cow."

"That's it."

"What's it?"

"A lease."

Tommy swung her around and brought her back to the cat guy.

"I want to rent the cat," Tommy said. "You could use a

break and I want to show the huge cat to my aunt who is an invalid and can't come down here."

"No."

"One night. One hundred and thirty-two dollars and thirty seven cents."

The cat guy raised an eyebrow, the grime over that eye cracked a little. "One fifty."

"I don't have one fifty, you know that."

"Then I want to see the redhead's hooters."

Tommy looked at Jody, then back at the cat guy, then back at Jody.

"No," Jody said calmly.

"No," Tommy said indignantly. "How dare you suggest it?"

"One hooter," countered the cat guy.

Tommy looked at Jody. She gave him the wide, green-eyed expression that she would have described as *I will slap you so far into next week that it will take a team of surgeons just to get Wednesday out of your ass.*

"No way," Tommy said. "The redhead's hooters are not on the table." He grinned, looked back at Jody, then looked away, really fast.

The cat guy shrugged. "I'll need some kind of security deposit, like your driver's license—"

"Sure," Tommy said.

"And a credit card."

"No," Jody said, pulling her jacket closed and zipping it up to her neck.

"Nothing kinky," said the cat guy. "I'll know."

"Going to show him to my aunt, and I'll have him back tomorrow, this time."

"Deal," said the cat guy. "His name is Chet."

You first," Tommy said. They stood in the great room of their loft on either side of the futon, where the huge cat, a crossbreed between a Persian, a dust mop, and possibly a water buffalo, was actively shedding. Tommy had decided that he was going to be very cool about the whole blood-drinking thing, despite the fact that he was so amped he felt as if he could run up and down the walls. In fact, he wasn't sure that he couldn't run up and down the walls, that was part of what was freaking him out. Still, since coming to San Francisco a couple of months ago, he had spent entirely too much time overreacting, and he wasn't going to do it now— not in front of his girlfriend. Not at all, if he could help it.

"You should go first," Jody said. "You've never fed before."

"But you gave the old vampire some of your blood," Tommy said. "You need it." It was true, she had given the vampire her blood to help heal him from the damage Tommy and his friends had caused by blowing up his yacht and so forth, but he hoped she would say no again.

"No, no, no, after you," Jody said, with a very bad French accent. "I insist."

"Well, if you insist."

Tommy leapt to the futon and bent over the huge cat. He wasn't sure how he was supposed to go about this, but he could see the healthy red life aura around Chet, and he could hear his little kitty heart pounding. There was a crackling noise inside of his head, like someone was popping bubble wrap in his ear canal, and then there was pressure on the roof of his mouth, painful pressure, and more crackling. He felt something give and two sharp points poking his lower lip. He pushed back from the cat and grinned at Jody, who yelped and jumped back a step.

"Fangth," Tommy said.

"Yes, I can see that," Jody said.

"Why'd you jump? Do they look thupid?"

"You startled me, is all," Jody said, looking away from him like he was an arc welder or a total eclipse and full eye contact might blind her. She waved him on. "Go, go, go. Be careful. Not too hard."

"Right," Tommy said. He grinned again and she shied away.

Tommy turned back, braced the cat, who seemed much less freaked by this process than the two vampires in the room, and bit.

"Thuppt, thuppt, ack!" Tommy stood up and started brushing at his tongue to remove cat hair. "Yuck!"

"Hold still," Jody said, going to him and brushing the loose, damp cat hair away from his face. She went to the kitchen counter and came back with a glass of water and a paper towel, which she used to wipe at Tommy's tongue.

"Just use the water to rinse. Don't swallow it. You won't be able to keep it down."

"I'm not going to thwollow it, my mouf is full of cat hair."

Once he had rinsed, Jody picked the last of the hairs from his mouth, and in doing so, she pricked one of her fingers on Tommy's right fang.

"Ouch." She pulled her finger away and put it in her mouth.

"Oh, jeez," Tommy said. He pulled her finger out of her mouth and put it in his. His eyes rolled back in his head and he moaned through his nose.

"Oh, I don't think so," Jody said. She grabbed his hand and bit into his forearm, attaching herself to him like a remora to a shark.

Tommy growled, flipped her around, and threw her facedown on the futon, his arm still in her mouth. She flipped her hair to the side and he sank his teeth into her neck. She screamed, but the shriek was muted, bubbling out on Tommy's bloody forearm. Chet, the huge cat, hissed and bolted across the room, through the bedroom door, to wedge himself under the bed, as the sounds of straining leather, tearing denim, and screaming predators filled the loft.

The irony, that it sounded like a huge catfight, was completely lost on the huge cat.

Red and White and Dead All Over

Kapoc stuffing and chicken feathers lay in great, fluffy drifts across the room, along with the shreds of their clothing, the futon cover, pieces of a fuzzy, Muppet-skin rug, and the crushed remains of a couple of cheap-ass Pier 1 paper lanterns. Sparks crackled from the bare wires over the breakfast bar, where the pendulum light fixtures used to hang. The loft looked as if someone had thrown a hand grenade into the middle of a teddy-bear orgy and the only survivors had had their fur blown off.

"Well, that was different," Jody said, still a little breathless. She was lying across the coffee table, looking out the window at a streetlight from an upside-down angle, naked except for one sleeve of her red leather jacket. She was smeared with blood from head to toe, and even as Tommy watched, the scratches and fang marks on her skin were healing over.

"If I'd known," Tommy said, panting, "I'd have grown a foreskin a long time ago." He lay across the room where she had thrown him, sprawled on a pile of books and kindling that had once been a bookshelf, also smeared with blood and covered in scratches—wearing only a sock.

As he pulled a pencil-sized splinter of bookcase out of his thigh, Tommy thought that he might have been a little hasty about yelling at Jody for turning him into a vampire. Although he couldn't really remember much of it, he was pretty sure he'd just had the most amazing sex ever. Apparently what he had read about vampire sex being all about drinking the blood and nothing else—it was just another myth like the changing into a bat and the inability to cross running water.

"Did you know that was going to happen?" Tommy asked.

"I had no idea," Jody said, still on the coffee table, and looking more to Tommy every minute like a murder victim, except that she was talking, and smiling. "I was going to make you buy me dinner and take me to a movie first."

Tommy chucked the bloody bookcase splinter at her. "I don't mean did you know we were going to do it, I mean did you know that it was going to be like that?"

"How would I know that?"

"I thought maybe the night you spent with the old vampire . . ."

Jody sat up. "I didn't *do* him, Tommy, I just spent the

night with him trying to find out about how to be a vampire. And his name is Elijah."

"Oh, so now you're on a first-name basis."

"Oh, for the love of God, Tommy, would you stop thinking? You're taking what was an amazing experience and sucking all the life out of it."

Tommy fidgeted on his pile of rubble and started to pout, but winced when he tried to push out his lower lip and it caught on his fangs. She was right. He'd always been like that, always overthinking, overanalyzing. "Sorry," he said.

"You have to just be part of the world now," Jody said softly. "You can't put everything into categories, separate yourself from experience by putting words on it. Like the song says, *let it be*."

"Sorry," Tommy said again. He tried to push the thoughts out of his head, closed his eyes, and listened to his heartbeat, and Jody's heartbeat coming from across the room.

"It's okay," Jody said. "Sex like that does sort of beg for a postmortem."

Tommy smiled, his eyes still closed. "So to speak."

Jody stood up and crossed the room to where he was sitting. She offered him her hand to help him up. "Careful, the back of your head is kind of stuck in the drywall."

Tommy turned his head and heard plaster cracking. "I'm still starving."

She pulled him to his feet. "I'm feeling a little drained myself."

"My bad," Tommy said. He could remember now, her

blood pulsing into him, at the same time that his was pulsing into her. He rubbed a place on his shoulder where the punctures from her fangs hadn't quite healed yet.

She kissed the spot he was rubbing. "You'll heal faster when you've had fresh blood."

Tommy felt an ache, like a sudden cramp in his stomach. "I really need to eat."

Jody led him into the bedroom, where Chet the huge cat was cowering in the corner, hiding unsuccessfully behind the wicker hamper.

"Wait," Jody said. She padded back out into the great room and came back a few seconds later wearing what was left of her red leather jacket (really more of a vest now) and her panties, which she had to hold together on one side where they'd been torn off. "Sorry," she said, "I'm not comfortable being naked in front of strangers."

Tommy nodded. "He's not a stranger, Jody. He's dinner."

"Uh-huh," Jody said, nodding and shaking her head at the same time, making her appear like a bloodstained, bobble-head doll. "You go. You're new."

"Me? Don't you know some superanimal hypnotism to call him to you?"

"Nope. Go get him. I'll wait."

Tommy looked at her. On top of the blood that streaked and smeared her pale skin, there were gobs of futon stuffing stuck to her here and there, as well as white chicken feathers in her hair from one of the exploded cushions. He had feathers and cat hair stuck to his chest and legs. "We're going to have to shave him first, you know?"

Jody nodded, not looking away from the huge cat. "Maybe a shower first."

"Good idea." Tommy put his arm around her.

"But just washing. No sex!"

"Why, we already lost the cleaning deposit?"

"Those shower doors are glass."

"Okay. But can I wash your—"

"No," she said. She took his hand and dragged him into the bathroom.

It turned out that superhuman vampire strength came in handy when shaving a thirty-five-pound cat. After a couple of false starts, which had them chasing Chet the huge shaving-cream-covered cat around the loft, they discovered the value of duct tape as a grooming tool. Because of the tape, they weren't able to shave his feet. When they were finished, Chet looked like a big-eyed, potbellied, protohuman in fur-lined, duct-tape space boots—the feline love child of Gollum and Dobby the house-elf.

"I'm not sure we needed to shave all of him," Tommy said, sitting on the bed next to Jody as they considered the bound and shaven Chet on the floor before them. "He looks creepy."

"Pretty creepy," Jody said. "You'd better drink. Your

wounds aren't healing." All her scratches, bruises, and love bites were completely healed, and except for a fleck of shaving cream here and there in her hair, she was as good as new.

"How?" Tommy asked. "How do I know where to bite him?"

"Try the neck," Jody said. "But sort of feel around for a vein with your tongue before you bite, and don't bite hard." She was trying to sound confident in her instructions, but she was in unexplored territory as much as he was. She was enjoying teaching Tommy about the particulars of vampirism, just as she enjoyed teaching him how to do grown-up human things like how to get the power and phone turned on in the loft—it made her feel sophisticated and in charge, and after a series of boyfriends for whom she had been little more than an accoutrement, whose lifestyles she had affected, from heavy-metal anarchists to financial-district yuppies, she liked being the pacesetter for a change. Still, when it came to teaching him about feeding on animals, she couldn't have been winging it more if she really could turn into a bat. The only time she'd ever considered drinking animal blood was when Tommy had brought her two large, live snapping turtles from Chinatown. She hadn't been able to bring herself to even try biting into the armored reptiles. Tommy had named them Scott and Zelda, which hadn't helped. Now Zelda was functioning as a lawn ornament in Pacific Heights and Scott was encased in bronze and standing next to the old vampire in the great room. The biker sculptors downstairs had bronzed them, which is what had given Tommy the idea to bronze Jody and the old vampire in the first place.

"Are you sure this is okay?" Tommy said, bending over Chet the huge shaved cat. "I mean, you said that we were only supposed to hunt the sick and the weak—the black auras. Chet's aura is shiny and pink."

"It's different with animals." She had no idea if it was different with animals. She'd eaten a moth once, whole—snatched it out of the air and downed it before she could think about it. She realized now that there were a lot more questions she should have asked Elijah when she had had the chance. "Besides, you're not going to kill him."

"Right," Tommy said. He put his mouth on Chet's kitty neck. "Like thith?"

Jody had to turn away to keep from laughing. "Yeah, that looks good."

"He tathes like thaving cream."

"Just go," Jody said.

"'Kay." Tommy bit and started to moan almost immediately. Not a moan of pleasure, but the moan of someone who has his tongue stuck on the ice-cube tray in the freezer. Chet seemed strangely calm, not even struggling against his kitty bonds. Maybe there was something to the vampire's power over his victims, Jody thought.

"Okay, that's enough," Jody said.

Tommy shook his head while still feeding on the huge shaved cat.

"Tommy, let off. You need to leave some."

"Nu-ih," Tommy said.

"Stop sucking the huge cat, Tommy," Jody said sternly. "I'm not kidding." She *was* kidding, a little bit.

Tommy was breathing hard now, and a little color had come into his skin. Jody looked around for something to get his attention. She spotted a vase of flowers on the night-stand.

She pulled out the flowers and tossed the water on Tommy and the huge cat. He kept feeding. The cat shuddered but otherwise remained immobile.

"Okay, then," Jody said. It was a heavy, stoneware vase, something Tommy had picked up to hold some apology flowers he'd brought her from the grocery store where he worked. He'd been good that way, sometimes bringing home apology flowers before he'd even done anything to apologize for. Really, you couldn't ask for more than that from a guy—which is why Jody slowed to half speed as she brought the vase around in a wide arc that ended with it smacking Tommy in the forehead and knocking him back about six feet. Chet the huge shaved cat yowled. Miraculously, the vase did not break.

"Thanks," Tommy said, wiping the blood from his mouth. There was a crescent-moon-shaped dent in his forehead that was rapidly filling in, healing.

"Sure," Jody said, staring at the vase. *Great vase,* she thought. Elegant, fragile porcelain was all well and good for the collector's case or the tea party, but for the girl who finds herself in need of a vessel that can deliver a wallop, Jody was suddenly sold on the sturdy value of stoneware.

"Tastes like cat breath," Tommy said, pointing to Chet. The punctures from Tommy's fangs had already healed. "Is it supposed to?"

Jody shrugged. "What's cat breath taste like?"

"Like tuna casserole left out in the sun for a week." Being from the Midwest, Tommy thought everyone knew what tuna casserole tasted like. Having been born and raised in Carmel, California, Jody knew it only as something eaten by the extinct people on *Nick at Nite*.

"I think I'm going to pass," Jody said. She was hungry, but not cat-breath hungry. She wasn't sure what she was going to do about feeding. She couldn't very well try to live off Tommy anymore, and regardless of the rush and the sense that she was serving nature's cause by taking only the weak and the sick, she didn't like the idea of preying on humans— strangers anyway. She needed time to think, to figure out what their new life was going to be like. Things had been happening too quickly since Tommy and his friends had taken down the old vampire. She said, "We should get Chet back to his owner tonight if we can. You don't want to lose your driver's license—we may need a valid ID to rent a new place."

"A new place?"

"We have to move, Tommy. I told Inspectors Rivera and Cavuto that I would leave town. You don't think they'll check?" There had been two homicide detectives who had

followed the trail of bodies to the old vampire, and ulti-
mately the discovery of Jody's delicate condition. She'd
promised them that she'd take the old vampire and leave
town if they'd let her go.

"Oh yeah," Tommy said. "That means I can't go back to
work at the Safeway either?"

He wasn't stupid, she knew he wasn't stupid, so why was
he so slow to see the obvious? "No, I don't think that would
be a good idea," Jody said. "Since you're going to pass out
cold at sunrise, just the way I do."

"Yeah, that'd be embarrassing," Tommy said.

"Especially when sunlight hits you and you burst into
flames."

"Yeah, there's got to be company policy against that."

Jody screamed in frustration.

"Jeez, kidding," Tommy said, cringing.

She sighed, realizing that he'd been goofing on her. "Get
dressed, cat breath, we don't want to run out of dark. We're
going to need some help."

Out in the great room, the vampire Elijah Ben Sapir was
trying to figure out exactly what was going on around him.
He knew he had been constrained—bound inside a vessel,
and whatever held him was immovable. He'd even turned
to mist, which relieved his anxiety somewhat—there was
an ethereal mind-set that accompanied the form, it took
concentration to not let yourself just float off in a daze—but

the bronze shell was airtight. He could hear them talking, but their comments told him little except that his fledgling had betrayed him. He smiled to himself. What a foolishly human mistake to let hope triumph over reason. He should have known better.

It would be days before the hunger was on him again, and even then, without any movement, he could last indefinitely without blood. He could live a very, very long time constrained like this, he realized—it was his sanity that would suffer. He decided to stay in mist form—drift as in a dream at night, sleep like the dead during the day. This way, he would wait, and when the time came, and it would come (if nothing else, living for eight hundred years had taught him patience), he would make his move.

The Emperor of San Francisco

Two in the morning. Normally, the Emperor of San Francisco would have been tucked in behind a Dumpster with the royal guard snuggled around him for warmth, snoring like a congested bulldozer, but tonight he had been undone by the generosity of a Starbucks froth slave in Union Square who had donated a bucket-sized Holiday Spice Mochaccino to the cause of royal comfort, thus leaving the Emperor and his two companions jangled, wandering the wee hours on a nearly deserted Market Street, waiting for breakfast time to roll around.

"Like crack with cinnamon," said the Emperor. He was a great, boiler tank of a man, an ambling meat locomotive in a wool overcoat, his face a firebox of intensity, framed with a gray tempest of hair and beard such as are found only on gods and lunatics.

Bummer, the smaller of the troops, a Boston terrier,

snorted and tossed his head. He'd lapped up some of the rich coffee broth himself, and felt ready to tear ass out of any rodent or pastrami sandwich that might cross his path. Lazarus, normally the calmer of the two, a golden retriever, pranced and leapt at the Emperor's side as if it might start raining ducks any minute—a recurring nightmare among retrievers.

"Steady, gents," the Emperor chided. "Lets us use this inopportune alertness to inspect a less frantic city than we find in the day, and determine where we might be of service." The Emperor believed that the first duty of any leader was to serve the weakest of his people, and he made an effort to pay attention to the city around him, lest someone fall through the cracks and be lost. Clearly he was a loon. "Calm, good fellows," he said.

But calm was not coming. The smell of cat was tall in the air and the men were jacked on java. Lazarus barked once and bolted down the sidewalk, followed closely by his bug-eyed brother-in-arms, the two descending on a dark figure that lay curled up around a cardboard sign on the traffic island at Battery Street, beneath a massive bronze statue that depicted four muscular men working a metal press. It had always looked to the Emperor like four guys molesting a stapler.

Bummer and Lazarus sniffed the man beneath the statue, sure that he had to have a cat concealed among his rags somewhere. When a cold nose hit a hand, the Emperor saw the man move, and breathed a sigh of relief. With a closer look, the Emperor recognized him as William with the Huge Cat. They knew each other to nod hello, but because of racial tensions between their respective canine and feline companions, the two had never become friends.

The Emperor knelt on the man's cardboard sign and jostled him. "William, wake up." William groaned and an empty Johnny Walker Black bottle slid out of his overcoat.

"Dead drunk, perhaps," said the Emperor, "but fortunately, not dead."

Bummer whimpered. Where was the cat?

The Emperor propped William up against the concrete base of the statue. William groaned. "He's gone. Gone. Gone. Gone."

The Emperor picked up the empty scotch bottle and sniffed it. Yes, it had recently held scotch. "William, was this full?"

William grabbed the cardboard sign off the sidewalk and propped it in his lap. "Gone," he said. The sign read I AM POOR AND SOMEONE STOLE MY HUGE CAT.

"My deepest sympathies," said the Emperor. He was about to ask William how he had managed to procure a fifth of top-shelf scotch, when he heard a long, feline yowl echo down the street, and looked up to see a huge shaved cat, in a red sweater, heading their way. He managed to catch hold of Bummer and Lazarus's collars before they darted after the cat, and dragged them away from William. The huge cat leapt into William's lap and the two commenced a drunken reunion embrace that involved quantities of purring, baby talk, and drool, enough that the Emperor had to fight down a little nausea at the sight of it.

Even the royal hounds had to look away, the two realizing instinctively that a maudlin and shaved, thirty-five-pound cat in a red sweater was clearly above their pay grade. There was just no doggy protocol for it, and presently they began to turn in circles on the sidewalk, as if looking for a good place to feign a nap.

"William, I believe someone has shaved your cat," said the Emperor.

"That would be me," said Tommy Flood as he came around the side of the traffic island, scaring the bejeezus out of everyone there. A pale and delicate hand reached out from behind the island, grabbed the collar of Tommy's coat, and snatched him back around the corner as if he were a rag doll.

"Tommy?" called the Emperor. The big man stalked around the concrete art bunker. Bummer and Lazarus had headed back down the street toward the waterfront, as if they had just seen a particularly fetching porterhouse steak hopping around down there that needed to be investigated. The Emperor found his friend C. Thomas Flood, held tight in the clutches of his girlfriend, Jody Stroud, the vampire, who had her hand pressed tightly over Tommy's mouth and was furiously giving him noogies with the knuckle of her other hand. There was a hollow popping each time she connected, and muted cries from Tommy.

"Jody, I must insist that you unhand the young man," insisted the Emperor.

And she did. Tommy twisted out of her grasp.

"Ow!" Tommy said, rubbing his head.

"Sorry," Jody said. "Couldn't be helped."

"I thought you were going to leave the city with that fiend," said the Emperor. He had been there, with the royal hounds and Tommy's crew from the Safeway, when they'd done battle with the old vampire at the St. Francis Yacht Club.

"Well, yes, of course. He left already and I'm going to join him," Jody said. "Just like I promised Inspector Rivera. But I wanted to make sure that Tommy was going to be all right before I left."

The Emperor liked Jody, and had been a little disappointed when he found that she was a bloodsucking fiend, but she was a pleasant girl nonetheless, and had always been generous with treats for the men, despite Bummer's dropping into yapping fits in her presence. "Well then, I suppose that will have to do," said the Emperor. "It appears that our young writer does require some adult supervision before being set loose on the City."

"Hey, I do okay," Tommy said.

"You shaved the cat," said the Emperor, raising a wild eyebrow that looked like a gray squirrel with a Mohawk.

"I—uh, we were testing him out, to see if I should get a cat to keep me company after Jody leaves." He looked at Jody, who nodded enthusiastically while trying to look wide-eyed and sincere.

"And . . . and," Tommy continued, "I was chewing some

bubble gum, you know, the kind that you can blow really big bubbles with—well, long story short, before I knew it, Chet had lunged at one of my bubbles and was completely covered with bubble gum."

Jody quit nodding and just stared at him.

"So you shaved him," the Emperor added.

Now it was Tommy's turn to nod and look sincere. "Regrettably."

Jody was nodding again, too. "Regrettably," she echoed.

"I see," said the Emperor. They certainly seemed sincere. "Well, the sweater was considerate."

"My idea," Jody said. "You know so he doesn't get chilled. It's actually my sweater. Tommy washed it and put it in the dryer, so it's a little too small for me."

"And don't think it was easy getting a cat that size into a sweater," Tommy said. "It was like trying to dress a ball of razor wire. I'm cut to ribbons." He pushed his sleeves up to expose his forearms, which were distinctly not cut to ribbons. They were, in fact, unmarked, if a little pale.

"Well, good show, then," the Emperor said, backing away. "The men and I will be on our way, then."

"Do you guys need anything, Your Majesty?" Jody asked.

"No, no, we have been most fortunate this evening. Most fortunate indeed."

"Well, take care, then," Jody said, even as the Emperor backed around the corner and headed up the street.

She can be deceptively pleasant for a blood-drinking agent of evil, the Emperor thought.

Bummer and Lazarus were almost out of sight, four blocks ahead. They had known, the rascals. The Emperor was disgusted with himself, leaving William there like that, at the mercy of the fiends. There was no telling what they might do, the two of them, but he felt fear chilling his spine and he couldn't make himself turn around. Perhaps they wouldn't hurt poor William. After all, they had been sweet children in life, both of them. And even in her current state, Jody had shown a certain quality of mercy by waiting until now to turn Tommy. Still, he had a city he was responsible for, and he could not shirk that responsibility.

It was a long walk to the Marina Safeway, but he had to reach it before the night crew left. As knavish as they might be, they were the only people in his city who actually had experience hunting vampires.

Bite him," Tommy said. He was standing over the huge cat guy, who had passed out again under the statue.

Jody shook her head and shuddered. "He's filthy. Don't tell me you can't smell that." Since she'd become a vampire, she'd only experienced nausea when she tried to eat real food, but she was nauseated now, despite the hunger grating in her core.

"Here, I'll clean off a spot." Tommy fished a tissue out of his coat pocket, licked it, and cleaned a spot on William's neck. "There. Go for it."

"Yuck."

"I bit the cat," Tommy said. "You said yourself that you were starving."

"But he's hammered." Jody said. She was taking little steps in place like a little kid who has to pee.

"Bite him."

"Quit saying 'bite him.' I don't think of it like that."

"How do you think of it?"

"I don't really think of it. It's sort of an animal thing."

"Oh, I see," Tommy said. "Bite him before some cops come along and take him away and you miss your chance."

"Ewww," Jody said, kneeling beside William. Chet the huge cat looked up at her from William's lap, then put his head down and closed his eyes. (Blood loss had mellowed him.) Jody pushed William's head aside and reared back with her mouth open wide as her fangs extended. She closed her eyes and bit.

"See how easy that was," Tommy said.

Jody glared at him without letting go, her breath rasping through her nose as she fed. She thought, *I should have hit him harder when I had the chance.* Finally, when she felt she'd taken enough to sustain her, but not enough to hurt the huge cat guy, she pulled away, sat down, and looked up at Tommy.

"You've got a little—" Tommy gestured to the corner of her mouth.

She wiped her mouth with her hand, came away with a little lipstick and a little blood. She looked at William's neck. It was sort of a dirt-gray color, with a white spot rimmed in lipstick. The punctures from her fangs had already healed, but the lipstick sort of stood out like a target. She reached over and wiped the lipstick off with her palm, then wiped her palm off on the huge cat's sweater. Chet purred. William snored. Jody climbed to her feet.

"How was it?" Tommy asked.

"How do you think it was? It was necessary."

"Well, I mean, when you used to bite me it was kind of a sexual thing."

"Oh, right," Jody snapped. "I planned all this because I wanted to fuck the huge cat guy." She was feeling a little light-headed for some reason.

"Sorry. We should get him off of Market Street," Tommy said, "before he gets robbed or arrested. He's got to have some of the money left. That much alcohol would have killed him."

"The hell do you care, writer boy? You shaved and ate his cat. Or was that a sexual thing?" She was definitely feeling light-headed.

"That was a mutual—"

"Oh, bullshit. Bite him. See how sexual it is. Get a taste of that down-home human hemoglobin goodness, Tommy. Don't be a wuss," Jody said. Well, he *was* being a wuss.

Tommy stepped back. "You're drunk."

"And you're being a wuss," Jody said. "Wuss, wuss, wuss."

"Help me. Take his feet. There's a sheltered alcove over

by the Federal Reserve building across the street. He can sleep it off there."

Jody bent to take the guy's feet, but they seemed to move as she reached for them, and when she corrected, she missed, and fell forward, catching herself so that she was on all fours with her ass in the air.

"Yeah, that worked," Tommy said. "How about you take Chet and I'll carry the huge cat guy?"

"Whadever, Mr. Wussyman," Jody said. Maybe she was a little tipsy. In the old days, prevampire days, she'd tried to stay away from alcohol, because it turned out that she was sort of an obnoxious drunk. Or that's what her ex-friends had told her.

Tommy picked up Chet the huge cat, who squirmed as he held him out to Jody. "Take him."

"You are not the head vampire here," Jody said.

"Fine," Tommy said. He slung Chet under his arm and, in a single movement, scooped up the huge cat guy and threw him over his shoulder with the other arm. "Careful crossing the street," Tommy called back to her as he crossed.

"Ha!" Jody said. "I am a finely tuned predator. I am a superbeing. I—" And at that point she bounced her forehead off a light pole with a dull twang and was suddenly lying on her back looking at the streetlights above her, which kept going out of focus, the bastards.

"I'll be back to get you," Tommy called.

He's so sweet, Jody thought.

Do Animals Get the Blues?

Clint was the only one of the Animals still left at the Marina Safeway. He was tall, with a wild mop of dark hair and thick, horn-rimmed glasses that were held together with medical tape, and he had a look of deep panic on his face. He'd been trying to keep the store together for nearly a week with only a couple of stock boys from the day crew, and a porter from a temp service (even Gustavo, the Mexican porter with five kids, had taken off with the Animals), but now a huge order had come in on the truck and he knew he needed professionals. He dialed Tommy's number for the fifth time that night. It was four in the morning, but Tommy was their leader—and perhaps the best frozen-turkey bowler the world had ever known. He knew what it meant to be an Animal; he would be awake.

The machine beeped. Clint said, "Dude, they're all gone. I need your help. It's just me, some temps, and the Lord tonight." Clint had been recently reborn after five years in a drug-induced haze. He swore that the Lord would forever be on his night crew. "The guys took off for Vegas. Call me. No, just bring your box cutter and come to work. I'm buried."

Once they had been nine strong, the Animals. Nine men, all under the age of twenty-five, left alone in a grocery store for eight hours with only Tommy to supervise them. They'd been given their name by the day manager, who had come in one morning to find them drunk, hanging from the giant Safeway letters on the front of the store, pelting one another with marshmallows. Tommy had recruited them to fight the old vampire. They'd found the vampire, sleeping inside a vault on his yacht, and they had also found his art collection. After selling it for ten cents on the dollar, each of them had netted a hundred thousand dollars. Tommy went home with Jody, Clint went home to pray for the vampire's soul. Simon had been killed. The rest of the Animals headed for Vegas.

Clint hung up the phone, then sat down hard in the manager's chair. It was too much responsibility. The weight of it would drive him over the edge. Even now he could hear dogs barking in his head.

"Front door," the temp night porter called over the half wall of the office.

Clint stood up to see the Emperor and his dogs at the double electric doors. He grabbed the keys, disarmed the alarm, and opened the door. The Boston terrier shot by him, heading for the beef-jerky display.

"Your Majesty," Clint said. "You're out of breath."

The big man held his chest as he panted. "Gather the troops, young man. C. Thomas Flood has been turned to a bloodsucking fiend. Gather your weapons, we must charge again into the breach."

"It's just me and noobs," Clint said. "Did you say that Tommy's a vampire?"

"Indeed. I saw him not two hours ago. As pale as death."

"Well, that's not good."

"Your talent for stating the obvious is unprecedented, young man."

"Come in." Clint stepped away from the door. "We are going to need to pray on this."

"Well, there's a start," said the Emperor.

"Then I need to call Tommy and tell him to never mind about coming to work," Clint said.

"Splendid," said the Emperor, without a hint of sarcasm. "I believe we've achieved a new level of doomed."

"You've always been good to me," Jody said.

"Well, I try," Tommy said.

He was going up the narrow stairway to their loft. She was slung over his shoulder, her forehead bounced off his belt with every step. She seemed so light. Tommy was still amazed at his newfound strength. He'd carried her ten blocks already and he wasn't even feeling it. Well, he was a little tired of listening to her, but physically he wasn't fatigued at all.

"I can be such a bitch sometimes."

"That's not true," Tommy said. Yes, it was.

"Yes it is, yes it is. Yes I am. I am a total bitch sometimes."

Tommy stopped at the top of the steps and dug in his pocket for his keys.

"Well, maybe a little, but—"

"So I am a bitch? You're saying I'm a bitch?"

"Oh my God, is the sun never going to come up?"

"Listen, you're lucky to have me, you wuss."

"Yes I am," Tommy said.

"You are?"

He swung her over to her feet, then caught her before she went over backwards into the wall. She had a big goofy smile on her face. Sometime during the evening, blood had dripped down the front of her blouse and there was some smeared on her lip. She looked a little like she'd been punched out. Tommy tried to rub away the blood with his thumb. The cloud of alcohol breath she let go on him made him wince.

"I love you, Tommy." She fell into his arms.

"Right back at you, Jody."

"I'm sorry I gave you noogies. I'm still learning to harness my powers, you know."

"That's okay."

"And called you a wuss."

"No problem."

She licked the side of his neck, nipped at him. "Let's make love before the sun comes up."

Tommy looked over her shoulder at the destruction they had wrought on the loft the last time they'd done it, and he said something he never thought he would hear coming out of his own mouth. "I think I've had enough for tonight. Maybe we should just lock down."

"You think I'm fat, don't you?"

"No, you're perfect."

"It's because I'm fat." She pushed him away and stumbled into the bedroom, then tripped and tumbled face-first into the shredded remains of their bed. "And old," she added, although it was only through his acute vampire hearing that Tommy understood this, since she was speaking directly into the mattress. "Fat and old," she said.

"You're going to get whiplash from those mood swings, Red," Tommy said quietly as he climbed into bed with his clothes on.

Then he lay there beside her thinking about all that they had to do, about how they were going to have to find a place and move without going out during the day, and beyond that, just exactly how were they going to survive and stay hidden? The Emperor could tell. Tommy could tell he could tell. And as much as he liked the Emperor, it wasn't a good sign. And so even as he worried, and listened to his girlfriend yell at him, C. Thomas Flood became the first vampire in history to actually pray for the sun to come up.

A few minutes later, his prayers were answered, and the two of them went out.

Since becoming a vampire, Jody had always hated the way consciousness came on at dusk like the streetlights coming on. There was no groggy twilight between sleep and wakefulness, just "bam, welcome to the night, here's your to-do list." Not tonight. Tonight she got her twilight, her grogginess, and a headache as well. She sat upright in bed so fast she nearly somersaulted off the end, then, when her head didn't seem to follow her, she lay back down with such force that her pillow exploded, sending out a snowstorm of feathers to whirl around the room. She moaned and Tommy came bounding into the room.

"Hey," he said.

"Ouch," Jody said, grabbing her forehead with both hands as if to hold her brains in.

"That's new, huh? Vampire hangover?" Tommy waved some feathers out of the air in front of him.

"I feel like death warmed over," Jody said.

"Cute. I'll bet you're missing coffee right now."

"And aspirin. I've fed off of you when you'd been drinking. Why did it affect me now?"

"I think maybe the huge cat guy had a little more in his blood than I did. Anyway, I have a theory about that. We can test it later, when you feel better, but right now we have a ton of stuff we have to do. We've got to figure out the move. Clint called me from the store last night. Wanting me to work. Then he called back all freaked out, saying I shouldn't come in."

Tommy played the message for her. Twice.

"He knows," Jody said.

"Yeah, but how does he know?"

"Doesn't matter. He knows."

"Fuck!"

"Little bit softer now," Jody said, holding her hair like it was hurting her.

"Too loud?"

Jody nodded. "You know, for your notebook, Tommy. Vampire senses when you're hungover? Not so good."

"Really? That bad?"

"Your breath is nauseating me from across the room."

"Yeah, we need toothpaste."

"There's someone at the door?" Jody covered her ears. She could hear sneakers scraping the sidewalk from all the way downstairs.

"There is?"

The door buzzer sounded.

"Yep," she said.

Tommy ran to the front windows and looked down to the street.

"There's a Humvee limo out there that's about a block long."

"You'd better answer it," Jody said.

"Maybe we should just hide. Pretend we're not home."

"No, you need to get it," Jody said. She could hear the shuffling at the door, the rock and roll playing in the limo, the bong bubbling, lines being chopped on a CD case, and a male voice repeating the phrase "sweet blue titties" over and over like a mantra. She grabbed the pillow from Tommy's side of the bed and pulled it over her head. "Answer it, Tommy. It's the fucking Animals."

Dude," said Lash Jefferson, a wiry black man with a newly shaved scalp, wearing mirror shades. He pulled Tommy out of his doorway and hugged him furiously—crazed, back-slamming, good-to-see-you guy hugs. "We are so fucked, dude," Lash continued.

Tommy pushed away, trying to reconcile that he was glad to see his friend with the fact that Lash smelled like a beer-bar urinal filled with mackerel.

"I thought you guys went to Vegas," Tommy said.

"Yeah. Yeah. We did. Everyone's in the limo. It's just that I need to talk to you. Can we go inside?"

"No." Tommy almost said that Jody was sleeping, which had been his excuse for keeping the Animals out of his loft in the past, but Jody was supposed to have left town. "Step in the stairway, I've got something happening upstairs."

Lash nodded and looked over the top of his shades and bounced his eyebrows. His eyes were bloodshot and glazed over. Tommy could hear his heart racing. Coke or fear, he guessed. Both maybe.

"Look, dude," Lash said. "First thing, we need to borrow some money."

"What? You guys have over a hundred grand each from the art we sold."

"Yeah, we did. We had a big weekend."

Tommy figured in his head. "You guys blew over six hundred grand in what—four days?"

"No," Lash said. "No, not all of it. We're not completely broke."

"Then why do you need to borrow money?"

"Just twenty grand or so, to get us through to tomorrow," Lash said. "Luckily I almost have my MBA and have mad business skills. Otherwise we'd have been broke yesterday."

Tommy nodded. Twenty grand was about six months' salary for him at the Safeway. He'd been a little intimidated by Lash's almost-MBA up until now. Now he was just worried that Lash would be able to tell he had changed. He said, "So, like you were saying, you're fucked."

"We were doing fine, only down like ten grand each, until we met Blue." Lash looked at the ceiling wistfully, like it was a distant memory he was trying to conjure, instead of something that had happened a couple of nights ago.

"Blue?"

"You know that group they have in Vegas? The Blue Men?"

"Yeah, the guys who paint themselves blue and pound on pipes and stuff?" Tommy was lost.

"Yeah," Lash said. "Well, it turns out there are blue women, too. Or at least there's one. And dude, she's sucking us dry."

In the back seat of the limo, Blue held Barry's face between her boobs, snugly enough to keep him under control, but not so snug that he couldn't breathe. While the other Animals had drunk, smoked, and fucked themselves into a zombielike stupor—and now lay sprawled about the glittery interior of the limo—Barry had opted to do two hits of XTC, a line of coke, and a bong load of sticky skunk weed, which had put his brain into some sort of redundant tribal loop that had him kneeling naked before her, chanting "sweet blue titties" for the last twenty minutes. She just couldn't take it anymore, so she had grabbed his curl-fringed bald head and pulled his face into her cleavage just to shut him up. Mercifully, he had gone quiet, because she really didn't want to suffocate him as long as he still had money.

It takes a meandering road of wrong turns to take a girl from being the milky-skinned Cheddar princess of Fond du Lac, Wisconsin, to a blue-dyed call girl turning tricks at downtown casinos in Vegas, but Blue would be damned if she'd add yet another wrong turn by smothering a golden goose between her proportionally improbable silicon joy orbs. The Animals were her way out, and if she had to stay in character as an Alien Pleasure Unit or a blueberry muffin to keep them on the hook, she would.

Blue was a method hooker. Early in her adventures, after she'd left cocktailing due to a propensity for spilling drinks, and before she'd begun stripping, where her lack of balance was mitigated by the presence of a sturdy pole, she had a short career acting in low-budget porn. She befriended a promising actress named Lotta Vulva, who gave her a book on the Stanislavski Method. "If you can find your sense memory," Lotta said, "it will keep you from barfing on the actors. Directors hate that." The "Method" had served Blue well since then, as it allowed her to calculate betting odds or figure her checkbook while her character was performing acts that she herself would have found unpleasant or outright disgusting. (How much better to reside in her sense memory of the budding Cheddar princess, coaxing the hearty, whole-milk goodness from the udders of a Holstein, than to face the harshly lit reality of her actions?)

After six months Blue was driven out of the film business by a "defect" one director called "not enough tits to fill a shot glass," which no amount of Method was able to remedy. She returned to cocktailing, albeit at a strip club, where she seldom had to carry more than one ten-dollar beer at a time, until she saved enough money for breast-augmentation surgery and made her way to the pole. She danced her way through her twenties, before she was driven off the stage by younger, more gravity-resistant girls, and because she had skipped personal typing class in high school and had therefore besmirched her permanent record, she landed in the employ of an outcall escort service.

"I feel like I'm doing Domino's delivery blow jobs," Blue told her roommate. "Satisfaction in twenty minutes or less or your money back. And the agency is taking most of the money. I'll never get out of this business at this rate."

"You need a gimmick," said her roommate, a cocktail waitress at the Venetian. "Like those Blue Men guys in the show. I swear they'd just be a bunch of frat boys beating on garbage cans if they weren't painted blue."

And so it began. The fallen Cheddar princess of Fond du Lac found some semipermanent skin dye, opened credit-card deposit accounts, had some pictures taken, placed ads in all the free sleaze rags around the city, and Blue was born. It wasn't as if she wouldn't have been able to make a living without the gimmick—most guys will shag a snake if you hold it steady for them. But it turned out they would pay a lot for the exotica of a blue woman.

She worked as much as she could handle, and her savings had climbed to the point where she could actually see the possibility of an exit. But about that same time, she realized that by going blue, she had opted out of the pipe dream of every hooker, stripper, and telemarketer: the rich guy who would take her away from it all. The whale who would drop a fortune on her to become his personal pet. There would be no big score for the blue chick, or so she thought, until the Animals called her in for a combination strip show and fuckfest. Where they got the money didn't matter. What mattered was that they had a lot of it, and it appeared that they would keep giving it to her until it was all gone. She had nearly half a million dollars in her makeup case, and Blue—the *character* Blue—could put up with a lot of attention from the Animals while *she* hid in the back of her mind and formulated an investment strategy. The tall, skinny one, Drew, had opened the hotel-room door and said, "Hi. We discussed it and agreed that when we were kids, we all really wanted to bone a Smurf."

"I get that a lot," said Blue.

Ψe just wanted to bone a Smurf," Lash said.

"Understandably," said Tommy.

"She's really nice," Lash said.

"Important quality in a ho," said Tommy.

"But now we can't seem to quit."

"So you want me to do what—hold an intervention?"

"No, you're our leader. We look to you for other things. So we want you to give us money so we can keep partying, and pay our rents and stuff."

"And when all of *my* money is gone, then I can intervene."

"Sure, if you feel you have to," said Lash. "How's your credit?"

"Lash, are you high?"

"Of course."

"Right. Of course. What was I thinking?" Tommy was relaxing now about Lash noticing that he was a vampire. Clearly the former stewards of Safeway night stock, in addition to being wasted, had gone collectively out of their minds. "Lash, I don't almost have an MBA like you, but isn't there sort of some business principle that you're violating? I mean, isn't there a class about not spending your rent money on hookers or something?"

"Step off, Flood," Lash said. "You hooked up with a vampire."

"She was cute," Tommy said.

"An important quality in a vampire," Lash said, looking over the top of his shades.

"She had sex with me," Tommy countered. He wanted to say that she was nice, but Lash had already used "nice" for his blue hooker.

"I think I've made my point," Lash said. "Give me your money."

"You haven't made your point. You completely haven't made your point." Tommy reared back as if to punch Lash in the chest, as the Animals did to one another all the time, but remembered that now he might crush some of the Animals' ribs. Instead, he said, "Don't make me cave in your skinny chest, bee-yotch."

"Your redheaded vampire kung fu is no match for the fearsome blue booty kung fu." Lash made a howling chicken noise and waved his hands around as he fell back into a fighting stance, then went right back onto his ass on the steps. He laughed until he choked, then coughed and said, "Seriously, dude, if you don't give us money, we're going to be totally broke in about six hours. I did the math."

"You could go back to work," Tommy said. "Clint called here last night. They're buried at the store. They need night stockers."

"No?" Lash said, pulling down his sunglasses.

"Yes," Tommy said.

"Then we're not fired?"

"Evidently not," Tommy said.

"That's it. We could go back to work. That's what we'll tell her. We have to go back to work."

"Why didn't you just tell her to go away before she did you all the way here from Vegas."

"We didn't want to be rude."

"Oh, right. Well then, off you go."

Lash pushed to his feet and steadied himself on the banister long enough to look Tommy in the eye. "You okay? You look pale."

"I'm heartbroken and shit," Tommy said. He hated it, but Lash's bloodshot eyes peering over the sunglasses had actually given him a twinge of hunger.

"Right." Lash went through the security door.

Tommy watched him as he paused at the rear door of the limo and turned back.

"You need some blue nooky to cheer you up?" Lash asked. "Our treat."

"No, I'm good," Tommy said.

"All for one, and whatnot," Lash said.

"Appreciate it." Tommy shrugged. "Heartbroken."

"Okay." Lash threw open the limo's door and two of the

Animals, Drew and Troy Lee, rolled out onto the pavement, followed by a great storm cloud of pot smoke.

"Fuck, dude. Did you know there was a door there?" said Drew, the scruffy thin one.

"Look," said Troy Lee, the Asian guy who actually did know kung fu. "Hey, look, it's fearless leader."

"Go to work," Tommy said. "It's only seven. You guys can get sobered up and be completely ready for your shift at eleven." *Not a chance,* Tommy thought.

"Yeah, we can do it," Lash said, peeking into the limo. "Hey, Barry, climb off, motherfucker, I'm up next, then it's Jeff's turn. I put it on the board. Blue, don't let him do that to your ear, baby, you won't hear for a month."

Tommy closed the security door and sat down hard on the steps, hiding his face in his hands to try to make it all go away. The Animals had been his friends, his crew. They had taken him in when he was alone in the city, made him their leader, and if he got the tone of Clint's second message right, in about four hours, when they got to the store, they were going to turn on him.

The List

While Jody showered, Tommy made a list.

Feed
Laundry
New Apartment
Toothpaste
Sweet Monkey Love
Windex
Dispose of Vampire
Minion

"What do we need an onion for?" Jody asked. She was having a little trouble getting her vision to focus.

"Minion, minion," Tommy said.

"Mint-flavored onion? Why do we need that?"

"A minion! Someone who can move around during the day who can help us out. Like I was for you."

"Oh, my bitch."

Tommy dropped his list. "Nuh-uh."

Jody picked it up and walked over to the kitchen counter where the coffee machine stood. "I would sell my soul for a big cup of joe."

"I was not your bitch," Tommy said.

"Right, right, right. Whatever. So how long do we have to do this list?"

"I checked the almanac. Sunrise is at six fifty-three, so we have about twelve hours. It's almost the solstice, so we get a lot of darkness."

"Solstice? Oh my God, it's almost Christmas."

"So?"

"Hello? Shopping?"

"Hello? We have an excuse. We're dead."

"My mother doesn't know that. I have to find something for her that she'll disapprove of. And your family—"

"Oh my God! Christmas. I was supposed to go home to Indiana for Christmas. We need to redo the list."

"You do it. I'm going to dry my hair," Jody said.

The new list read:

Christmas Presents
Call Home
Feed

Minion (not our Bitch)
Hot Monkey Love
Windex
Write Literature
Dispose of Creepy Old Vampire
New Apartment
Laundry
Toothpaste

"I think you should take monkey love off of the list," Jody said. "What if we lose the list and someone finds it?"

"Well I think 'dispose of Creepy Old Vampire' would be a little more embarrassing, don't you?"

"You're right, cut monkey love and change 'vampire' to 'Elijah.'" Jody tapped the list with a pen. "And take off Windex and put in 'buy coffee.'"

"We can't drink coffee."

"We can smell it. Tommy, I desperately need coffee. It's like the blood hunger, only, you know, more civilized."

"Speaking of blood hunger—"

"Yeah, you'd better move that up the list."

"And add a bottle of whiskey. You're going to have to buy it."

"Sorry, writer boy, but we're doing this stupid list together."

"I'm not old enough to buy liquor."

Jody stepped away from him and shuddered. "That's right. Isn't it?"

"Yep," Tommy said, nodding—trying to look wide-eyed and innocent.

"Well, okay then. I should have checked IDs before picking my bitch."

"Hey!"

"Kidding. What are you going to do with a bottle of whiskey anyway?"

"Check something else off the list," Tommy said. "I have an idea. Get your purse."

"What did the Animals want, anyway?"

"Twenty grand."

"I hope you told them to fuck themselves."

"They did that already."

"Did they suspect, you know, about what you are now?"

"Not yet. Lash said I looked a little pale. I sent them to the store. If Clint knows, well—"

"Oh, good move. Maybe we should just take out an ad. 'Young vampire couple seeks angry village people to hunt them down and kill them.'"

"Ha. Village people. Funny. Put self-tanning lotion on the list. I think the pale thing is giving me away."

At seven in the evening, three days before Christmas, Union Square was awash in shoppers. There was a Santa's Village set up in the raised square, with a line of children and parents that wound five hundred deep through a labyrinth of red velvet cattle gates. Around the square, the street performers, who would normally have knocked off around five, lined the granite steps up to the square. A juggler here, a sleight-of-hand guy there, a half-dozen "robots"—people painted silver and gold who would move in machine-jerk rhythm for the drop of a coin or a bill—and even a couple of human statues. Jody's favorite was a gold guy in a business suit, who stood motionless for hours on end, as if he'd been frozen in midstep on the way to work. There was a small hole in his briefcase into which people stuffed bills and dropped coins after photographing him or trying to make him flinch.

"This guy used to freak me out," Tommy whispered. "But now I can see him breathing and the aura thing."

"I watched him for a whole lunch hour one time and he never moved," Jody said. "In the summer, you know he has to be suffering in that painted suit." Suddenly she shuddered at the thought of Elijah, the old vampire, still encased in bronze back at the loft. Yes, he had killed her, technically, but in a way he'd just opened a door for her, a door that, no matter how bizarre, was immediate, vital, and passionate. And yes, he'd done it for his amusement, he'd said, but also because he was lonely.

She wound her arm into Tommy's and kissed him on the cheek.

"What was that for?"

"Because you're here," she said. "What's first on the list?"

"Christmas presents."

"Skip down."

"Sweet monkey love."

"Yeah, we'll do it in the Santa's Workshop window at Macy's."

"Really?"

"No, not really."

"Okay, then we need liquor."

Jody snatched the list out of his hand so quickly that most people wouldn't have even seen her move. "You are no longer in charge of the list. We're getting me a new leather jacket."

I AM HOMELESS AND SOMEONE SHAVED MY HUGE CAT. William had changed his sign. Chet the huge cat was still wearing Jody's sweater. He eyed the two vampires suspiciously as they approached.

Tommy held the bottle of Johnny Walker out to William. "Merry Christmas."

William took the liquor and squirreled it away in his coat. "Most people just give money," he said.

"We're cutting out the middleman," Jody said. "How are you feeling today?"

"Great, why? Really good, you know, considering that I'm homeless and you guys shaved my cat."

"You were pretty hammered last night."

"Yeah, but I feel great today."

"That's how it used to affect me," Tommy said. "Remember. Kind of energizing."

Jody waved Tommy away. "You didn't get light-headed or anything?" Jody asked.

"I was a little hungover when I woke up, but I was fine after a couple of cups of coffee."

"Fuck!" Jody spat. Then she held her head.

"Calm," Tommy said, patting her shoulder. "Dr. Flood will make it all better. Maybe."

Jody growled, just loud enough for Tommy to hear.

"Ya know," said William, when there was a break in the pedestrian traffic and he didn't have to concentrate on looking pathetic, "I'm flush for cash, but since you're in the Christmas spirit, I'd still go for a look at Red's hooters."

"Bite me, dirtbag," Jody said as she rolled up on William.

"Honey." Tommy caught the back of her newly purchased red leather jacket, just in case. They'd never know if his idea was going to work if Jody snapped the bum's neck.

"I will not be sexually harassed by the entrée."

"Something you ate isn't agreeing with you?" Tommy grinned at her when she looked back at him, but the fire went out of her eyes.

"You can just cross sweet monkey love right off your list," Jody said.

"Jeez, what a bitch," said William. "Her time of the month?"

Tommy quickly wrapped his arms around Jody, lifted her off her feet, and carried her a few steps around the corner, even as she squirmed.

"Let me go, I'm not going to hurt him."

"Good."

"Much."

"That's what I thought," Tommy said, still holding her tight. "Why don't you head over to the Walgreens and I'll finish up with the huge cat guy?"

A family of Christmas shoppers smiled as they passed them, thinking they were young lovers indulging in a public display of affection. The father whispered "Get a room" under his breath to his wife, which a normal person wouldn't have heard.

"Count your lucky stars, buddy, we almost did it in the Santa's Workshop window. Hot, sweaty elf sex—in front of the kids. The kids would have liked that, huh?"

The father hurried his family on down the street.

"Nice," Jody said. "Way to stay under the radar."

"Well, you know, I like to stay sharp," Tommy said. Because he was nineteen and had only started having sex regularly since he met Jody, he still thought he had some sort of secret knowledge that was unavailable to other people. *How can they possibly be thinking about anything else?* he thought in the private part of his mind.

"I'll bet it smells like peppermint," Tommy said.

"What?"

"Elf sex."

"Would you please put me down."

"Okay, but don't hurt the huge cat guy."

"I'm fine. I'll meet you at the drugstore in five minutes. This had better work."

"Five minutes," Tommy said. "Cinnamon. Maybe it smells like cinnamon."

The pale couple stalked the aisles of the Walgreens, having a great time dismissing the crass accoutrements of bourgeois American life, and generally scoffing at all the conventions of traditional culture. They were elite, after all. Special. Chosen—if you will—if only by the nature of their heightened sensitivities and superior sensibilities. They both claimed the ability to look past the facade put on by most people, and see the very depths of the human soul. Strange, then, that they didn't see it coming when the skinny guy in a flannel shirt popped around the corner in front of them.

"Let's ask these guys," Flannel said. "They look like heroin addicts."

Jared White Wolf and Abby Normal backpedaled from the eyeliner display where they'd been looking for something hypoallergenic. Abby's eyes had been watering all night, causing her makeup to run and giving her more of a sad-clown-of-life look than she was going for.

Jared hid behind Abby, just a little, which was awkward, since he was nearly a foot taller than she. The guy in flannel was joined by a beautiful, pale redhead, carrying an armload of toiletries. *What amazing hair,* Abby thought, looking at the long red tresses. *I'd give anything for hair like that.*

"Tommy, leave these poor people alone," said the red-head.

"No, wait." Flannel turned to Abby and smiled. "Do you guys know where they keep the syringes?"

Abby looked at Jared, who looked at the guy in flannel. "Well, you can't just buy them," Jared said. He was fiddling with the leather straps on his bondage pants, looking coy. Abby slapped his hand.

"You need a prescription to buy syringes," Abby said.

"Do you really think I look like a heroin addict?" Jared threw his bangs out of his face dramatically. His head was shaved except for his bangs, which reached to his chin, specifically so he could throw them out of his face dramatically. "I was, like, thinking that maybe I should bulk up. You know, eat and stuff, but—"

"Well, thanks," said Flannel Shirt. The redhead moved off down the aisle. "I was going to try some heroin, but if you can't buy needles, well, there you go. See you guys. Nice shirt, by the way."

Abby looked down at her T-shirt, black, of course, with the image of a poet taken from a nineteenth-century etching. "Like you even know who it is."

" 'She walks in beauty, like the night,' " quoted the flannel-shirt guy. He winked at her, then grinned. "Byron's a hero of mine. See ya."

He turned and started to walk away. Abby reached out and snagged his sleeve. "Hey, there are needle exchange programs all over town. They're listed in the *Bay Guardian*."

"Thanks," said flannel. He turned and Abby grabbed him again.

"We're going to be at the Glas Kat. There's a Goth club tonight. Five-hundred block of Fourth Street. I know a dealer there. You know, for your heroin."

The flannel-shirt guy nodded, and looked at Byron's picture on her shirt again, then at her face. *Fucksocks. He's so looking at my streaking eye makeup.*

"Thanks, milady," said Flannel Shirt. And he was gone, off over the dark moors of the tampon aisle.

"What was that about?" whined Jared. "He's so, so *Happy Days.*" Jared White Wolf spent a lot of time watching *Nick at Nite* when he wasn't brooding or fussing with his appearance.

Abby walked into the flap of Jared's black duster and pounded his slight chest with her palms. "Didn't you see. Didn't you see?"

"What, you acting like a complete ho?"

"He had fangs," Abby said.

"Well, so do I," Jared said, reaching into his pocket and pulling out a pair of perfect, dentistry-quality vampire fangs. "Duh, everybody does."

"Yeah, but his grew! I saw them. Let's go," Abby said, pulling Jared White Wolf by his great bat-wing lapels. "I have to change into something hot before we go to the club."

"Wait, I want to get some Halls. My throat is raw from all the cloves we smoked last night."

"Hurry." The buckles of Abby's black platform boots

jangled as she dragged her friend past the lipsticks and hair products before he could get interested.

"Okay," said Jared, "but if I don't meet a cute guy to-night, you have to stay up all night and hold me while I cry."

You should try black lipstick sometime," Tommy said to Jody as they approached their building, their arms loaded with packages. He was still thinking about the kids at the drugstore. It was the first time since tenth grade that he'd used his knowledge of Romantic poetry. For a while he'd tried molding himself into the tragic Romantic hero, brooding and staring clench-jawed off into space as he composed dark verse in his head. But it turned out that trying to appear tragic in Incontinence, Indiana, was re-dundant, and his mother kept shouting at him and making him forget his rhymes. "Tommy, if you keep grinding your teeth like that, they'll wear away and you'll have to have dentures like Aunt Ester." Tommy only wished his beard was as heavy as Aunt Ester's—then he could stare out over the moors while he stroked it pensively.

"Yeah," Jody said, "because I need to make it more ob-vious that I'm an undead creature that feeds on the blood of the living."

"You make it sound so sordid."

"No, I meant it in a nice way."

"Oh."

"Because it's not like people wouldn't understand if they found out we were vampires, because we slipped up and, oh, I don't know, UNSHEATHED OUR FANGS IN THE FUCKING DRUGSTORE!"

Tommy almost dropped his packages. She hadn't said a word about that all night. He'd hoped she hadn't noticed. "It was an accident."

"You called that girl 'milady.'"

"She was impressed with my Byron."

"Yeah, well, your Byron was probably sticking out a little, too, wasn't he?"

"It wasn't like that."

"You drooled." Jody paused at their security door and dug into her jacket for her key.

Tommy stepped around her. "I'm still new at this. I think I'm doing pretty well. My ghastly pallor obviously impressed the lady at the needle exchange." He reached into his bag and fanned out a handful of sterile-wrapped and capped syringes.

"Congratulations, you can now pass as an HIV-positive heroin addict."

"*Très chic.*" He grinned like he imagined a sexy Italian man-whore might.

"Who drools in public," Jody said.

Damn, she's immune to my sexy Italian man-whore grin, Tommy thought. He said, "Be nice, I'm new. My lips don't fit together right when my fangs are out."

She turned the key and swung the door open. There,

passed out on the landing, was William the huge cat guy and sleeping on his chest, Chet the huge cat.

"I told you it would work," Tommy said.

Jody stepped into the stairwell and closed the door behind her. "You go first."

Fifteen minutes later, as he placed five syringes full of blood in their refrigerator, Tommy said, "This vampire thing is going to be great."

He'd had a moment when he'd bitten William—not just getting over the idea of being that close to someone who smelled that nasty, but also being close to another man period. But after cleaning William's neck with an alcohol swab they'd gotten from the drugstore, and consoling himself that most literary vampires seemed sexually ambivalent anyway, the blood hunger pushed him through.

He was feeling more relaxed, now that they had the food problem solved—for a while, anyway. If his friends didn't kill them in the next couple of days, he might even enjoy life as a vampire. Then he turned to Jody and frowned. "But I can't help but think that it may be wrong, taking advantage of a homeless alcoholic."

"We could just hunt and kill people," Jody said cheerfully. She had a little crust of William's blood in the corner of her mouth. Tommy licked his thumb and wiped it away.

"We did give him a nice sweater for his huge shaved cat," Tommy said.

"I loved that sweater," Jody said. "And we are giving him a warm landing to sleep on," she added, diving onto Tommy's rationalization dog pile.

"And if we only take a little bit each day, he'll actually feel better. I know I did."

"And we won't become alcoholics ourselves."

"How are you feeling, by the way?" Tommy said.

"Better. Hair of the dog. You?"

"Two-beer buzz, max. I'll be fine. You want to try the experiment?"

Jody checked her watch. "No time. We'll do it tomorrow night."

"Right. So, on to the list. Looks like hot monkey love."

"Tommy, we need to find a daytime person to help us. We have to move out of this place."

"I've been thinking about Alaska."

"Okay, good for you, but we still need to find a place to live where the Animals and Inspector Rivera can't find us."

"No, I'm thinking we should move to Alaska. For one thing, in the winter, it's dark for like twenty hours a day, so we'd have plenty of time. And I read somewhere that Eskimos put their old people out on the ice when they are ready to die. It would be like people were leaving snacks out for us."

"You're kidding."

"Eskimo Pies?" He grinned.

Jody put her hand on her hip and looked at him, her

mouth hanging open a little, as if she was waiting for something more. When it didn't come, she said, "Okay then, I'm going to change."

"Into a wolf?"

"Clothes, cadaver breath."

"I didn't know. I thought maybe you'd learned."

Tommy thought Alaska was a great idea. Just because she was a few years older, she always acted like his ideas were stupid. "The thing with William worked," he said defensively as he put away the supplies they'd bought at the drugstore.

"That was a good idea," Jody said from inside the closet. Now what? "Well, Alaska isn't a bad idea."

"Tommy, there's like nine people in all of Alaska. We'll stand out, don't you think?"

"No, everyone is pale there. They don't have sun for most of the year."

She came out of the closet wearing her little black cocktail dress and her strappy come-fuck-me pumps. "I'm ready," she said.

"Wow," Tommy said. He'd forgotten what they were talking about.

"You think the Ferrari-red lipstick would be too much?"

"No, I love the Ferrari-red lipstick on you." *Hot, sweet monkey love,* he thought. This was exactly why he loved her. In the midst of all of the pressure, the danger, really—she still took time to think of his feelings.

She lifted her breasts until they threatened to spill out of the plunging neckline of the dress. "Too much?"

"Perfect," Tommy said, walking toward her with his hands out. "Gimme."

She breezed past him into the bathroom. "Not for you. I need to get going."

"No, no, no," Tommy said. "Hot monkey love."

While Tommy watched from the doorway, Jody applied the Ferrari-red lipstick, checked it, then frowned and wiped it off, then grabbed a different tube off the vanity. "When I get back."

"Where?" Tommy said. Sexual frustration had reduced him to single syllables.

She turned to him with the new coat of maroon lipstick. "To get your minion."

"Not like that, you're not," Tommy said.

"This is how it works, Tommy. This is how I got you."

"Nuh-uh, you weren't wearing that when I met you."

"No, but the reason you pursued me is because you were interested in me sexually, wasn't it?"

"Well, that's how it started, but it's more than that now." And it was more, but that was no reason to leave him here all aroused and stuff.

She walked over to him and put her arms around him. He let his hands slip inside the low back of her dress. His pants were getting tight and he could feel the pressure of his fangs coming out.

"When I get back," she said. "I promise. You're my guy, Tommy. I picked you as my guy, forever. I'm going to find someone to help us move and do things for us in the day-time."

"They're just going to want to bone you, and when you don't do them, they'll turn on you."

"Not necessarily."

"Of course they will. Look at you."

"I'll figure it out, okay. I don't know how else to go about it."

"We could put an ad on Craig's List." (Craig's List was a classified Web site that had started in the Bay Area and was now the first place people checked for jobs, apartments, or nearly everything.)

"We're not putting an ad on Craig's List. Look, Tommy, we have more things to do than we have time. You can clean the loft and go get the laundry done and I'll get us an onion."

"Minion," he corrected.

"Whatever. I love you," she said.

Bitch! He was vanquished. *Unfair.* "I love you, too."

"I'll take one of the disposable cell phones you bought. You can call me anytime."

"They're not even activated yet."

"Well, get on that, buddy. The sooner I get out there and find someone, the sooner I can get back here for some hot monkey love."

She has absolutely no sense of ethics, he thought. *She's a monster. And yet, there she is, only a few dress straps from being naked.*

"Okay," he said. "Don't step on the huge cat on the way out."

Jody had only been gone twenty minutes before Tommy decided that cleaning and laundry sucked and that he could find a minion as well as she could, even if he didn't look as hot in a little black dress. He was careful not to wake Chet and William on his way out.

She Walks in Beauty

Jody moved down Columbus Avenue with long, runway-
model strides, feeling the windblown fog brush by her like
the chill ghosts of rejected suitors. What she could never
teach Tommy, what she could never really share with him,
was what it felt like to move from being a victim—afraid
of attack, the shadow around the corner, the footsteps
behind—to being the hunter. It wasn't the stalking or the
rush of taking down prey—Tommy would understand that.
It was walking down a dark street, late at night, knowing
that you were the most powerful creature there, that there
was absolutely nothing, no one, that could fuck with you.
Until she had been changed and had stalked the city as a
vampire, she never realized that virtually every moment
she had been there as a woman, she had been a little bit
afraid. A man would never understand. That was the reason for the dress and the shoes—not to attract a minion,

but to throw her sexuality out there on display, dare some underevolved male to make the mistake of seeing her as a victim. Truth be told, although it had come down to confrontation only once, and then she'd been wearing a baggy sweatshirt and jeans, Jody enjoyed kicking ass. She also enjoyed—every bit as much—just knowing that she could. It was her secret.

Without fear, the City was a great sensual carnival. There was no danger in anything she experienced, no anxiety. Red was red, yellow didn't mean caution, smoke didn't mean fire, and the mumbling of the four Chinese guys standing by their car just around the corner was just the click and twang of empty swinging dick talk. She could hear their hearts speed up when they saw her, could smell sweat and garlic and gun oil coming off them. She'd learned the smell of fear and imminent violence, too, of sexual arousal and surrender, although she'd have been hard-pressed to describe any of that. It was just there. Like color.

You know . . .

Try to describe blue.

Without mentioning blue.

See?

There weren't a lot of people out on the street at this time of night, but there were a few, spread up the length of Columbus: barhoppers, late diners just wrapping it up, college boys heading down to the strip clubs on Broadway, the exodus from Cobb's Comedy Club up the street, people giddy and so into the rhythm of laughing that they found one another and everything they saw hilarious—all of them vibrant, wearing auras of healthy pink life, trailing heat and perfume and cigarette smoke and gas held through long dinners. Witnesses.

The Chinese guys weren't harmless, by any means, but she didn't think they'd attack her, and she felt a twinge of regret. One of them, the one with the gun, yelled something at her in Cantonese—something sleazy and insulting, she could tell by the tone. She spun as she walked, smiled her biggest red carpet smile, and without breaking stride, said, "Hey, nano-dick, go fuck yourself!"

There was a lot of bluster and shuffle, the smart one, the one with fear coming off him, held his friend Nano-dick back, thus saving his life. *She must be a cop, or just crazy. Something's wrong.* They clustered around their tricked-out Honda and huffed out great breaths of testosterone and frustration. Jody grinned, and detoured up a side street, away from traffic.

"My night," she said to herself. "Mine."

Now off the main drag, she saw only a single old man shuffling ahead of her. His life aura looked like a burned-out bulb, a spot of dark gray around him. He walked stooped over, with a dogged determination, as if he knew that if he stopped, he would never start again. From what she could tell, he never would. He wore baggy, wide-wale corduroys that made the sound of rodents nesting when he walked. A wisp of breeze off the Bay brought Jody the acrid smell of failing organs, of stale tobacco, of despair, of a deep, rotting sickness, and she felt the elation leave her.

She slipped comfortably into the new slot the night had made for her, like tumblers of a lock slipping into place.

She made sure that she made enough noise so that he could hear her approaching, and when she was beside him, he paused, his feet still moving in tiny steps that turned him to the side, as if his motor was idling.

"Hi," she said.

He smiled. "My, you are a lovely girl. Would you walk with me?"

"Sure."

They walked a few steps together before he said, "I'm dying, you know."

"Yeah, I kind of figured," Jody said.

"I'm just walking. Thinking, and walking. Mostly walking."

"Nice night for it."

"A little cold, but I don't feel it. I got a whole pocketful of painkillers. You want one?"

"No, I'm good. Thanks."

"I ran out of things to think about."

"Just in time."

"I wondered if I'd get to kiss a pretty girl once before the end. I think that would be all I'd want."

"What's your name?"

"James. James O'Mally."

"James. My name is Jody. I'm pleased to meet you." She stopped and offered her hand to shake.

"The pleasure is all mine, I assure you," said James, bowing as best he could.

She took his face in her hands, and steadied him, then kissed him on the lips, softly and for a long time, and when she pulled away they were both smiling.

"That was lovely," James O'Mally said.

"Yes it was," Jody said.

"I suppose I'm finished now," James said. "Thank you."

"The pleasure was all mine," Jody said. "I assure you."

Then she put her arms around his slight frame, and held him, one hand cradling the back of his head like an infant, and he only trembled a little when she drank.

A little later, she bundled his clothes together under her arm, and hooked his old wing tips on two fingers. The dust that had been James O'Mally was spread in a powdery-gray pile on the sidewalk, like a negative shadow, a bleached spot. She brushed it flat with her palm, and wrote, *Nice kiss, James,* with her fingernail.

As she walked away, an hourglass trickle of James trailed out of his clothes behind her and was carried off on the chill bay breeze.

The guy working the door of the Glas Kat looked like a raven had exploded on his head, his hair plastered out in a chaos of black spikes. The music coming from inside sounded like robots fucking. And complaining about it. In rhythmic monotone. European robots.

Tommy was a little intimidated. 'Sploded raven-head guy had better fangs than he did, was paler, and had seventeen silver rings in his lips. (Tommy had counted.)

"Bet it's hard to whistle with those in, huh?" Tommy asked.

"Ten dollars," said 'Sploded.

Tommy gave him the money. He checked Tommy's ID and stamped his wrist with a red slash. Just then a group of Japanese girls dressed like tragic Victorian baby dolls breezed by behind Tommy, waving their wrist slashes like they'd just returned from a joyful suicide party instead of smoking cloves on the street. They, too, looked more like vampires than Tommy did.

He shrugged and entered the club. Everyone, it appeared, looked more like a vampire than he did. He'd bought some black jeans and a black leather jacket at the Levi's store while Jody was off finding something hideous for her mother for Christmas, but evidently he should have been looking for some black lipstick and something cobalt- or fuchsia-colored to weave into his hair. And in retrospect, the flannel shirt may have been a mistake. He looked like he'd shown up at the sacrificial mass of the damned ready to fix the dishwasher.

The music changed to an ethereal female chorus of

Celtic nonsense. With a techno beat. And robots complaining. Grumpy robots.

He tried to listen around it, the way Jody had taught him. With all the black light, strobes, and black clothing, his newly heightened senses were overloading. He tried to focus on people's faces, their life auras, look through the haze of heat, hairspray, and patchouli for the girl he'd met at Walgreens.

Tommy had felt alone in a crowd before, even inferior to everyone in a crowd, but now he felt, well, different. It wasn't just the clothes and the makeup, it was the humanity. He wasn't part of it. Heightened senses or not, he felt like he had his nose pressed against the window, looking in. The problem was, it was the window of a donut shop.

"Hey!" Someone grabbed his arm and he wheeled around so quickly that the girl nearly tumbled over backwards, startled.

"Fuck! Dude."

"Hi," Tommy said. "Wow." Thinking, *Ah, jelly donut.* It was the girl from Walgreens. She was nearly a foot shorter than he, and a little skinny. Tonight she'd gone with the waifish look, wearing striped stockings with holes ripped in them and a shiny red PVC miniskirt. She'd traded in her Lord Byron shirt for a tank top, black, of course, with dripping red letters that read GOT BLOOD?, and fishnet gloves that went halfway up her biceps. Her makeup was sad-clown marionette: black tears drawn streaming down either side of her face. She crooked her finger to get him to bend down so she could shout into his ear over the music.

"My name's Abby Normal."

Tommy spoke into her ear; she smelled of hairspray and what was that? Raspberry? "My name is Flood," he said. "C. Thomas Flood." It was his pen name. The *C* didn't really stand for anything, he just liked the sound of it. "Call me Flood," he added. Tommy was a stupid name for a vampire, but Flood—ah, Flood—there was disaster and power there, and a hint of mystery, he thought.

Abby smiled like a cat in a tuna cannery. "Flood," she said. "Flood."

She was trying it on, it seemed to Tommy. He imagined that she'd have a black vinyl binder at school and she'd soon be writing *Mrs. Flood* surrounded by a heart with an arrow through it on the cover in her own blood. He'd never seen a girl so obviously attracted to him, and he realized that he had no experience in dealing with it. For a moment he flashed on the three vampire brides of Dracula who try to seduce Jonathan Harker in Stoker's classic novel. (He'd been studying all the vampire fiction he could get his hands on since meeting Jody, since it didn't appear that anyone had written a good how-to book on vampirism.) Could he really deal with three luscious vampire brides? Would he have to bring them a kid in a sack the way Dracula does in the book? How many kids a week would it take to keep them happy? And where did you get kid sacks? And although he hadn't discussed it with Jody, he was pretty sure she was not going to be happy sharing him with two other luscious vampire brides, even if he brought her sacks and sacks full of kids. They'd need a bigger apartment. One with a washer and dryer in the building, because there'd be a lot of bloodstained lingerie to be washed. Vampire logistics were a nightmare. You should get a castle and a staff when you got your fangs. How was he going to do all of this? "This sucks," Tommy finally said, overwhelmed by the enormity of his responsibilities.

Abby looked startled, then a little hurt. "Sorry," she said. "You want to get out of here?"

"Oh, no, I didn't mean—I mean, uh, yes. Let us go."

"Do you still need to get your heroin?"

"What? No, that matter is taken care of."

"You know, Byron and Shelley did opiates," Abby said. "Laudanum. It was like cough syrup."

Then, for no reason that he could think of, Tommy said, "Those scamps, they loved to get wrecked and read ghost stories from the German."

"That is so fucking cool," Abby said, grabbing his arm and hugging his biceps like it was her newest, bestest friend. She started pulling him toward the door.

"What about your friend?" Tommy said.

"Oh, someone made a comment about his cape being gray when we first got here, so he went home to redye all of his blacks."

"Of course," Tommy said, thinking, *What the fuck?*

Out on the sidewalk, Abby said, "I suppose we need to find somewhere private."

"We do?"

"So you can take me," Abby said, stretching her neck to the side, looking more like a stringless marionette than ever.

Tommy had no idea what to do. How did she know? Everyone in that club would have scored higher on the "are you a vampire?" test than he would. There needed to be a book, and this sort of thing needed to be in it. Should he deny it? Should he just get on with it? What was he going to tell Jody when she woke up next to the skinny marionette girl? He hadn't really understood women when he was a normal, human guy, when it seemed that all you had to do was pretend that you didn't want to have sex with them until they would have sex with you, but being a vampire added a whole new aspect to things. Was he supposed to conceal that he was a vampire *and a dork*? He used to read the articles in *Cosmo* to get some clue to the female psyche, and so he deferred to advice he'd read in an article entitled "Think He's Just Pretending to Like You So You'll Have Sex with Him? Try a Coffee Date."

"How 'bout I buy you a cup of coffee instead," he said. "We can talk."

"It's because I have small boobs, isn't it?" Abby said, going into a very practiced pout.

"Of course not." Tommy smiled in a way he thought would be charming, mature, and reassuring. "Coffee won't help that."

. .

As Jody pushed the bundle of clothes into the storm sewer, a silver cigarette case slid out of the jacket pocket onto the pavement. She reached for it and felt a light shock—no, that wasn't it. It was a warmth that moved up her arm. She kicked the clothes into the opening and stood under the streetlight, turning the silver case in her hands. It had his name engraved on it. She couldn't keep it, like she had the folding money from his pockets, but she couldn't throw it away either. Something wouldn't let her.

She heard a buzz, like an angry insect, and looked up to see a neon "Open" sign flickering above a shop called Asher's Secondhand. That was it. That's where the cigarette case had to go. She owed it to James. After all, he'd given her everything, or at least everything he'd had left. She quickstepped across the street and into the shop.

The owner was working the counter at the back by himself. A thin guy in his early thirties, with a look of pleasant confusion not unlike the one she'd first noticed on Tommy's face. Normally, this guy would be prime minion material, or at least based on her minion recruitment of the past he would, except apparently, he was dead. Or at least not alive like most people. He had no life aura around him. No healthy pink glow, no crusty brown or gray corona of illness. Nothing. The only time she'd ever seen this before was with Elijah, the old vampire.

The shopkeeper looked up and she smiled. He smiled back. She moved to the counter. While he tried not to stare at her cleavage, she looked more closely for some life aura. There was heat, or at least there appeared to be some heat coming off him.

"Hi," said the shopkeeper. "Can I help you?"

"I found this," she said, holding up the cigarette case. "I was in the neighborhood and something made me think that this belonged here." She set the case down on the counter. How could he have no life aura? What the hell was he?

"Touch me," she said. She held out her hand to him.

"Huh?" He seemed a little frightened at first, but he took her hand, then quickly let go.

He was warm. "Then you're not one of us?" But he wasn't one of them either.

"Us? What do you mean us?" He touched the cigarette case and she could tell that this was exactly why she had brought it here. It was supposed to be here. Whatever part of James O'Mally had been left in that cigarette case had led her here. And this thin, confused-looking guy was supposed to have it. He took what was left of people all the time. It's what he did. Jody felt some of the confidence she'd felt earlier draining away. Maybe the night wasn't hers after all.

Jody backed away a step. "No. You don't just take the weak and the sick, do you? You take anyone."

"Take? What do you mean, take?" He was furiously trying to push the cigarette case back to her across the counter.

He didn't know. He was like she was when she'd awakened that first night as a vampire and had no idea what she had become. "You don't even know, do you?"

"Know what?" He picked up the cigarette case again. "Wait a second, can you see this thing glowing?"

"No glow. It just felt like it belonged here." This poor guy, he didn't even know. "What's your name?" She asked.

"Charlie Asher. This is Asher's."

"Well Charlie, you seem like a nice guy, and I don't know exactly what you are, and it doesn't seem like you know. You don't, do you?"

He blushed. Jody could see his face flush with heat. "I've been going through some changes lately."

Jody nodded. He really would have been perfect as a minion—if he hadn't been some bizarre supernatural creature. She'd just gotten used to the idea of vampires being real, and it took some serious blood drinking to drive that reality home, and now there were other—other—things? Still, Jody felt bad for him, "Okay," she said. "I know what it's like, uh, to find yourself thrown into a situation where forces beyond your control are changing you into someone, something you don't have an owner's manual for. I understand what it is to not know. But someone, somewhere, does know. Someone can tell you what's going on." *And hopefully they aren't just fucking with you,* she wanted to add, but thought better of it.

"What are you talking about?" he asked.

"You make people die, don't you Charlie?" She didn't

know why she said it, but as soon as she said it, she knew it was true. Like when all her other senses had been dialed to eleven, she could sense something new, like noise on the line, and it was telling her this.

"But how do you—?"

"Because it's what I do," Jody said. "Not like you, but it's what I do. Find them, Charlie. Backtrack and find whoever was there when your world changed."

She shouldn't have said that, she knew it as she was saying it. She'd just handed him an item that had been owned by someone she'd taken not twenty minutes ago. But even as regret for passing out incriminating evidence hit her, she also realized that she had left Tommy out there to wave in the wind just like this guy. Even if it was only for a few hours, Tommy had no idea how to go about being a vampire—truth be told, he hadn't really been that good at being a human. He was just a doofy guy from Indiana and she'd abandoned him to the merciless city.

She turned and ran out of the shop.

Cocoa?" Tommy said. "You look cold." He'd given her his jacket out on the street.

He's so gallant, Abby thought. *He probably wants me to drink cocoa to get my blood sugar up before he sucks the life from my veins.*

Abby had lived much of her life waiting for something extraordinary to happen. No matter where she had been, there was a world somewhere that was more interesting. She'd progressed from wanting to live in a fantastic, *kawaii-*cute plastic world of Hello Kitty, to being a Day-Glo, Manga lollipop space girl in platform sneakers, and then just a couple of years ago she had moved into the dark gothic world of pseudo vampires, suicidal poets, and romantic disappointment. It was a dark, seductive world where you got to sleep really late on the weekends. She'd been true to her dark nature, too, trying to maintain an aspect of exhausted mopeyness while channeling any enthusiasm she felt into a vehicle for imminent disappointment, and above all, suppressing the deep-seated perkiness that her friend Lily said she'd never shed when she'd refused to throw away her Hello Kitty backpack or let go of her Nintendog virtual beagle puppy.

"He has virtual parvo," Lily had said. "You have to put him down."

"He doesn't have parvo," Abby had insisted. "He's just tired."

"He's doomed, and you're cute, and hopelessly perky," Lily taunted.

"I am not. I'm complex and I'm dark."

"You're perky and your e-dog has i-parvo."

"As Azrael is my witness, I will never be perky again," said Abby, her wrist set tragically to her forehead. Lily stood with her as she threw her Nintendog cartridge under the tire of the 91 midnight express bus.

And now she had been chosen by a real creature of the night, and she would be true to her word: she had shed her perkiness. She sipped her hot chocolate, and studied the vampire Flood across the table. How clever, that he could appear as just a simple, clueless guy—but then, he could probably take many shapes.

"I could be a slave to your darkest desires," Abby said. "I can do things. Anything you want."

The vampire Flood commenced a coughing fit. When he had control again, he said, "Well, that's terrific, because we have a lot of laundry piled up and the apartment is a wreck."

He was testing her. Seeing if she was worthy before bringing her into his world. "Anything you desire, my lord. I can do laundry, clean, bring you small creatures to quench your thirst until I am worthy."

The vampire Flood snickered. "This is so cool," he said. "You'll do my laundry, just like that?"

Abby knew she had to tread carefully here, not fall for his trap. "Anything," she said.

"Have you ever gone apartment hunting?"

"Sure," she lied.

"Okay, you can start tomorrow first thing. You need to find us an apartment."

Abby was horrified. She hadn't really tried on the idea of leaving her old life so quickly. But all that would mean nothing when she became immortal, and ran with the children of the night. But her mom was going to be pissed. "I can't move in right away, my lord. I have affairs to put in order before I make the change."

The vampire Flood smiled, his fangs barely visible now.

"Oh, it's not for you. There's another." He paused and leaned across the table. "An elder," he whispered.

There was another? Was she to become the sacrifice to a whole coven of the undead? Well, whatever. Lily would be so jealous. "As you please, my lord," she said.

"You might want to chill with the 'my lord' stuff," Flood said.

"Sorry."

"It's okay. You know this all has to be completely secret, right?"

"Right. Secret."

"I mean, I'm okay with it, but the other, the elder, she has a terrible temper."

"She?"

"Yeah, you know, an Irish redhead."

"A Celtic countess, then? The one who was with you at Walgreens?"

"Exactly."

"Sweet!" Abby blurted out. She couldn't help it. She immediately tried to hide her latent perkiness by biting the edge of her cocoa cup.

"You've got chocolate, here." The vampire Flood gestured to her lip. "Kind of a marshmallow mustache."

"Sorry," Abby said, wiping her mouth furiously with the back of her fishnet glove, smearing her black lipstick across the side of her face.

"It's okay," said the vampire Flood. "It's cute."

"Fuck!" Abby said.

It's Like Time Travel, Only, You Know, Slower...

THE CHRONICLES OF ABBY NORMAL:
Tortured Victim of the Daylight Dwellers

So here I am again, to open my veins and spill my pain onto your pages. My dark friend, after sixteen years of totally boring existence, I come to you at last with a glimmer of hope to break through the gloomth that is my miserable life. OMG! I have found him! Or I should say, he has found me.

That's right, my Dark Lord has found me. A for-real vampyre. He is called the vampyre Flood, and he didn't say, but I think he is descended from European royalty—a viscount or a discount or one of those.

I was in Walgreens with Jared when we saw him—and OMFG he's so hot, in a totally stealth way. I would have thought he was just a totally mainstream geek or something, with his flannel shirt and jeans, but he asked us about buying syringes and I totally saw his fangs come out. So, I was like, "I can hook you up with my dealer," like that, and then he looked at my T-shirt and saw Byron's picture on it and he quoted "She Walks in Beauty," which is like my favorite poem next to the one by Baudelaire about his girlfriend being nothing but worm food, except that Lily called that one first because Baudelaire is her fave poet and so she got the shirt with him on it, even though Byron is way more scrumptious and I would do him on sharp gravel if I had the chance.

So I went home and changed my clothes and fixed my makeup, and when we got to Glas Kat we breezed by the door like we were twenty-five or something. Jared made our IDs himself at Kinkos and we both look so mature in our pictures, although I think he overdid it with the mustache. Anyway, we were there like ten minutes, and this song came on that I really like—"Boning You in the Ossuary," by Dead Can Dub—which is so cool and macabre. And I tried to get Jared to dance, but this guy comes by and grabs Jared's cape and says, "Blacks fade much?" and that was it. Jared went into a level-five freak-out, and turned into a total fuckwit, trying to get me to hide him and stuff, and then just saying he couldn't take it anymore and he had to go home and redye right then. So he abandoned me to the dank loneliness that is the night and I bought a bottle of water and some chips and got ready to grieve my lost youth, when HE showed up. OMG!

Check it, he actually knew Byron and Shelley! He used to party with them in Switzerland when they were all young. They all did laudanum and read ghost stories and stuff, and then they actually invented Goth, right there in this villa on some lake. He is like THE SOURCE! He took me for coffee and I wanted to give myself to him right there in Starbucks. Lily will be totally jealous.

So he said I have to wait. He is connected to some ancient Celtic vampire countess and I'm supposed to find them an apartment in the morning. He even gave me the name of a rental agent to call and a big wad of cash. I have to prove myself worthy of his trust, otherwise there's like no way he'll bestow the dark gift on me, and I'll totally have to finish my sophomore year and probably end up in junior college or working at Old Navy or something.

So, since we're off for Christmas break, I'm going to call this woman and go find an apartment for the vampyre Flood and the Celtic vampyre countess. And when Flood rises from the grave at sunset, I will get my reward.

I'm totally freaked about meeting the Celtic vampyre countess. Flood says she has a temper. What if she hates me? Flood says he's not really into her—it's not like that. It's like, she's his vampyre sire, and they've been together for like five hundred years, so, you know, they have history, and I can respect that.

NOTE: Make sure to find out if I need to move their native soil to the new apartment before we move their coffins.

NOTE: Do I need to have a coffin made? Is it okay if it's purple?

Oh yeah, my sister Ronnie has head lice.

Red, White, and Blue,
Not Necessarily in That Order

*S*now White, thought Blue.

With the seven to look after me, and me them, I could be just like Snow White. Granted, the Animals weren't exactly dwarves, Jeff Murray, the ex-high-school-basketball star was at least six five, and Drew, their resident pharmacologist, was pretty close to that height, but she wasn't exactly Snow White either. Still, they were all kind to her, considerate, and basically respectful of her, within their limits as a bunch of pot-head punani hounds. They did seem to have a decent work ethic, were loyal, didn't fight among themselves, and were relatively clean, as guys this age went.

In a few days, she'd have the rest of their money, she knew it, and they knew it, but then what? It was a ton of money, to be sure, but it wasn't fuck-you money. (Defined as having so much money that you can say "fuck you" to anyone, anywhere, anytime, and not have to worry about the consequences.) She'd have to find something to do, somewhere to go. As the possibility of her getting out of the life finally loomed large, she realized that she was going to need a new life to live, and frankly, it was scaring the hell out of her. Time isn't kind to a girl living on her looks, and she'd already extended her sell-by date by going blue, but what now? Who knew that the future she'd been hoping for would show up with such sharp teeth. So Blue asked herself the question . . .

Can a fallen Cheddar princess of Fond Du Lac make a life with seven perpetually adolescent party animals from the Bay Area? Maybe it could happen, but she had her misgivings about dwarf number seven: Clint.

In her experience, it took a lot of work to fuck the Jesus out of a guy, and even then, he was prone to come down with a bad case of the guilts a day or two later. Not really a problem when you were working outcall, but if you were going to high-ho a whole pack of dwarves on a semipermanent basis, one of them having a high-maintenance, holy-ghost haunting was going to be a problem.

"Whore of Babylon," Clint said as the Animals led her into the Safeway like they were presenting her at the palace.

She paused in the automatic doors, despite the fact that she felt like she was turning blue under her blue, dressed as she was in a silver lamé minidress and six-inch clear Lucite heels, none of it protecting her from the frigid wind coming off the Bay, whipping through the Marina

Safeway parking lot. Thinking she'd probably spend most of her time naked, she hadn't packed for San Francisco weather.

"I've never even been to Babylon," she said. "But I'm open to new experiences." She licked her lips and stepped to where her breasts were within an inch of Clint's chest.

He turned and bolted to the office, chanting, "Get thee behind me, get thee behind me, get thee behind me," the whole way.

"However you want it, baby," said Blue. She decided she'd think of him as Freaked, the paranoid dwarf.

"Barry will show you to the break room," Lash said. He'd become the new leader of the Animals, mainly because he tended to be the most sober. "Jeff, send the limo back and lock the doors. Drew, make some coffee. Gustavo, see what the situation is on the floors. We may need you to throw stock on the shelves."

They stood there, looking at him. Stoned. Drunk. Baffled. Blue would think of Barry, the little, prematurely bald guy, as her special dwarf, Baffled. She smiled.

Clint peeked over the three-quarter wall of the office. "Hey, you guys. You should know that the Emperor was here last night. He says that Tommy Flood is a vampire."

"Huh?" Lash said.

"He's a vampire. That girl of his, she didn't leave town. She changed him."

"Get the fuck outta here," said Jeff.

Clint nodded furiously. "It's true."

"Well, fuck," said the others, in an unsynchronized chorus.

"Meeting," Lash announced. "Gentlemen, take your seats." He looked apologetically to Blue. "This shouldn't take long."

"I'll make coffee," she said.

"Uh . . ." Lash seemed concerned. "Blue, we're kind of on a budget from here on out."

"Coffee's free," Blue said. She turned and started heading to the back of the store. "I'll find it."

The Animals watched Blue walk away and, when she turned the corner, gathered by the registers. Clint unlocked the office door and came out. "So, we have to notify those cops, so they can help us hunt him down."

Lash looked at the Animals, who looked back. Lash raised an eyebrow. The others nodded. Lash put his arm around Clint's shoulders. "Clint, the guys and I have discussed it, and we'd all like to do something for you."

Clint ran back in the office and slammed the door. "No! We have to destroy the agents of Satan."

"Right. Of course. We'll get right on that. But first I'd like you to ask yourself something, Clint. And I'd like you to answer not as the born-again man that you are now, but from that little boy that's inside of all of us."

"Okay," Clint said, peeking over the office door.

"Clint, haven't you ever wanted to bone a Smurf?"

. .

Jody heard Tommy come in the security door downstairs and met him on the stairs with a big hug and a backbreaking kiss.

"Wow," Tommy said.

"Are you okay?"

"I'm really good now. I was just checking on William. I think he pooped himself."

"I'm so sorry, Tommy. I shouldn't have left you on your own this soon."

"It's okay. I'm okay. Hey, you have something on your dress."

Jody was still wearing the little black dress. Some of the dust that was James O'Mally was still clinging to it near the hemline. "Oh, I must have bumped up against something."

"Let me get that for you," Tommy said, brushing at her thigh, then starting to raise the dress up past her waist.

Jody caught his hand. "Horndog!"

Chet the huge shaved cat looked up for a second, then put his head back down on William's chest and went back to sleep.

"But you left me on my own," Tommy said, trying to sound sad, but smiling too much to make it work.

"You're fine." She looked at her watch. "We only have about forty minutes till sunup. We can talk while we get ready for bed."

"I'm ready for bed now," Tommy said.

She led him up the stairs into the loft, through the great room, the bedroom, and into the bathroom. She grabbed her toothbrush off the sink and tossed Tommy his. She pasted, then chucked the tube to him.

"Do we still have to floss?" Tommy asked. "I mean, what's the point of being immortal if we have to floss?"

"Yeah," Jody said, through a mouthful of pinkish foam, "you should just go lie in the sun and get it over with, rather than suffer the torture of flossing."

"Don't be sarcastic. I didn't think we could get sick at all, but your hangover proved that to be wrong."

Jody nodded and spit. "Don't swallow any when you rinse. The water will come right back up."

"How come your foam is pink? My foam isn't pink. And I went last."

"My gums might be bleeding," Jody said.

Jody wasn't ready to tell him that she'd taken someone tonight. She would tell him, just not now. So, to change the subject, she summoned her superhuman strength and pantsed him.

"Hey!"

"When did you get skull-and-crossbones boxers?"

"I bought them tonight, when you were getting Christmas presents. I thought they would seem dangerous."

"You bet," Jody said, nodding furiously to keep from laughing. "And you'll blend in—in case you're ever caught with your pants down in the pirate locker room."

"Yeah, there's that," Tommy said, a little toothpaste

foam dribbling down his chest as he looked at his boxers. "I have the whitest legs in the universe. My legs are like great white carrion worms."

"Stop, you're making me horny."

"I've got to use that tanning lotion we bought. Where is it?"

Jody moved with catlike speed out to the kitchen, snatched the lotion off the counter, and was back sitting on the edge of the bed in only a couple of seconds. If she could just keep Tommy from asking any questions until sunup, she was sure she'd figure out a way to tell him about the old man. "Come over here, worm legs, let me put some lotion on you." To emphasize her commitment to lotionization, she stood, pulled the straps of her dress off her shoulders, and let it fall to the floor at her feet. She stepped out of her dress and stood there, in just her pumps and a silver necklace with a tiny heart that he had given her.

Tommy hopped out of the bathroom—his pants still around his ankles—one long hop, and he stood in front of her. Jody smiled. Give a geek supernatural agility and speed, and what you get is a superagile, speedy geek.

"You went out commando, in that dress?"

"Never again," Jody said, grabbing the waistband of his boxers and pulling him toward her. "These are mine, now. I want to be dangerous."

"That's so, so slutty," he said, lisping a little, his fangs coming out now.

"Yep. Where do you want to start with the lotion?"

He pulled her close and kissed her neck. "We have to be careful not to break the furniture this time."

"Fuck it, less to move," she said, her own fangs coming out now. She raked them down his chest. "If we figure out a way to get a place before someone kills us."

"Oh, yeah, I found us a minion," he said as she bit into his side and tore his boxers off in a single swift pull.

"What?"

But Tommy was finished talking for a while.

Blue watched as the Butterball rocketed by her and slammed into a triangle of two-liter soft-drink bottles—the front bottle burst, sending a cola-brown eruption of foam across the floor by the meat case.

"Strike!" Barry shouted. He danced in a tight circle among the Animals, pointing and chanting, "I own you, and you, and you," to each as he passed.

Blue looked to Lash, and raised a cobalt eyebrow.

Lash shrugged. "It happens. That's why we use diet soda. It's not as sticky." He had decided that they all needed to sober up some more before they started stocking the shelves; thus the turkey bowling.

"Can someone bring a mop?" Clint said. Because he would not gamble, he was the designated pin setter. He was scrambling around trying to retrieve soda bottles even as Jeff Murray was warming up at the other end of the aisle, swinging a Foster's Fresh Frozen Homestyle in each hand. He be-

lieved that he got better pin action off the Foster's because of
the savory gravy packet stuffed in its center. He claimed
that Foster's had mastered superior poultry technology, and
was, in fact, working on an oversized titanium turkey. The
other Animals were forced to point out to him that he was
completely full of shit as they sprayed root beer on him.

"So you guys hunted vampires?" Blue asked Lash. She
had come back to the front with coffee for everyone just in
time to hear Lash lay out the scenario for the Animals.
She'd held off asking any questions until now. A Fresh
Frozen meat missile zipped down the aisle between them.
Lash didn't even blink.

"Yep. We didn't kill him. We just blew up his yacht and
took his art. That's where we got the money."

"Yeah, right," said Blue. "I got that part. It's the vampire
part I'm not clear on. Like a real vampire. A real, blood-
drinking, can't-go-out-in-the-day, live-forever vampire."

"We figured he had to be at least six hundred years old,"
Troy Lee added, joining in the conversation. "Blue, you
wanna skid the buzzard?" He nodded to the end of the aisle,
where Jeff was offering his spare Fresh Frozen turkey like a
sacrifice.

"So you guys, who work in a grocery store, have seen a
vampire?"

"Two of them," Lash said. "Our night-crew leader,
Tommy, was living with one of them."

"She was hot," Troy Lee added.

"Vampire hunters?" Blue couldn't believe it.

"Well, not anymore," Lash said.

"Yeah," Troy Lee said. "Clint says that Tommy's a vampire now. We're not going to mess with him."

"Spawn of Satan!" Clint shouted from the end of the aisle.

Drew, who Blue had decided to think of as Doc, because he always carried the pot, ran down the aisle and shot-putted a twelve-pound self-basting at Clint's head. "Shut the fuck up!" Clint ducked and covered. The turkey went over the meat counter and stuck in the drywall by the window at the back of the meat department. To Blue, Drew said, "Sorry, couldn't be helped."

"Well, that's gonna take all night to patch," said Clint.

Lash looked at Troy Lee. "Could you kill him?"

"On it," Troy Lee said, falling into a fighting stance, before taking off and chasing Clint around the corner. "Prepare to die, White Devil!"

"So," said Blue. "You were saying?"

"Well, Clint says Tommy is a vampire now, and we should go stake him out or something, but he's one of us, so we've decided to pursue a policy of Buddhist tolerance."

Just then Troy Lee dragged Clint back around the corner in a headlock. Despite being six inches shorter and forty pounds lighter than Clint, he'd studied martial arts since he was six and that took size out of the equation.

"Should I hypnotize the chicken?" Troy asked.

"Make it so," said Lash.

Troy Lee adjusted his chokehold on Clint. The larger

man's eyes bugged out, his mouth moved like a gasping fish out of water, and he went limp in Troy's arms, who then dropped him in the puddle of diet soda on the floor.

"He'll come around in a second or two." Lash leaned into Blue to explain. "We used to call it *choke* the chicken, but that sounded kind of gayish."

"Of course," said Blue. That trick would come in handy in her work. She'd have to ask Troy Lee to teach it to her.

"And you think that your friend and this girl are really vampires."

"I suppose. Clint said he heard it from the Emperor, and he was the one that turned us on to the old vampire guy in the first place. Either way, they're not our problem."

"What if I said they were?" Blue said. Her mind was putting it together like a sewing machine on crack. It was insane, but for once she could see a future stretching out before her, welcoming her. "What if I said I wanted you to go after them?"

Lash blinked at her like she was speaking Klingon. "Huh?" He looked at the other Animals, who had stopped bowling and moved into range of the conversation. They stood there with frosty gobblers steaming in their hands like they were on wet-nurse duty for a group of headless infant snowmen.

"Flood is our friend," Lash said.

"I don't want you to kill him," Blue said. "Just catch him."

Lash looked to the others, who looked away—at the

floor, at the cabbage and lettuce counter, at the turnips, at their frozen charges.

"I'll make it worth your while," Blue said.

Jody lay on the bed watching Tommy turn slowly, back and forth in the air like a pale white-boy mobile. The loft had twenty-foot ceilings with open, industrial-style beams, and sometime during their lovemaking, they had both ended up hanging from them. Jody dropped to the bed after she came, but Tommy still hung by one hand. The bright side was that with the exception of the set of shredded sheets upon which she lay, they had kept the destruction to a minimum. The downside—well, she really could have gone a couple of lifetimes without seeing him from this angle.

"We did good," Jody said. "Hardly anything broken."

"You think that monkeys really do it that way?" Tommy replied.

"I always thought you were just using that as an expression." She'd thought she could remain detached enough about their lovemaking to stay in control—to enjoy it, but to use it, as it were—but since Tommy had changed, it wasn't like that anymore. She lost herself in it, she didn't just make love with him, she fucked him like a crazed monkey girl. It was good, but disconcerting. She had liked being in control.

"You look amazing from this angle," Tommy said.

"You look like a man-shaped fluorescent lightbulb," Jody said, grinning at him, then noticing a change. "Do not get wood, Thomas Flood. You will not get wood, do you hear me?"

"You sound like my mom," Tommy said.

"Ewwwww," Jody said, shuddering and covering her eyes.

"Ewwwww," Tommy said, realizing what he had just said and about what and whom.

He dropped to the bed and bounced. "Sorry. Quick, put the self-tanning lotion on me, we only have a few minutes before sunup."

"Okay, but just the lotion."

"Right, go."

Jody took the lotion and squirted some on her hands. "Turn around, I'll get your back."

"But—"

"Just point that thing the other way, writer boy, you have had all the monkey love you're going to get tonight." She said it, but she didn't mean it—she'd go another round if he wanted, if they had time before sunrise. Then she remembered.

"Did you say you found us a minion?"

"Yeah, I did. She's going to start tomorrow—er, today. I gave her money to get us an apartment. Told her what we needed."

"Her?"

"Yeah, you remember that girl we saw in the drugstore?"

Jody stopped rubbing, grabbed his shoulders, and spun him around. "You gave our deposit money to a nine-year-old?"

"She's not nine. She's sixteen."

"Still, Tommy. You trusted our secret to a sixteen-year-old girl?"

"She already knew."

"Yes, because you let your fangs show like some doofus of the night. You could have explained that somehow, or better yet, never seen her again."

"Look, she's smart, and she'll be loyal. I promise."

"You could have just gotten us killed."

"What would you have done? Huh? You have to trust someone."

"But a sixteen-year-old kid?"

"I'm only nineteen, and I was a great minion. Besides, she thinks I'm her dark lord."

"Did you even tell her about me?"

"Of course, she knows all about you. Knows that you're my sire—that's what they call the vampire who made you. I even told her that you were older, that you had vast experience."

"Vast? Vast experience sounds like I'm a slutty old divorcée. How old does she think I am?"

"Five hundred."

"What?"

"But you look great for five hundred. I mean, look, you got my attention. Do my front."

"Do your own front." She threw the lotion bottle at him and he snatched it out of the air.

"Love you," Tommy said, slathering self-tanning goo all over his face and chest.

"I'm going to lock the bedroom door," Jody said as the alarm on their watches started beeping, signaling ten minutes before sunrise. She'd gotten the alarm watches for both of them, just in case. "You didn't give her keys, did you?"

"Not to the bedroom."

"Great. What if she finds William in the stairwell and stakes him out? You could have given our key to a Buffy wannabe—"

"This stuff is supposed to take like eight hours to work, so by sundown I'll be sexy bronze."

"There's a bronze vampire in the living room. Why don't you go ask him how that's working out for him?"

"He's impersonal bronze, not sexy bronze like I'll be."

"Come to bed. And put on a T-shirt. I don't want a sexy bronze stain on the sheets, even if they are torn up."

Tommy sniff-tested a half-dozen shirts, finally decided on one, climbed into bed, and was kissing Jody good morning when the sunrise put them out.

Then, When They Woke Up

"Oh my God, that stuff turned me completely orange."

"Not completely."

"I look like the Great Pumpkin."

"Good grief, Tommy, you do not."

Blood, Coffee, Sex, Magic— Not Necessarily in That Order

Just after sundown.

They watched the coffee dripping out of the filter like they were distilling nitroglycerine and the slightest bit of inattention might cause an explosion. "It smells really good," Jody said.

"It's like I never noticed it before," Tommy said.

"You'd think it would smell sickening, since it's indigestible," Jody said. The last time she'd taken a sip of coffee, her vampire system had rejected it so violently that she ended up convulsively dry-heaving on the floor, feeling like forks were twisting inside of her.

"This might work," Tommy said. "You ready?"

"Ready."

He poured a tablespoonful or so of coffee into a glass cup. Then he uncapped one of the syringes that held William's blood and squirted a few drops into the coffee.

"You first," he said, swishing the cup around in front of her.

"No, you," Jody said. As good as the coffee smelled, the memory of her nausea held her back.

Tommy shrugged and threw the coffee back like a tequila shooter, then set the cup down on the counter.

Jody stepped back and snatched a tea towel off the fridge handle in preparation for the coffee's return trip. Tommy rolled his eyes, shuddered, then grabbed his throat and fell to the floor, twitching and choking. "Dying," he croaked. "Suffering and dying."

Jody was barefoot and didn't want to stub her toe, so she pulled the kick to his ribs. "You suck, you know that."

Tommy rolled on the floor giggling, curling himself around her foot. "It works! It works! It works!" He sort of dog-humped her leg in rhythm and tugged at the hem of her robe. "You never have to be grumpy again!"

Jody grinned. "Pour cups, grommet! Full cups."

Tommy climbed to his feet. "We don't even know the blood-to-coffee ratio yet."

"Pour!" Jody was in the fridge in an instant, grabbing another syringe. "We'll wing it."

The she heard the downstairs door open and spun on her heel. "William?"

Tommy listened to the footfalls coming up the steps and shook his head. "Nope, too light."

They could hear the key fitting into the lock. "You said you didn't give her a key," Jody said.

"I said I didn't give her a key to the bedroom," Tommy said.

"Lord Flood, there's a stinky dead guy with a huge cat on your landing," said Abby Normal as she came through the door.

THE CHRONICLES OF ABBY NORMAL:
Dedicated Servant of the Vampyre Flood

I have been to the lair of the vampyre Flood. I am part of the coven! Kinda. Okay, back up. So I like slept till eleven, because we're on Christmas break, only it's called winter break now because Jesus is AN OPPRESSIVE ZOMBIE BASTARD AND WE DO NOT BOW DOWN TO HIS BIRTHDAY! At least not at Allen Ginsberg High School, we don't. (Go, Fighting Beatniks!) But it's all good, 'cause I'm going to have to get used to getting up later if I'm going to be a creature of the night.

So, like first thing, I made some toast, and it burned, as black as my soul, and I was so bummed that my tears of despair fell like cold bits of crystal, to be destroyed on the unforgiving rocks of this miserable life. But then I saw that Mom had left a twenty out on the counter with a note:

Allison (Allison is my day-slave name—my mom named me after some song by some Elvis guy, so I totally refuse to accept it), *here's your lunch money, and please stop at Walgreens and pick up some RID shampoo for Ronnie's head lice.* (Veronica is my sister, who is twelve and a total tumor on the ass of my existence.)

So, I was like, Sweet! Starbucks!

It took forever to pick what I was going to wear, and not just because I'd never rented an apartment before. The lightbulb burned out in my closet and we didn't have any extras, so I had to take everything out in the living room to look at it in the light. Like the song says, I wear black on the outside to reflect the black I feel on the inside, but OMG, it's impossible to tell one thing from another in a dark closet. Since it was going to be a business thing, I decided on my striped tights with my red PVC mini, my skull-and-crossbones hoodie, and my lime Converse All Stars. I went with just a plain stud in my nose, a barbell in my eyebrow, and a simple silver ring in my lip—understated and elegant. I carried my hot-pink biohazard messenger bag.

Ronnie was all, "I wanna come with you, I wanna come with you," but I pointed out that she was a scourge on humanity and that if she came along I would tell everyone on the bus she had lice, so she elected to stay home and watch toons. It was then that I ventured into the undiscovered country, and called the number that the vampyre Flood had given me.

And the woman was totally a bitch.

She was like, "Hello. Blah Blah Property Management."

And I was like, "I need to rent an apartment."

And she was all, "How many bedrooms and did you have an area in mind?"

And I was all, "What's with all the questions, bitch? Are you some kind of thought police or something?"

And she was like, "I'm just trying to help."

"Right, help. Like tuberculosis."

So she's all, "I beg your pardon," like the queen of freakin' France or something.

And then I remembered that I was supposed to ask for a specific person, so I was like, "Oh, I need to speak to Alicia DeVries, Is she there?"

And the bitch connected me.

So it turns out that Alicia DeVries is this crusty hippie who is like as old as my grandma, but wants to be all Earth Mother and everything, which I'm not against, because old hippies have the best pot and they'll just give it to you if you pretend not to notice that they're crusty and old. So Alicia picks me up in her crust-mobile rainbow peace-and-love Jeep CJ and I give her the requirements of the vampyre Flood, which were bedroom with no windows, a washer and dryer, private entrance with lockout, and, at least above the ground floor, windows looking down on the street.

And she's all, "We have to have a Social Security number and driver's license number for the paperwork—you have to be eighteen."

So I'm, "My client will provide all the information you need, it's just that he's very busy and can't deal with pissant details during the day." Then I waved the cash that Flood gave me and she went all spacey, overmeditated, *"namaste"* on me, like it's not about the money when it's really about the money. Then she takes me to this loft, which it turns out is only like a half a block from the address where Flood said to meet him at sundown. Sweet!

So I'm all, "Excellent, the master will be pleased."

And she's like, "I'll make you out a receipt."

Then she starts to lecture me about respecting myself as a woman, and not allowing myself to be subjugated to the desires of an older man and shit—like I'm this corporate fuck-puppet for some creepy businessman or something. I didn't want her to get suspicious and try to rescue me, so I'm like, "No, you misunderstand, I call him the master because he's the sensei of my jujitsu dojo—he's not boning me or anything."

Luckily I have an extensive martial-arts background from watching anime with Jared and I knew that one must never bone the sensei.

So she like reaches over and pats my knee. All, "That's okay, sweetheart."

And I'm like, "Step off, rug-muncher!" I mean, I'm as bi as the next person, but not with some crusty old hippie—I need music and some X, and then only if some guy has rejected me and thrown my heart into the gutter like an abandoned vegetarian burrito—and even then I draw the line at making out.

So she gave me the keys and took my money and just,

like, left me there. So I called Lily, who came over with a two-liter of Diet Green Tea, a bag of Cheese Newts (I still hadn't had breakfast), and some book she found called *The Big Book of Death*. So we looked at the book, which is this how-to thing with great art, and drank tea and ate Cheese Newts until she had to go to work. I wanted to tell her about the vampyre Flood, but I promised that I would keep his secret, so all I told her was that I had dis-covered my Dark Lord, and he would soon satisfy my ev-ery desire and I couldn't tell her anything else. So she was all, "whatever, ho," which is what I like about her—Lily is *très noir*.

So I walked over to the Sony Metreon and watched the flat-screens until it started to get dark. I was already about ready to pee with nervousness when I got to Flood's door, but then, just as I get my key in the door, this big Hummer limo pulls up, and these three college-age guys climb out followed by this blue woman in a silver dress with ginor-mous fake boobs. And they're all, "Where is Flood? We need to find Flood?" And she's all, "Where did you get the key? You need to let us in before it gets dark."

I'm not intimidated—because I know that her boobs are fake. And it's so obvious that they hunt the nosferatu that it's not even funny. Inside, I was like: "Ha, suck my spiky rubber strap-on, vampyre hunter!"

But on the outside I was totally chill. And I'm like, "I don't know who you're talking about. This is my apart-ment." Then I opened the door and inside, lying on the landing, there's this dead guy with a huge bald cat in a red sweater on his chest. And the cat hissed at me and I screamed just a little bit and slammed the door. "You have to go," I said. "My boyfriend is naked and he gets mad if strangers see his enormous unit." I looked right at the blue bitch when I said that, like: *Oh yeah, some of us are confident enough in our own femininity that we don't need fake tits to get a guy with a huge unit.*

And the black guy is like, "I just talked to Flood here last night."

And I was like, "Yeah, he moved."

Then the Asian guy checked his watch and was like, "Dude, too late, it's officially sunset."

And it was like it was on cue or something, the cat on the dead guy let out a long scary yowl, and even the blue skank backed away toward the limo.

"You'd better go now," I said, all ominous and full of foreboding and dread.

And she was all, "We'll be back."

And I was like, "So?"

So they went. But then I had to get past the cat and the dead guy and go up the steps. I have to say, that as much as I'm all about the peace of the grave and the glorious gloomth of the nonliving and all, it's different when there's a real dead guy you have to walk over, not to mention a really big, angry cat in a sweater.

NOTE TO SELF: Always carry Kitty Treats for Self-Defense (because evidently they don't like Skittles, which I tried).

. .

Since I didn't have any kitty treats, I got by the preternaturally big-ass cat by opening the door wide and yelling, "Hey, kitty, go away!" Much to my amazement, the cat ran out of the doorway and hid under a parked car. It was like I already had vampyre powers to command the Children of the Night. Then I had to get past the dead guy on the landing, which was sort of like dead-guy hopscotch, but I got up the stairs and managed only to step on one of his arms. I was hoping he really was dead, and not one of the nosferatu, because then he might be pissed off when he rose. He certainly smelled dead, the fetid stench of the charnel house emanated from him like a foul miasma of evil, as they say in the books.

So I opened the door, and I go, "Lord Flood, there's a stinky dead guy with a huge cat on your landing." Thinking that I would get total loyal-servant brownies.

Then I saw her, the ancient vampyre mistress—her skin like alabaster, or you know, no zits at all, and she seemed to glow with inner power. I could see why even a powerful vampyre like Flood might be helpless under her awesome strengths, gathered over the ages by sucking the lifeblood of thousands of helpless victims, probably kids. And she was like, drinking a cup of coffee out of a Garfield mug, as if flaunting her immortality in the face of us petty, insignificant mortals. She had on only a bathrobe, which was partly open in front, so you could see that she had like great cleavage, ancient total skank that she was.

So I'm like, "Hi."

And she's like, "So, Wednesday, you know Buffy's not a real person, right?"

Bitch.

Uhat do you mean, dead?" Tommy said. He ran to the door and flung it open. "He's not here." He bolted down the steps in his bare feet, leaving Jody standing across the breakfast bar from Abby. "I'm going to look for him," Tommy called. The downstairs door closed, the lock clicked.

Jody pulled her robe closed when she saw Abby Normal staring. She could hear the girl's heart pounding, could see her pulse beating in her neck, could smell nervous sweat, clove cigarettes, and some kind of cheese snack.

They stared at each other.

"I found you an apartment, Mistress," Abby said. She dug into the pocket of her hoodie and came out with a rent receipt.

"Call me Jody," Jody said.

Abby nodded conspiratorially, like she was acknowledging it was only a code name. She was a cute kid, in a scary, will-probably-poison-the-dog-and-then-molest-him kind of way. Jody had never really had a problem with younger women as competition. After all, she was only twenty-six, and with the extreme antiaging treatment she'd gained from her vampirism, right down to her baby toes straightening out and every freckle she'd ever had disappearing, she felt superior, even a tad maternal toward Abby, who was a little knock-kneed in her red plastic skirt and green sneakers.

"I'm Abby," Abby said, and she curtsied.

Jody choked, sprayed coffee out her nose, and turned quickly so as not to laugh in Abby's face.

"Are you okay, Mistress—I mean, Jody?"

"No, I'm fine." It was strange just how sensitive the vampire sinus is to hot liquids. Jody was sure that she might never smell anything but bloody French roast again, and her eyes were watering, or so she thought, but when she turned back around, Abby jumped back six feet and yelped.

"Holy shit!" Abby had backed against the futon frame and was about to tumble over backwards.

Jody was around the breakfast bar, steadying the girl in less than a tenth of a second—which caused Abby to jump straight into the air about three feet.

Jody could tell the girl was going to fall. Abby was going to come down with one foot on the back of the futon frame, one in midair, and she was going to tumble over and land on her shoulder and head on the hardwood floor. Jody saw this coming, could have caught Abby and set her gently on her feet, but instead, she felt that maternal instinct kick in—the realization that if the child didn't take a knock or two, she'd never learn—so Jody stepped back into the kitchen, where she picked up her coffee and watched as the kid hit.

"Ouch!" Said Abby, now a black-and-red heap on the floor.

"Boy, that looked like it hurt," Jody said.

Abby was on her feet, limping and rubbing her head. "What the fuck, Countess? I thought you had my back."

"Yeah, sorry," Jody said. "Why the freak-out?"

"There's blood running down your face. I guess it startled me."

Jody dabbed at her eyes with the sleeve of her robe, leaving little red spots on the white terry cloth. "Well, would you look at that?" She was trying to be casual, trying to act like someone four or five hundred years old might behave, but the blood tears were disturbing her more than a little.

Change the subject. "So, this apartment you found, where is it?"

"Don't you want to wait for Flood?" Abby asked.

"Flood? What Flood?"

"Flood, the orange-colored vampire who just ran out the door."

"Oh, him," Jody said. Tommy and his tanning lotion. He was out running around on the street with no shirt or shoes. Orange. "Was he orange?"

Abby threw out her nearly nonexistent hip. "Hello? You're crying blood and your partner is orange and you didn't notice? Do you guys get senile over the years or what?"

Jody set her cup down on the counter, just to make sure that it didn't shatter in her hand. She drew on her experience working in the claims department at Transamerica, where her immediate supervisor was a complete ass-bag, and it took everything she could do, every minute of the day, not to bang the woman's skull repeatedly in a filing drawer. She liked to think of it as her professional face. So instead of snapping Abby's pale little neck, she smiled, counting to ten as she did. At ten, she said, "Go get him. Bring him back." Another smile. "Okay, sweetie?"

"But why is he orange?"

"The shedding is upon him," Jody said. "Every hundred years or so, we shed our skin, and a few weeks prior we turn orange. It's a very dangerous time for us. So please, go find him."

Abby nodded furiously and backed away toward the door. "Really?"

"Really," Jody said, nodding gravely. "Quick, away with you, the time of the shedding is upon him." She waved toward the door the way she thought a five-hundred-year-old countess might. (*Where did the countess thing come from, anyway?*)

"Right," Abby said, and she took off out the loft door and down the steps after Tommy.

Jody went to the bathroom and used a damp washcloth to wash the blood tears off her face. *I may actually be evil*, she thought. She knew it should bother her more, being evil and all, but after she put on a little mascara and some lipstick and poured herself another cup of blood-laced coffee, she found that she was okay with it.

Moving Day

Jody sipped her coffee and sighed, satisfied, like she'd just had a gentle coffee orgasm, the sort of pleasurable release you only see people have in commercials for froufrou coffee and hemorrhoid cream. This blood-beverage phenomenon added a whole new twist to their lives. A glass of wine? A diet cola maybe—wait, screw diet—a sugary, teeth-rotting cola. What about solid food? Sure, being a godlike creature of the night was great, but what about a jelly donut? French fries? She was Irish, she felt a deep-seated need for potatoes.

She was musing on the idea of heading up to McDonald's on Market Street and spooging a syringe full of William's blood all over a supersized box of deep-fried nirvana when the phone rang. The caller ID number was blocked, it just said *mobile*. It might be Tommy. He'd activated the disposable mobile phones they'd bought, but he probably hadn't written down the numbers.

"Hey, pumpkin," Jody said.

She heard a clattering at the other end of the line. "Sorry, I dropped the phone."

Oops. Not Tommy. "Who is this?"

"Uh, it's, uh, it's Steve. I'm the med student who called you about your condition."

He'd found her when she'd gone to a Blood Drinkers Anonymous meeting in Japan Town, which turned out to be a bunch of nerds with problems distinguishing fantasy from reality. Had watched her from a distance and called her on a pay phone from blocks away, ready to jump in his car and bolt if she came near him. He knew what she was.

He'd said that he had examined one of the bodies left by the old vampire. Elijah had snapped their necks so the bodies would be found, instead of turning to dust.

"What do you want?"

"Well, like I said, I'm a med student at Berkeley. Actually, I'm in research. Gene therapy."

"Yeah, next lie, please." Jody's mind was going ninety miles and hour. Too many people knew about her. Maybe she and Tommy *should* have left town.

"What lie?" Steve asked.

"Berkeley doesn't have a med school," Jody said. "So what do you want?"

"I don't want anything. I've been trying to tell you, I've studied the blood of the victims. I think I may be able to reverse your condition. Turn you back. I just need some time in the lab with your blood."

"Bullshit, Steve. This isn't biology."

"Yes it is. I told your boyfriend the night you turned him."

"How did you know . . . ?"

"I was on the phone with him when you told him you were going to be together for a very long time."

"Well, that was rude, just listening like that."

"Sorry. I've managed to get cloned cells from the throats of victims to revert to their natural human state."

"Which is dead," Jody said.

"No, living cells. I just need to meet with you."

He'd pressed this before, and Jody had been willing to meet with him, but unfortunately, while she was sleeping, Tommy had put her in the freezer for a few days and she'd missed the appointment. "No meeting, Steve. Forget you know anything about this. You'll have to write your dissertation on something else."

"Well, take my number if you change your mind, okay?"

He gave her the number and Jody wrote it down.

"It's a burner cell phone," Steve said, "So you can't find me through it."

"I don't want to find you, Steve."

"I promise I won't reveal your—your condition to anyone, so you don't need to find me."

"Don't worry," Jody said. "I don't want to find you." *Get over yourself,* she wanted to add.

"What about the other one you warned me about?"

Jody looked at the bronze statue that held Elijah Ben Sapir. "He won't bother you either."

"Oh, good."

"Steve?"

"Yeah?"

"If you tell anyone, I'll find you, and I'll slowly snap every bone in your body before I kill you." Jody tried to make it sound cheerful, but the threat sort of cut through the bright, friendly lilt in her voice.

"Okay then. Bye."

"Yeah," Jody said. "You take care."

The shedding?" Tommy said as he came through the door. Jody stood at the counter in her new red leather jacket, boots, and mist-tight black jeans.

Jody could hear Abby locking the downstairs door, so they had a few seconds alone.

"Look, did you want me to tell her you were just a big orange doofus?"

"I guess not. Hey—"

"She calls you Flood?"

"I couldn't tell her 'Tommy.' I'm her dark lord. Your dark lord can't be named Tommy. 'Flood' has an air of power."

"And dampness."

"Yeah, it's got the dampness thing going for it, too."

Abby came in, breathing hard. She'd been sweating and

her eyeliner was running in two black streaks down her cheeks. "We didn't find him. I could have sworn he was dead. He smelled like it."

"You got something against dead people?" Jody said— tough-guy voice. "Are you saying there's something wrong with dead people? Is that what you're saying? Are you saying you're too good for the dead, is that what you're saying?"

Abby stepped behind Tommy and peeked around. The kid was still out of breath from trying to keep up with Tommy, and now she was frightened, too. "No, Mistress, I think the nonliving are great. I'm all about dead people. I have a 'I Fuck the Dead' T-shirt even. I can wear it tomorrow if you want. I didn't mean . . ."

"It's okay, Abby," Jody said, waving it off. "Just fucking with you."

"Jody!" Tommy said, scolding. "Don't scare the minion."

"Sorry," Jody said, thinking, once again, that she might be evil. "What about the new apartment. Did you look at it?"

"We went by it. It's only a few doors down. We don't even have to cross the street."

"You think that's far enough? They won't find us there?"

"Well, at least they won't find us *here*. I don't think anyone's going to think that we'd only move a few doors down. They'll think we've at least left the City. What kind of idiot would only move a few doors away? It's brilliant."

"Plus an easy move," Jody said. "You guys can do it without a truck."

"You guys?"

"Well, I've got to find William, and you can't exactly run around until the shedding has subsided. Abby, do you have enough makeup to cover his face and hands?"

"Tons," Abby said. She held up her messenger bag. "But I can only help for a little while. I have to get home."

"Why?" Tommy asked. "We require your services." He meant to sound sophisticated and European, but it came out sounding lecherous.

"He means moving," Jody said. "I've got his other services covered."

"I can't," Abby said. "My sister has lice."

So," Abby said, "the countess is kind of a bitch."

"No, she's just a dark creature of unspeakable evil," Tommy said. He had the futon on his back and was making his way down the street as Abby followed him with a lamp in one hand and a blender in the other. "In a nice way," he added—thinking that maybe he'd already made enough of an impression on Abby.

Although it was early in the evening, and it was a little unusual to see a guy walking down the street carrying a futon, followed by a Goth girl carrying a lamp and a blender, it was just unusual enough that people would have felt stupid if they asked what was going on and someone pointed out it was modern dance, or performance art, or people robbing an apartment. San Francisco is a city of sophisticates,

and except for a homeless guy who remarked on the tacki-
ness of Tommy's Pier 1 Imports decor, they had moved half
of the furniture and clothing without comment.

"Do you need to feed?" Abby asked when they got back
to the old loft. They were standing in the living room,
where there was little left except some bookcases and the
three bronze statues.

"Huh?" Tommy replied.

"I'm guessing that you need to feed," Abby said, pulling
her hoodie aside and offering up her neck. "And I have to get
going. I have to get to Walgreens and catch the bus home
before the parental unit goes critical. Go ahead. I'm ready."

She closed her eyes and started breathing hard, as if
bracing for the pain. "Take me, Flood. I'm ready."

"Really?" Tommy said.

Abby opened one eye. "Well yeah."

"You're sure?" Tommy hadn't bitten another woman.
He wasn't sure if it might not be cheating. What if the
whole sex thing went off the way it did with Jody? That
kind of activity would kill a normal human woman, plus,
he was pretty sure that Jody would not approve. "Maybe a
little from the wrist," Tommy said.

Abby opened her eyes and pulled up her sleeve. "Of
course, so you don't leave the mark of *nosferatu*." She said it
with a hiss—*nasss*—*sssss*—*fer-a-too*—like she was speaking
snake.

"Oh, it won't leave any marks," Tommy said. "You'll
heal up like instantly." He was starting to feel the hunger

rise in him, he could feel his fangs pressing down from the roof of his mouth.

"Really?"

"Oh yeah, Jody bit me almost every night before I changed over, and no one ever noticed down at the store."

"The store?"

Oops. "The ye olde porridge and leeches store, where I worked, in the ye old days."

"I thought you were a lord?"

"Well, yeah, I mean, I owned the store, and some serfs, and scullery maids—couldn't get enough of the scullery maids—but I put in a shift now and then. You know, help to stir the porridge and inventory the leeches. Serfs will steal you blind if you don't watch them. Well, enough business, let's get to that feeding."

He took her wrist and pulled it to his mouth, then stopped. She was looking at him, one eyebrow sort of cocked in the air, and there was a silver ring in it, so it felt more incredulous than a normal eyebrow.

He dropped her arm.

"You know, maybe you should get home before you get in trouble. I wouldn't want my minion on restriction."

Abby looked hurt now. "But, Lord Flood, have I offended you? Am I not deserving?"

"You were looking at me like you thought I was fucking with you," Tommy said.

"Weren't you?"

"Well no. This is a two-way street, Abby. I can't ask for

your loyalty if I don't give you trust in return." He couldn't believe the bullshit that was coming out of his mouth.

"Oh, okay then."

"Tomorrow night," Tommy said. "I'll bleed you within an inch of your life, I promise." The things you never think you'll hear yourself say.

Abby rolled down her sleeve. "Okay then. Will you be able to get the rest by yourself?"

"Sure. Vampire powers. Duh." He laughed, waving at the heavy bronze statues like they were nothing.

"You know," Abby said, "the man and the turtle are cool, but that woman statue, you should get rid of that. She looks kind of skanky."

"You think?"

Abby nodded. "Yeah. Maybe there's some church or something that you could donate it to. Like, to show how you don't want your daughter to grow up. Oh, sorry, Lord Flood, I didn't mean to say church."

"No, I'm okay," Tommy said. "I'll walk you out."

"Thanks," Abby said.

He followed her downstairs and held the door to the street, then at the last minute, as she was walking away, she turned and kissed him quickly on the cheek. "I love you, Lord Flood," she whispered in his ear. Then she turned and ran up the sidewalk.

Tommy felt himself blush. Dead as he was, he felt heat rise in his cheeks. He turned and trudged back up the steps, feeling the full weight of his four, maybe five hundred years of life. He needed to talk to Jody. How long could it take to find one drunk guy with a giant cat?

He dug his cell phone out of his pocket and dialed the number of the phone he'd given Jody. He could hear it ringing on the kitchen counter where she had left it.

Powers for Good

The Emperor was sitting on a black marble bench just around the corner from the great opera house, feeling small and ashamed, when he saw the striking redhead in jeans coming toward him. Bummer lapsed into a barking fit and the Emperor snatched the Boston terrier up by the scruff of the neck and stuffed him into the oversized pocket of his coat to quiet him.

"Brave Bummer," said the old man. "Would that I could still hold that kind of passion, even if it were fear. But my fear is weak and damp, I've barely the spine for a dignified surrender."

He'd felt like this since he'd seen Jody outside the secondhand store, where she'd warned him away from the owner. Yes, now he knew her to be one of the undead, a bloodsucking fiend—but then, not so much a fiend. She had been a friend, a good one, even after he had betrayed Tommy to the Animals. He could feel the City's eye on him, could feel her disappointment in him. What does a man have, if not character? What is character, if not a man's measure of himself against his friends and enemies? The great city of San Francisco shook her head at him, ashamed. Her bridges slumped in the fog with disappointment.

He remembered a house somewhere and that same look on the face of a dark-haired woman, but mercifully, in an instant that memory was a ghost, and Jody was bending to scratch behind the ears of the steadfast Lazarus, who had never been agitated by her like his bug-eyed brother, who even now squirmed furiously in the woolen pocket.

"Your Majesty," Jody said. "How are you?"

"Worthless and weak," said the Emperor. She really was a lovely girl. He'd never known her to hurt a soul. What a cad he was.

"I'm sorry to hear that. You have plenty to eat? Staying warm?"

"The men and I have this very hour vanquished a corned beef on a sourdough roll the size of a healthy infant, thank you."

"Tommy's Joynt?" Jody said with a smile.

"Indeed. We are not worthy, yet my people provide."

"Don't be silly, you're worthy. Look, Emperor, have you seen William?"

"William of the huge and recently shaven cat?"

"That's the one."

"Why yes, we crossed his path not long ago. He was at

the liquor store at Geary and Taylor. He seemed very enthusiastic about purchasing some scotch. More energetic than I've seen him in many years."

"That was how long ago?" She stopped petting Lazarus and stood.

"Little more than an hour ago."

"Thank you, Your Majesty. You don't know where he was going?"

"I should think to find a safe place to drink his dinner. Although I can't claim to know him well, I don't think William passes the evening in the Tenderloin often."

Jody patted the Emperor's shoulder, and he took her hand.

"I'm so sorry, dear."

"Sorry? About what?"

"When I saw you and Thomas the other night, I noticed. It's true, isn't it? Thomas has changed."

"No, he's still a doofus."

"I mean he is one of your kind now?"

"Yes." She looked up the street. "I was alone," she said.

The Emperor knew exactly how she felt. "I told one of his crew from the Safeway, Jody. I'm sorry, I was frightened."

"You told the Animals?"

"The born-again one, yes."

"And how did he react?"

"He was worried for Thomas's soul."

"Yeah, that would be Clint's reaction. You don't know if he told the other Animals?"

"I would guess yes, by now."

"Okay, don't worry, then, Your Highness. It's okay. Just don't tell anyone else. Tommy and I are leaving the City just like we promised those police detectives. We just have to get things in order."

"And the other—the old vampire?"

"Yes. Him, too."

She turned and strode away, heading into the Tenderloin, her boot heels clacking on the sidewalk as she kept her pace just below a run.

The Emperor shook his head and rubbed Lazarus behind the ears. "I should have told her about the detectives. I know that, old friend." There was only so much weakness he could confess to at one time—that, too, a fault. The Emperor resolved to sleep somewhere cold and damp tonight, perhaps in the park by the Maritime Museum, as penance for his weakness.

There was no way she was going to remember his new mobile number. It was five in the morning before Tommy had finished moving all of the furniture, books, and clothes. Now the new loft looked almost exactly like the old loft had looked, except that it didn't have a working phone line. So Tommy sat on the counter of the old loft, looking at the three bronze statues and waiting for Jody to call.

Just the three statues left to move: Jody, the old vampire, and the turtle. The old vampire looked fairly natural.

He'd been unconscious when he'd been bronzed, but Tommy had the biker sculptors downstairs pose him as if he was in midstep, out for a stroll. Jody was posed with her hand on her hip, her head thrown back as if she'd just tossed her long hair over her shoulder, smiling.

Tommy turned his head to the side, getting perspective. She didn't look skanky. What made Abby say the statue was skanky? Sexy, well yes. Jody had been wearing some very low-cut jeans and a crop top when he'd posed her for the electroplating, and the bikers had insisted upon exposing more of her cleavage than was probably decorous, but what could you expect from a couple of guys who specialized in making high-end garden gnomes acting out the Kama Sutra?

Okay, she looked a little skanky, but he didn't see how that was a bad thing. He had actually been delighted when she came streaming out of the ear holes to materialize, stark naked, in front of him. If she hadn't killed him, it would have been the fulfillment of a sexual fantasy he'd nurtured for a long time. (There had been this old TV show he'd watched as a kid, about a beautiful genie who lived in a bottle—well, Tommy had done some serious bottle polishing over that one.)

So the Jody statue stayed. But the old vampire, Elijah, that was a different story. There was a real creature in there. A real scary creature. Whatever bizarre events had brought them to this spot had been set off by Elijah Ben Sapir. He was a reminder that neither he—Tommy—nor

Jody had chosen to be vampires. Neither had chosen to live out the rest of their days in the night. Elijah had taken their choices away from them, and replaced them with a whole new set of scarier, bigger choices. The first of which was how the hell do you deal with the fact that you have imprisoned a sentient, feeling being in a shell of bronze, even if he is an evil dick-weed from the Dark Ages? But they couldn't let him out. He'd kill them for sure if they did. Really kill them, too, a complete death, the kind with no nooky.

Suddenly Tommy was angry. He'd had a future. He might have been a writer, a Nobel Prize winner, an adventurer, a spy. Now he was just a foul dead thing, and the furthest his ambition would reach was his next victim. Okay, that wasn't really true, but still, he was pissed off. So what if Elijah was trapped in a bronze shell forever. He'd trapped them in these monstrous bodies. Maybe it was time to do something monstrous.

Tommy picked up Jody's statue and threw it over his shoulder and, despite his great vampire strength, followed it over backward as it clanged against the floor. Okay, it had taken the two bikers and a refrigerator dolly to get the statues up here, maybe a little planning was in order.

It turned out he could move the statue pretty efficiently if he slung it over his back and let one of her feet drag, and so he did, down the steps, half a block down the sidewalk, and back up the steps of the new loft. Bronze Jody looked happy in the new place, he thought. The turtle took half as long. She, too, looked pleased with the surroundings.

As for Elijah, Tommy figured what was the point of being in a city on a peninsula if you didn't take advantage of the water now and then. And Elijah evidently liked the ocean, since he'd come to the City on his yacht, which Tommy and the Animals had managed to blow to smithereens.

The vampire statue was even heavier that Jody's, but Tommy felt energized by the idea of getting rid of it. Just a short twelve blocks to the sea and that would be that.

"From the sea ye came, and to the sea ye shall return," Tommy said, thinking that he might be quoting Coleridge, or maybe a Godzilla movie.

As Tommy dragged the bronzed vampire down Mission Street, he considered his future. What *would* he do? He had a lot of time to fill, and after a while, figuring out new ways to jump Jody would only fill up a part of his nights. He was going to have to find a purpose. They had money— cash the vampire had given Jody when he turned her—and what was left of the money from the sale of Elijah's art, but eventually that would run out. Maybe he should get a job. Or become a crime fighter.

That's it, he would use his powers for good. Maybe get an outfit.

After a few blocks Tommy noticed that Elijah's toe, the one that was dragging on the sidewalk, was starting to wear away. The bikers had warned Tommy that the bronze shell was pretty thin. It wouldn't do to unleash a claustrophobic and hungry ancient vampire when you were the guy who had imprisoned him, so Tommy stood the vampire on the corner for a minute while he dug through a trash bin until he found some heavy-duty plastic Big Gulp cups, which he fitted on the vampire's dragging foot as skid protection.

"Ha!" Tommy said. "Thought you had me."

A couple of guys in hip-hop wear walked by as Tommy was fitting the cups on the vampire's feet. Tommy made the mistake of making eye contact and they paused.

"Stole it from a building on Fourth," Tommy said.

The two nodded, as if they were saying, *Of course, we were just wondering,* and proceeded to move down the sidewalk.

They must sense my superior strength and speed, Tommy thought, *so they wouldn't dare mess with me.* In fact, the two had confirmed that the white boy in the ghost makeup was crazy—and what would they do with a four-hundred-pound statue anyway?

Tommy figured he'd drag the statue to the Embarcadero and toss it off the pier by the Ferry Building. If there was anyone around, he'd just stand at the rail like he was there with his gay lover, then shove the statue in when no one was looking. He felt enormously sophisticated about the plan. No one would ever think a guy from Indiana was pretending to be gay. That kind of thing just wasn't done. Tommy had known a kid once in high school who had gone up to Chicago to see the musical *Rent* and was never heard from again. Tommy reckoned he'd been disappeared by the local Kiwanis Club.

When he got to the Embarcadero, which ran all along

the waterfront, Tommy was tempted to just chuck Elijah in the Bay right there and call it a night, but he had a plan, so he dragged the vampire that last two blocks to the promenade at the end of Market Street, where the antique streetcars, the cable cars, and the cross-bay ferries all converged in a big paved park and sculpture garden. Here, away from the buildings, the night seemed to open up to his vampire senses, take on a new light. Tommy stopped for moment, stood Elijah by a fountain, and watched heat streaming out of some grates by the streetcar turnaround. Perfect. There was absolutely no one around.

Then the beeping started. Tommy looked at his watch. Sunrise in ten minutes. The night hadn't opened up to him, it had been shutting him down. Ten minutes, and the loft was a good twenty blocks away.

Jody was quickstepping along the alleyway that came out in front of their old loft. She still had twenty minutes until sunrise, but she could see the sky lightening, and twenty minutes was cutting it too close. Tommy would be freaked. She should have taken the cell phone with her. She shouldn't have left him alone with the new minion.

She'd finally found William, passed out in a doorway in Chinatown, with Chet the huge cat sleeping on his chest. They'd have to remember not to leave William with any money from now on, if he was going to be their food source. Otherwise he'd go elsewhere for his alcohol, and that wasn't going to work. He was making his staggering way home on his own. Maybe she'd let him take a shower at the old loft—they weren't going to get their deposit back anyway.

There was still a light on in the loft. Great, Tommy was home. She'd forgotten to get a key for the new place. She was about to step out of the alley when she smelled cigar smoke and heard a man's voice. She stopped and peeked around the corner.

There was a brown Ford sedan parked across the street from their old loft, and in it sat two middle-aged men. Cavuto and Rivera, the homicide detectives that she'd made a deal with the night they'd blown up Elijah's yacht. They'd moved just in time, but then, maybe not quite. She couldn't get to the new place either. It was only a half a block away, and she'd have to cross in the open. And even then, what if it was locked?

She jumped four feet straight up when the alarm on her watch went off.

It was toward the end of their second shift after returning to the Safeway that the Animals sobered up. Lash was sitting by himself in the wide backseat of the Hummer limo, his head cradled in his hands, hoping desperately that the despair and self-loathing he was feeling was only the effect of a hangover, instead of what it really was, which was a big flaming enema of reality. The reality was, they had spent more than a half a million dollars on a blue hooker. He let the hugeness of it roll around in his head, and looked up at the other Animals, who were sitting around the perimeter of the limo, similarly posed, trying not to make eye contact with one another. They'd had nearly two semi trucks of stock to put up that night, and they'd known it was coming because they'd ordered it to make up for the time they'd been away and Clint had let the shelves get low. So they'd sobered up, put their heads down, and thrown stock like the Animals that they were. Now it was getting close to dawn and it was dawning on all of them that they might have severely fucked up.

Lash risked a sideways glance at Blue, who was sitting between Barry and Troy Lee. She'd taken Lash's apartment on Northpoint, and made him sleep on the couch at Troy Lee's, where there were about seven hundred Chinese family members, including Troy's grandmother, who, every time she passed through the room during the day, when Lash was trying to sleep, would screech, "What's up, my nigga!" and try to get him to wake up and give her a pound or a high five.

Lash had been explaining to her that it's impolite to refer to an African American as a nigga, unless one was another African-American, when Troy Lee came in and said, "She only speaks Cantonese."

"She does not. She keeps coming in and saying, 'What's up, my nigga?'"

"Oh yeah. She does that to me, too. Did you give her a pound?"

"No, I didn't give her a pound, motherfucker. She called me a nigga."

"Well, she's not going to quit unless you give her a pound. It's just the way she rolls."

"That's some bullshit, Troy."

"It's her couch."

Lash, exhausted and already hungover, gave the wizened old woman a pound.

Granny turned to Troy Lee. "What's up, my nigga!" She offered and received a pound from her grandson.

"That shit is not the same!" Lash said.

"Get some sleep. We have a big load tonight."

Now half a million dollars was gone. His apartment was gone. The limo was costing them a thousand dollars a day. Lash looked out the blackout windows at the moving patchwork of shadows thrown by the streetlights, then turned to Blue

"Blue," he said. "We have to get rid of the limo."

Everyone looked up, shocked. No one had said anything to her since they'd finished stocking. They'd brought her coffee and juice, but no one had said anything.

Blue looked at him. "Get me what I want." Not a hint of malice, not even a demand, really, just a statement of fact.

"Okay," Lash said. Then to the driver he said, "Take a right up here. Head back to that building where we went last night."

Lash crawled over the divider into the front passenger seat. He couldn't see shit out the blackened windows. They'd only gone about three blocks into the SOMA district when he saw someone running. Running way, way too fast for a jogger. Running—like he was on fire—running.

"Pull up alongside of that guy."

The driver nodded.

"Hey, guys, is that Flood?"

"Yeah, it is," Barry, the bald one, said.

Lash rolled down the window. "Tommy, you need a ride, man?"

Tommy, still running, nodded like a bobble-head on crack.

Barry threw open the back door, and before the limo could even slow down, Tommy leapt in, landing across Drew and Gustavo's laps.

"Man, am I glad you guys came along," Tommy said. "In about a minute, I'm going to—"

He passed out in their laps as the sun washed over the hills of San Francisco.

Broken Clowns

Inspector Alphonse Rivera watched the broken clown girl—black-and-white-striped stockings and green sneakers—come out of Jody Stroud's apartment and head up the street, then turn and look back at their brown, unmarked sedan.

"We're made," said Nick Cavuto, Rivera's partner, a broad-shouldered bear of a man, who longed for the days of Dashiell Hammett, when cops talked tough and there were very few problems that couldn't be solved with your fists or a smack from a lead sap.

"We're not made. She's just looking. Two middle-aged guys sitting in the car on the city street—it's unusual."

If Cavuto was a bear, then Rivera was a raven—a sharp-featured, lean Hispanic, with just a touch of gray at the temples. Lately he'd taken to wearing expensive Italian suits, in raw silk or linen when he could find them. His partner was in rumpled Men's Wearhouse. Rivera often wondered if

Nick Cavuto might not be the only gay man on the planet who had no fashion sense whatsoever.

The knock-kneed kid with the raccoon eye makeup was making her way across the street toward them.

"Roll up your window," Cavuto said. "Roll up your window. Pretend like you don't see her."

"I'm not going to hide from her," Rivera said. "She's just a kid."

"Exactly. You can't hit her."

"Jesus, Nick. She's just a creepy kid. What's wrong with you?"

Cavuto had been on edge since they'd pulled up an hour ago. They both had, really, since the guy named Clint, one of the night crew from the Marina Safeway, had left a message on Rivera's voice mail that Jody Stroud, the redheaded vampire, had not left town as she had promised, and that her boyfriend, Tommy Flood, was now also a vampire. It was a very bad turn of events for the two cops, both of whom had taken a share of the money from the old vampire's art collection in return for letting them all go. It had seemed like the only option, really. Neither of the cops wanted to explain how the serial killer they'd been chasing had been an ancient vampire, and how he'd been tracked down by a bunch of stoners from the Safeway. And when the Animals blew up the vampire's yacht—well, the case was solved, and if the vampires had left, it would have all been good. The cops had planned to retire early and open a rare-book store. Rivera thought he might learn to golf.

Now he was feeling it all float away on an evil breeze. A cop for twenty years, without ever so much as fixing a traffic ticket, then the one time you take a hundred thousand dollars and let a vampire go, the whole world turns on you like you're some kind of bad guy. Rivera was raised a Catholic, but he was starting to believe in karma.

"Pull out. Pull out," Cavuto said. "Go around the block until she goes away."

"Hey," said the broken clown girl. "You guys cops?"

Cavuto hit the window button on his door but the ignition was off, so the window didn't budge. "Go away, kid. Why aren't you in school? Do we need to take you in?"

"Winter break, brain trust," said the kid.

Rivera couldn't hold the laugh in and he snorted a little trying to.

"Move along, kid. Go wash that shit off your face. You look like you fell asleep with a Magic Marker in your mouth."

"Yeah," said the kid, examining a black fingernail, "well, you look like someone pumped about three hundred pounds of cat barf into a cheap suit and gave it a bad haircut."

Rivera slid down in his seat and turned his face toward the door. He couldn't look at his partner. He was sure that if it was possible for steam to come out of someone's ears, that might be happening to Cavuto, and if he looked, he'd lose it.

"If you were a guy," Cavuto said, "I'd have you in handcuffs already, kid."

"Oh God," Rivera said under his breath.

"If I were a guy, I'll bet you would. And I'll bet I'd have to send you to the S and M ATM, because the kinky shit is extra." The kid leaned down so she was eye level with Cavuto, and winked.

That was it. Rivera started giggling like a little girl—tears were creeping out the corners of his eyes.

"You're a big fucking help," Cavuto said. He reached over, flipped the ignition key to "accessory," then rolled up his window.

The kid came over to Rivera's side of the car.

"So, have you seen Flood?" she asked. "Cop?" She added "cop" with a high pop on the *p*, like it was a punctuation mark, not a profession.

"You just came out of his apartment," Rivera said, trying to shake off the giggles. "You tell me."

"Place is empty. The douche nozzle owes me money," said the kid.

"For what?"

"Stuff I did for him."

"Be specific, sweetheart. Unlike my partner, I don't threaten." It was a threat, of course, but he thought he might have hit pay dirt, the kid's eyes opened wide enough to see light.

"I helped him and that redheaded hag load their stuff into a truck."

Rivera looked her up and down. She couldn't have weighed ninety pounds. "He hired you to help him move?"

"Just little crap. Lamps and stuff. They were like, in a hurry. I was walking by, he flagged me down. Said he'd give me a hundred bucks."

"But he didn't?"

"He gave me eighty. He said it was all he had on him. To come back this morning for the rest."

"Did either of them say where they were going?"

"Just that they were going to leave the City this morning, as soon as they paid me."

"You notice anything unusual about either of them—Flood or the redhead?"

"Just day dwellers, like you. Bourgeois four-oh-fours."

"Four-oh-Fours?"

"Clueless—Pottery Barn fucktards."

"Of course," Rivera said. He could hear his partner snickering now.

"So you haven't seen them?" the kid said.

"They're not coming, kid."

"How do you know that?"

"I know that. You're out twenty dollars. Cheap lesson. Go away and don't come back here, and if either of them contact you, or you see them, call me."

Rivera handed the kid a business card. "What's your name?"

"My day-slave name?"

"Sure, let's try that one."

"Allison. Allison Green. But on the street I'm known as Abby Normal."

"On the street?"

"Shut up, I have street cred." Then she added, "Cop!" like the chirp of a car alarm arming.

"Good. Take your street cred and run along, Allison."

She shuffled off, trying to swivel nearly nonexistent hips as she went.

"You think they left the City?" Cavuto asked.

"I want to own a bookstore, Nick. I want to sell old books and learn to golf."

"So that would be no?"

"Let's go talk to the born-again Safeway guy."

Four robots and one statue guy worked the Embarcadero by the Ferry Building. Not every day. Some days, when it was slow, there were only two robots and a statue guy, or on rainy days, none of them worked, because the silver or gold makeup they used to color their skin didn't hold up well in the rain, but as a rule, it was four robots and one statue guy. Monet was the statue guy—the ONLY statue guy. He'd staked his territory three years ago, and if some poseur ever showed up, he had to meet Monet on the field of stillness, where they would clash in the motion-free battle of doing absolutely nothing. Monet had always prevailed, but this guy—this new guy—was really good.

The challenger had been there when Monet arrived in the late morning, and he hadn't even blinked for two hours. The guy's makeup was perfect, too. He looked as if he had really been bronzed, so it was beyond Monet why he would choose to get his collections in Big Gulp cups that he'd jammed his feet into. Monet carried a small portfolio case, with a hole cut in it where tourists could stuff their bills. He had primed his money hole with a five today, just to show the challenger that he wasn't intimidated, but the truth was, after two hours, he hadn't made half of what he saw the newcomer take in, and he *was* intimidated. And his nose itched.

His nose itched and the new statue guy was kicking his ass. Normally Monet would change positions every half hour or so, then stand motionless while the tourists taunted him and tried to make him flinch, but with the new competition, he had to stay still as long as it took.

The robots on the promenade had all assumed poses from which they could watch. They only had to hold still until someone dropped cash into their cup, then they would do the robot dance. It was boring work, but the hours were good and you were outside. It looked like Monet was going down.

Sundown.

He felt like his ass was on fire.

Tommy came to to the sound of a riding crop being smacked against his bare butt and the rough bark of a woman's voice.

"Say it! Say it! Say it!"

He tried to pull away from the pain but couldn't move

his arms or legs. He was having trouble focusing his vision—waves of light and heat were rocketing around his brain and all he could really see was a bright red spot with waves of heat coming off of it and a figure moving around the edges. It was like staring into the sun through a red filter. He could feel the heat on his face.

"Ouch!" Tommy said. "Dammit!" He pulled against his bonds and heard a metallic rattling, but nothing gave.

The red hot light went away and was replaced by the blurry form of a female face, a blue face, just inches away from his own. "Say it," she whispered harshly, spitting a little on the "it."

"Say what?"

"Say it, vampire!" she said. She whipped the riding crop across his stomach and he howled.

Tommy squirmed against his bonds and heard the rattling again. With the spotlight moved away, he could see that he was suspended by very professional-looking nylon restraints to a brass, four-poster bed frame that had been stood on end. He was completely naked and evidently the blue woman, who was dressed in a black vinyl bustier, boots, and nothing else, had been whaling on him for some time. He could see welts across his stomach and thighs, and well, his ass felt like it was on fire.

She wound up to smack him again.

"Whoa, whoa, whoa, whoa," Tommy said, trying not to screech. He only realized then that his fangs were extended and he'd bitten his own lips.

The blue woman held up. "Say it."

Tommy tried to keep his voice calm. "I know you've been doing this for a while now, but I've only been awake for about a minute of it, so I have no idea what you are asking me. If you slow down and repeat the whole question, I'll be happy to tell you whatever I know."

"Your safety word," said the blue woman.

"Which is?" Tommy said. He noticed for the first time that she had enormous boobs spilling out of that bustier and it occurred to him that he had never seen big blue boobs before. They were kind of mesmerizing. He wouldn't have been able to look away even if he weren't strapped down.

"I told you," she said, letting the riding crop fall to her side.

"You told me what a safety word is?"

"I just told you what *it* is."

"So you know it, then?"

"Yes," she said.

"Then why are you asking?"

"To see if you're at your breaking point." She seemed to be pouting a little now. "Don't be a dick, this isn't my specialty."

"Where am I?" Tommy asked. "You're Lash's Smurf, aren't you? Are we at Lash's?"

"I'm asking the questions here." She snapped the riding crop against his thigh.

"Ouch! Fuck! Stop that. You have issues, lady."

"Say it!"

"What is it? I was asleep when you told me, you stupid bitch!" He was wrong, he *was* able to look away from the blue boobs. He snarled at her, something coming up from deep inside him that he didn't even recognize—something that felt wild and on the verge of out of control—like when he first made love with Jody as a vampire, only this felt—well, lethal.

"It's Cheddar."

"Cheddar? Like the cheese?" He was getting a beating because of cheese?

"Yes."

"So I said it. Now what?"

"You're broken."

" 'Kay," Tommy said, straining against the heavy nylon straps, understanding now what he was feeling. He was going to kill her. He didn't know how yet, but he was as certain of it as of anything he had ever known. Grass was green, water was wet, and this bitch was dead.

"So now you have to turn me," she said.

"Turn you?" he said. His fangs ached, like they were going to leap out of his mouth.

"Make me like you," she said.

"You want to be orange? Is this another Cheddar thing? Because—"

"Not orange, you nitwit, a vampire!" she said, and she snapped the riding crop across his chest.

He bit his lips again and felt the blood running down

his chin. "So for that you needed all the hitting?" He said. "Come over here."

She leaned up and kissed him, then pushed away hard and came away with his blood on her mouth. "I guess I'm going to have to get used to this," she said, licking her lips.

"Closer," Tommy said.

Being the Chronicles of Abby Normal: Completely Fucked Servant of the Vampyre Flood

OMFG-W00T! I have failed, left my duty undone, like so much dog poop on the gloaming sidewalk of the tragedy that is my life. Even as I sit here at the Metreon Starbucks, writing this, the froth slaves seem to move like silver-eyed zombies and my nonfat, soy Amaretto Mochaccino has gone as bitter as snake bile. (Which is like the bitterest bile you can get.) If there wasn't a totally hot guy two tables away, acting like he doesn't notice me, I would weep—but real tears make your mascara run, so I'm staying chilly in my despair. Your loss, cute guy, for I have been chosen. Suffer, bitch!

I had to leave Lord Flood to his own devices last night, but before I left, I confessed my undying love for him. I am a hopeless hose beast. All I had to do was say good-bye, but no, I just barked it out. It's like he has this power over me—like I have an eating disorder and he's a package of

Oreo Double Stuff cookies. (I don't have an eating disorder, I'm just skinny because I enjoy eating mass quantities and then yakking it back up. It's not a body-image problem. I think my system has always wanted to live on a liquid diet, and until I'm brought into my Dark Lord's loving embrace, then it's Starbucks for me.)

I have been trying to call my Dark Lord and the Countess all day on their cells, but I kept getting voice mail. Well, duh—they're vampires. They won't be answering the phone. I'm such a tard sometimes.

So I went to the old loft early this morning, in fact even before dawn. I should be, like, made a Brontë sister for coming up with a story to get out of the house that early, but I wanted to talk to the master before his slumber. Thing was, the scary drunk guy and his huge cat were gone, but so were my master and the Countess. Everything had been moved except the statue of the turtle and the Countess.

So I rolled out, headed for the new loft I rented, when I spotted two cops sitting in a POS brown car. I knew they were vampyre hunters right away. It must be the master's dark powers rubbing off on me. There was a big fat gay cop and a sharp-faced Hispano-cop.

So I was like, "Could you guys look any more like cops?"

And they were like, "Move along, little lady."

So I was forced to point out to them that they were not the boss of me and then I proceeded to humiliate them by verbally bitch-slapping them until they cried. What is it about the crusties? Their minds work so slowly that you have to, like, prompt them to stand up so you can slap them again until they faint like the little wuss-bags that they are. I never want to be crusty. And I won't be, because my Lord will bring me into the fold and I shall stalk the night for eternity, my beauty forever preserved as it is, except I'd like a little bigger boobs.

Anyway, I wandered around on Market Street and up in Union Square to give the cops enough time to slink off to lick their wounds, then I returned to the master's street to check the new loft. This time there was this Asian guy sitting across the street in a Honda, looking all Manga-cool, but it was obvious that he was watching the loft door. He didn't look like a cop, but he was definitely watching, so I stopped and pretended to watch the sculptors work who have the space under the master's old loft. They are these two crusty biker guys, but they do some amazing shit. They'd left the garage door open so I stepped in.

They were putting dead chickens on wires and dipping them in silver paint, then hanging them on sticks by the wires.

So I was all, "What the fuck, biker? What are you doing?"

And one of them was like, "It's almost the year of the cock."

And I was all, "Don't be gross, you crustacious fuck. You pull that thing out and I'll pepper-spray you until you fry." (You have to be stern with weenie waggers—I've been exposed to on the bus over seventeen times, so I know.)

And he was like, "No, it's the year of the cock in the Chinese zodiac."

Which I knew, of course.

"We're making statues," said the bigger biker, who was named Frank. (The other one's name was Monk. He didn't talk much, which might explain the name.)

So they showed me how they took real dead roosters they bought in Chinatown, ran wires through them to pose them, then dipped them in a thin metallic paint, then put them in this big tank and attached electric clips to them. They pass some current through the clips and the current attracts bronze molecules or something to the metallic paint. It's like instant bronze rooster. I thought about the statue of the Countess upstairs and got a little creeped out.

So I'm all, "You ever do a person?"

And they were like, "No way, that would be wrong. You'd better go now, because we're behind and don't you have school and stuff?"

So walking out, I saw the Asian guy checking me out and I was like, "Hey, it's almost the year of the cock. Shouldn't you be out shopping for one?"

He looked really nervous, but he kinda grinned. Then started his car and drove off, but he wants me, I can tell, so he'll be back. I hope he wants me. He was so cute—in that Final Fantasy Thirty-Seven way. What I'm saying is, the Sex Fu is strong with this one.

So there was no sign of my Dark Lord or the Countess at the new place. I wonder if they have crawled under the earth in some park and satisfied their perverse desires with each other among the worms and the tree roots. Eww!

Oh well, almost dark. I'd better go back to the loft and wait for them.

Addendum: The lice shampoo didn't work on my sister. Looks like we might have to shave her head. I'm going to try to talk her into getting a pentagram tattooed on her scalp. I know a guy in the Haight who will do it for free if you verbally abuse him while he's tattooing. More later.

Sundown. Jody awoke to pain and the smell of cooking meat. She rolled away from the source of the pain and went crashing through the acoustical ceiling tiles to land in a commercial sink full of dishes and soapy water. A Mexican guy was backing across the dish room crossing himself and invoking saints in Spanish as Jody climbed out of the sink and brushed suds off her jacket and jeans. When she touched the front of her thighs she nearly leapt back through the ceiling the pain was so sharp.

"Mother-fuck-that-hurts!" she said, hopping around on one foot, because that will generally help all manner of pain, regardless of where it's located on the body. Her boot heel clicking against the tiles sounded like a limping flamenco dancer.

The dishwasher turned and bolted out of the dish room into the bakery.

The bakery. When the alarm on her watch had threatened dawn she ran down the alley checking doors as she went, and the only one she found unlocked led into the stockroom of a bakery. She needed a place to hide where she'd be undisturbed while she slept, and although she considered hiding under a couple of the fifty-pound bags of flour, she had no way of knowing if the bakers would be using them today. She'd already awakened in a morgue once before (when Tommy had frozen her), and finding a rotund necrophiliac morgue attendant rubbing his hands and other bits over her seminaked body while she thawed had soured her to the whole morgue experience. No, she had to find someplace more secluded.

One of the bakers had been coming into the stockroom, she could hear his voice and footfalls outside the door. She looked around for somewhere to hide, then spotted the grimy acoustic ceiling tiles suspended above. She leapt onto the pallet of flour, lifted a tile to see that the ceiling was suspended a full four feet below the structural ceiling. Bless old buildings. She grabbed a water pipe, pulled herself through the ceiling, jackknifed her legs up and around the pipe, then used her free hand to pull the ceiling tile back in place, all in less than two seconds.

She listened as the man moved around below her, then scooped up one of the big bags of flour and left the room. That was a good call.

She checked her watch. Less than a minute before she'd go out. She spotted four pipes running together parallel to the floor. They were slightly warm, which was why she could see them at all in the darkness, but each was two inches around and braced to the ceiling every few feet. They'd hold her.

She scrambled over to the pipes, squirmed out of her leather jacket, and put it across the pipes, then lay facedown on top of it. This way, even if one of her legs slipped off, it wouldn't pull her off the pipes. She was trying to wedge the toes of her boots into the gap between the pipes when she went out.

The problem was that the pipes weren't used that early in the morning. As the building awoke, hot water began coursing through them, and Jody had been subjected to the heat all day. Her jacket had protected her face and torso, but her thighs had been slow-cooked inside her jeans.

She gritted her teeth and bolted through the dish room door into the back room of the bakery. So *now* it's deserted. Of course, bakers work in the middle of the night and the early morning. At sundown the dishwasher would be the only guy still in the building.

She found her way to the stockroom, then out into the alley. She could see the entries to both of their lofts from the end of the alley, and fortunately, no one appeared to be watching from the street. There were lights on in the new loft and she made her way to the door, her legs burning with every step.

She listened at the door—did what she thought of as "reaching out." If she focused she could almost hear shapes, depending on the ambient noise. There was someone in the loft—she could hear the heartbeat, industrial music playing in headphones, the shuffling of a body—a light body dancing. It was the kid, Abby Normal. Where in the hell was Tommy? He couldn't be far from the loft—the sun had gone down only five minutes ago.

Jody pounded on the door, but the shuffling sounds upstairs didn't change rhythm, and she pounded again, this time leaving a dent in the metal door. *Fuck, the kid has the headphones cranked and can't hear a thing.*

Jody shivered, although not because of the cold, but because the hunger was rising in her. Her body telling her she needed to feed so she could heal.

She'd only done it once before, and wasn't sure she could pull it off again, but she needed to get into the loft and leave a lockable door intact. She concentrated as the old vampire had taught her, and gradually, she felt herself fading—going to mist.

Monet was no longer dressed as the statue guy, no longer in character—not *that* character, anyway. Now he was the masta-blasta, gansta-rappa, full-ninja-badass and a bag of mo-thafuckin' chips, bi-yatch—bent on revenge and whatnot. He'd given up midafternoon on making any money and had gone home to remove his makeup and lick his wounds. He'd taken a vicious ass-whuppin' today, even if it was only to his ego. But now he was rolling with his homies, P.J. and Fly, they would put that bronze muthafucka down—if he was still around. If he didn't run away like a little bitch.

"You strapped?" Fly said, adjusting his do-rag as he drove his ten-year-old Honda Civic with rims worth more than the rest of the car.

"Huh?" Monet inquired.

"Do you have a weapon?" Fly said, enunciating all Royal Shakespeare Company precise.

"Oh, yeah." Monet pulled the Glock out of his waistband and showed it to Fly.

"Nigga, put that shit down," said P.J., who was in the backseat, wearing a Phat Pharm tracksuit that was four sizes too big for him.

"Sorry," Monet said, tucking the gun back into the waistband of his jeans. He'd borrowed the Glock—rented it, really—from a real gangsta in Hunter's Point, who needed it back in two hours or he'd charge another twenty-five bucks. Before he gave Monet the gun, he made him swear that no one would be wearing gang colors, so nothing Monet did could come back on him. Monet had made the assurance, then, after P.J. did a Google search for gang colors, they settled on orange do-rags, since no gang seemed to claim that one.

"Highway Safety Posse, yo," Monet had said.

"Yo, Stone Tangerine Thugs, yo," suggested Fly.

"Yo, yo, yo, check it out," said P.J., with enough hand gestures that any deaf person watching would have thought he had ASL Tourette's syndrome. "Cheesy Goldfish Crew."

"Yo, dog, that's so stupid it's not stupid," Monet said.

"Is that good?" asked Fly.

"Yo, dog, get in character." Fly was a bad actor. They were all in the same acting class.

He should have just hired real gangsters to do this. P.J. was probably going to trip over the legs of his track pants and completely ruin their intimidation.

"This is it," Fly said, pulling off the street, right up onto the sidewalk of the Embarcadero by the Ferry Building. "That him?"

"That's him," Monet said. There was no one around but the occasional passing car, but the new statue guy still stood there.

"Remember," Fly said. "Walk. Don't run up. Just walk, like you got all the time in the world. Use your sense memories."

"Right, right, right," Monet said. He and P.J. got out of the car and quickstepped across the bricks to where the statue guy was running his game. Damn, he was good, didn't even flinch.

As he reached the statue guy, Monet raised the Glock and the barrel connected with the statue's forehead. "Bi-yatch!" There was a dull clank.

"Whoa," P.J. said. "Nigga really is a statue."

Monet tapped the statue, three dull clanks. "Yep."

"But he got all that money in his shoes," P.J. said.

"Well, take it, stupid," Monet said.

"Yo, step off, Monet. I'm not the one that got upstaged by a statue."

"Shut up," Monet said.

P.J. was grabbing handfuls of bills out of the Big Gulp cups at the statue's feet and shoving them into his pockets. "Must be a G here, G."

"Yo," Monet said. "Help me get the statue into the car."

P.J. stood and got one shoulder under the statue and tried to lift it, while Monet tucked the gun in his pants and got under the other. They dragged the statue only a couple of feet before they had to set it down and catch their breath.

"Motherfucker heavy," P.J. said.

"Would you guys come on!" Fly screamed from the car, totally out of character now.

"Fuck this," Monet said. This whole thing was just too embarrassing. He'd paid rent on the gun, hadn't he? He drew the Glock from his waistband and squeezed one off at the statue.

"Shit," P.J. said, ducking. "Are you crazy?"

"Bi-atch need to learn a—" Monet's comment was choked off.

P.J. stood up and looked back. There was smoke streaming out of the bullet hole in the statue, and in the second he watched, it had formed into a hand and grabbed Monet by the throat. P.J. turned to run, but something caught the hood of his tracksuit and yanked him back off his feet. He could hear Monet gagging and choking. Then he felt a sharp pain in the side of his neck and he felt suddenly light-headed.

The last thing he saw was Fly peeling away in the Honda.

Being the Chronicles of Abby Normal: Newly Baptized Minion of the Children of the Night

Bow before me, skeezy mortals, for now I see you for the pathetic little rodents that you are. Scurry before my dazzling darkness, daysters, for I am your mistress, your queen, your goddess—I have been brought into the fold—I am Abigail Von Normal, NOSFERATU, bitches!

Sort of.

OMG. It was so fucking cool—like coming twice with Skittles and a Coke. I was in the loft, spacing into my jams on my MP3 player. I had downloaded the latest Dead Can Dub CD (*Death Boots Badonka Mix*) at the Starbucks and it was totally transcendent. I was transported to an ancient Romanian castle, where everyone had done X and was dancing totally chill and sensuous (with perfect hair). I was grinding a free-form booty dance on the armchair—perfecting my dance gestalt—when I saw some smoke coming in under the door.

(I can't wait to dance with Jared to this new CD. He's so going to love this move I do. That's what I love about dancing with gay guys. If they get wood during a booty dance, you can just take it as a compliment, not an agenda. Jared said that if I was a guy, he would totally suck my dick. He can be so sweet.)

So I pulled out one of my headphones and I was like, "Whoa, fire in the staircase—sucks to be me." There's only one exit, so, you know, blackened Abby coming up.

But the smoke formed into a pillar, and then it started growing arms and legs. When I saw it had eyes I ran into the bedroom and shut the door. I wasn't trippin' or anything, just totally calm. But it wasn't like when your friends hold your hair while you puke and tell you it's just the drugs and you'll be okay—so I went for the safe thing of locking the door so I could assess the situation. Then the door just 'splodes into splinters and there's the Countess, totally naked, standing in the doorway with the knob in her hand. And she was totally hot, except that her legs were all fucked up, like they were burned or rotted or something.

So I'm all, "You totally wrecked your deposit."

And the Countess like grabs my hair and pulls me to her and bites my neck, just like that. It didn't really hurt—it was more surprising—like you woke up from getting a root canal to find your dentist going down on you. Well, not exactly like that—more mystical. But still, surprising. (Okay, it hurt, but not as much as the time Lily tried to pierce our nipples with a compass from geometry class and an ice cube. Youch!)

She smelled like burning meat, and I tried to push her away, but it was like my limbs were paralyzed or there was a fat guy sitting on me—like I was buried alive or something, just watching it happen. And then I started to get light-headed and I thought I was going to pass out. That's when the ho dropped me.

She goes, "Go downstairs and get my clothes off the sidewalk. And make coffee."

And I'm like, *Wait a minute, I just lost my mortality virginity, shouldn't I get a cigarette and a fucking towel or something?* But I just said, "Okay," because where the Countess was all burned was healing while I watched, and it was kind of freaking me out to be looking at her naked, burned-up thighs and her totally red pubes anyway. So I went downstairs and just outside the door there was a homeless guy digging through a pile of clothes. Well, really, he was sniffing her panties. And because I don't feel we always do enough to help the homeless, I was like, "Take them, and tell no one what you witnessed here tonight."

(I was already feeling the superiority of my Nosferatitude, so it only seemed appropriate that I go all noblesse oblige on his ass.) So off he went to sniff the lacy crotch of the undead while I went back upstairs to find coffee filters.

So when I get up there the Countess is dressed and hair brushed and she's all, "Where is Tommy? Have you seen Tommy? Did you talk to those cops? And where's Tommy?"

And I was all, "Countess, begging your pardon and shit, but you need to chill. The vampyre Flood was gone when

I got here this morning, and so was that bronze statue from the other side. I thought you guys went off to sleep in the damp womb of your native soil or something."

"Yuck!" goes the Countess. Then she tightens down all of sudden. "Make me a cup of coffee, two sugars, and squeeze one of those vials of blood into it—and call us a cab."

And I was like, "Hey, step off, Countess. I'm one of you and you are not the boss of me and—"

And she said, "I said for *us,* didn't I?"

So I did her bidding—well, *our* bidding, really—and we took a cab over to the Marina Safeway, but why we didn't transform into bats and fly is beyond me. Anyway, we were there in ten minutes. But as we start to pull in, the Countess tells the driver to keep going.

She was all, "It's Rivera and Cavuto. This is not good."

The POS brown cop car was parked in front of the store. I was all, "Cops? Their shit is weak."

She seemed surprised that I knew the cops, but I told her how I had owned them like the little wussy-boys that they are and I could tell that the Countess was feeling pretty good about bringing me into the dark fold of the coven.

Then she was all, "Fucking Clint—he's telling them about Tommy."

But I couldn't even see what she was looking at beyond the big glass front of the Safeway. I guess my powers will develop as time goes on. Five hundred years is a long time to get your vampyre kung fu down.

The Countess had the driver drop us at Fort Mason, so

we could still see the front of the Safeway, and we stood in the fog like the creatures of the night that we were while we waited for the cops to leave.

Then the Countess put her arm around my shoulders and she was all, "Abby, I'm sorry I, uh, attacked you like that. I was hurt really badly and to heal I needed fresh blood. I wasn't really in control of myself. It won't happen again."

"No worries," I told her. "I'm honored to be promoted. Besides, it was kind of hot." Which it was, you know, except for the smell of burning flesh and stuff.

And she was all, "Well, thanks for looking out for us."

And I was all, "Pardon, Countess, but why are we at the Safeway?" Because it's not like we needed groceries.

And she was all, "These guys used to work with Tommy, and one of them knows that he is, uh, one of the children of the night. I think they might know something about where he is now."

Then, over at the Safeway, we saw this goofy-looking guy with frizzy hair and glasses unlock the front door and let the cops out. They got in their car and the frizzy guy locked the front door behind them.

"Showtime," said the Countess. She zipped up her leather jacket, took a pair of sunglasses out of her jacket pocket, and put them on. She goes, "Stay back, Abby. I'll be right back." Then she started across the parking lot toward the Safeway, taking big strides and looking all angel of vengeance, with her red hair flying out behind her, and the lights shining down on her through the fog.

I was like, "Oh shit!"

She didn't even slow down. When she got about ten feet from the front window she snatched up one of the steel-reinforced trash cans like it was made of cardboard and flung it through the window. And she just kept walking! Little cubes of safety glass rained down on her and she just walked through the front of the store like she owned it and everyone in it—which she did.

Before I even got in the store, she was coming back around the corner, dragging the frizzy-haired guy by the throat. She threw him up against a rack of wine bottles, which shattered, spilling red all over the floor and splattering the registers and stuff.

I was all, "Oh, dog, Countess gonna crack open a forty of whup-ass on you now. Oh, you in the shit now, wigga!" (I am not inclined to use hip-hop vernacular often, but there are times when, like French, it just better expresses the sentiment of the moment.)

Just then the whole crowd of guys I'd seen in the limo came running around the corner. The Countess snatched a wine bottle off the rack, and without a second of hesitation, she threw it and it hit the first guy, a tall, hippie-looking guy, right in the middle of the forehead and he went down like he was shot.

She goes, "Back!" and they all headed back around the corner the way they came, except the hippie-looking guy, who was out cold.

Then the Countess picked up the guy with glasses by

the throat. And even though he was like a foot taller than her, she whipped him around like a rag doll until he was screaming stuff about Satan and Jesus and telling her to get behind him and shit. And the Countess was all, "Where is Tommy?"

And he was all, "I don't know. I don't know."

And the Countess grabbed him by the hair and held his head steady against the wine rack. Real chilly, she says, "Clint, I'm going to take your right eye now. Then if you don't tell me where Tommy is, I'm going to take your left. Ready. On three. One . . . Two . . ."

Then he's all, "I didn't have anything to do with it. She's the spawn of Satan, I told them that."

"Three!" goes the Countess.

"He's in Lash's apartment on Northpoint. I don't know the number."

And the Countess just yells "Number?" out to the whole store.

And the black guy pops up from behind a display of Cheerios and is all, "Six ninety-three Northpoint, Apartment 301." And one of the other guys pulls him back down.

Then the Countess is all, "Thank you. If he's hurt, I'll be back." And she throws the Clint guy through a rack of Doritos, which exploded their nacho cheesy goodness all over the place.

Then she's all, "Well, that's a nice surprise."

And I'm all, "That Lord Flood is in an apartment on Northpoint?"

"I didn't think they would really know. I just didn't know where else to start."

"Probably your senses attuned to Lord Flood's presence over the eons," I said, like a total tard.

And she's all, "Let's go, Abby."

And I don't know why, I guess because I had like low blood sugar or something from blood loss, but I was like, "Can I get some gum?"

And she was all, "Sure. Grab some coffee, too. Whole beans. We're almost out."

So I did. And when I caught up with her, she was half-way across the parking lot, headed back toward Ghirardelli Square, and little pieces of safety glass were still shining in her hair and she smiled at me when I caught up and I just couldn't help myself, because that was the coolest thing I'd ever seen. Ever! And I was all, "Countess, I love you."

And she put her arm around me and kissed me on the forehead and goes, "Let's get Tommy."

I guess I'll start feeling my vampyre powers tomorrow night, but right now I feel like a total fucking loser. But I am so going to rule when school starts again.

Nobody Likes a Dead Whore

Finding her boyfriend tied naked to an upright bed frame, covered in blood, with a dead, blue dominatrix at his feet would be enough to rattle some women's confidence in the stability of their relationship. Some women might even take it as a sign of trouble. But Jody had been single for a number of years—she'd dated rock musicians and stockbrokers—and was conditioned to unusual bumps on the road of romance, so she simply sighed and kicked the hooker in the ribs—more as a conversation opener than a confirmation that the ho was dead—and said, "So, rough night?"

"Awk-ward," Abby sang, peeking in the door, then immediately swinging back into the hallway.

"I forgot my safety word," Tommy said.

Jody nodded. "Well, that had to be embarrassing."

"She beat me."

"You okay?"

"Yeah. But it hurt. A lot." Tommy looked past Jody toward the door. "Hi, Abby!"

Abby swung around the corner. "Lord Flood," she said, with a nod and a little grin. Then she looked down at the body, her eyes went wide, and she swung back out into the hall.

"How're your sister's lice?" Tommy said.

"Shampoo didn't work." Abby called, without looking in. "We had to shave her head."

"Sorry about that."

"It's okay. She looks kind of cool, in a 'Make a Wish kid' kind of way."

Jody said. "Abby, why don't you come in and shut the door? If someone walks by and looks in, it might, oh, I don't know, freak them out a little."

" 'Kay," said Abby. She stepped in and palmed the door shut behind her, as if the clicking of the door latch might actually be the thing that would attract attention.

"I think I killed her," Tommy said. "She was beating me, and she wanted me to bite her, so I did. I think I drained her dry."

"Well, she's dead all right." Jody reached down and tossed the blue hooker's arm up. It fell back to the floor. "But you didn't drain her."

"I didn't?"

"She'd be dust if you did. Heart attack or stroke or something. Looks like most of her blood went on you and the carpet."

"Yeah, I sort of tore her throat out and she fell before I could finish."

"Well, what did she expect? You were tied up."

"You don't seem that bothered by it. I thought you'd be jealous."

"Did you ask her to bring you here and beat you until you snapped and killed her?"

"Nope."

"Did you encourage her to beat you until you snapped and killed her?"

"Of course not."

"And you didn't get off on her beating you until you snapped and killed her."

"Honestly?"

"You're naked and chained to a bed frame, and I'm just inches away from both a riding crop and your genitals. I think honesty would be a good policy."

"Well, honestly, the killing part was kind of a turn-on."

"But not sexual."

"No way. It was totally homicidal lust."

"Then we're okay."

"Really, you're not mad?"

"I'm just glad you're okay."

"I should feel bad about it, I know, but I don't."

"That happens."

"Some bitches just need killing," Abby said, looking briefly at Tommy, then realizing he was naked under all that blood, looking away quickly.

"There you go," Jody said. She stepped up and began to undo his restraints. They were double bands of fleece and nylon, with heavy metal shackles locked over them. "What did she buy these for, to handcuff a grizzly bear? Abby, check the body for a key."

"Nuh-uh," Abby said, staring down at the dead blue hooker.

Jody noticed that the kid was focused on the breasts, which were defying gravity, and apparently death itself, by standing there at complete attention. "Those aren't real," Jody said.

"I knew that."

"She was a very mean woman," Tommy said, trying to help. "With really big but insincere boobs. Don't be afraid."

Abby tore her gaze from the dead woman's chest and looked from Tommy, to Jody, to Jody's chest, and back to the body. "Fucksocks! Does everybody have big boobs but me? God, I hate you guys!" She ran out the door and slammed it behind her.

"I *do not* have big boobs," Jody said.

"Perfectly proportioned," Tommy said. "Perfect, really."

"Thanks, sweetie," Jody said, kissing him on the lips lightly so as not to get a taste of the whore's blood.

"I think I saw her hang the key in Lash's Forty-Fucking-Niners hat rack by the door."

"I really need to teach you how to go to mist," Jody said, retrieving the key.

"Yeah, that would have helped me avoid a lot of this."

"You know the Animals sold you out, right?"

"I can't see them doing that. She must have blackmailed them or something."

"Clint told the cops, too. Rivera and Cavuto had our loft staked out."

"Clint doesn't really count, though. He traded in all his moral credibility in this world when he committed to live forever."

"Amazing how badly the promise of immortality makes people behave."

"Like it doesn't matter how you treat people," Tommy said.

"There!" Jody finally got the shackle on Tommy's right wrist unlocked and started working on the left. They were heavy, but she thought that given the motivation of torture, she could have broken loose, or at least torn apart the bed frame. "You couldn't just snap these?"

"I guess I need to work out." He scratched his nose furiously. "So, should we hide the body or something?"

"No, I think it's a good warning for your buddies."

"Right."

"What about the cops?"

"Not our problem," she said as she twisted the key in the lock and snapped the restraint off his left wrist. "We don't have a dead blue hooker in *our* apartment."

"That's an excellent point," Tommy said, rubbing his wrist. "Thank you for rescuing me, by the way. I love you." He grabbed her and pulled her to him, nearly tumbling over on his face when she stepped back and he encountered the resistance of his ankle restraints.

"I love you, too," she said, palming his forehead and pushing him back on balance, "but you are covered with skank oil and you will not get it on my new leather jacket."

In the cab, Abby pouted—sticking out her lower lip far enough that pink was showing above her black lipstick, making her look vaguely like a cat eating a plum.

"Just drop me at my house."

Tommy, who sat in the middle, wearing one of Lash's Forty-Niners jerseys, put his arm around Abby's shoulders to comfort her.

"It's okay, kid. You did great. We are most pleased with you."

Abby snorted and looked out the window. Jody, in turn, put her arm around Tommy's neck and dug her nails into his shoulder. "Shut up," she whispered, so soft that only Tommy would be able to hear it. "You're not helping."

"Look, Abby," Jody said, "it's not something that happens all at once, like in the movies. Sometimes you have to eat bugs for years before you become one of the chosen."

"I know I did," Tommy said. "Beetles, bugs, spiders, mice, rats, snakes, marmosets, OUCH! Stop that, I've been tortured already tonight."

"You two are just into each other," Abby said. "You don't care about anyone else. We're like cattle to you."

The cabdriver, who was a Hindu, looked in the rear-view mirror.

"So what's your point?" Jody said.

Tommy elbowed her in the ribs.

"Kidding. Jeez. Abby, we care very deeply about you. We've trusted you with everything. In fact, you may have saved my life tonight."

Tommy reared back and looked at Jody.

"Long story," the redhead said. Then to Abby again: "Get some rest and come to the loft tomorrow at dusk. We'll talk about your future."

Abby crossed her arms. "Tomorrow is Christmas. I'm trapped with the family."

"Tomorrow is Christmas?" Tommy said.

"Yeah," Jody said. "So?"

"The Animals won't be working. I have some issues with them."

"You were thinking revenge?"

"Well, yeah."

Jody patted the flight bag on the seat, which held all of the money that the Animals had paid to Blue, almost six hundred thousand dollars. "I think you have that covered."

Tommy frowned. "I'm beginning to doubt the steadiness of your moral compass."

"Sure, I'm the one with skewed ethics, when you spent the whole night tied up and beaten by a blue dominatrix and then ripping her throat out."

"You make everything sound so sleazy."

Abby put her fingers in her mouth and whistled—shrill and nearly deafening in the enclosed space. "Hello, there's a cabdriver here. Would you two shut the fuck up."

"Hey," Jody said.

"Hey," Tommy said.

"Hey, you, little creepy girl," said the cabdriver, "you will not be whistling in my cab again or I will be putting you out on the curb."

"Sorry," Abby said.

"Sorry," Tommy and Jody said in unison.

With the exception of the odd serial killer, and car salesmen who think of them as the perfect unit for measuring trunk space, nobody likes a dead whore. ("Yeah, you can get five-maybe six dead hookers in this baby.")

"She looks so natural," said Troy Lee, looking down on Blue. "Except for the way her arm is bent under her—and the riding crop—and the blood everywhere, I mean."

"And she's blue," said Lash.

The other Animals nodded mournfully.

It was turning out to be a stressful morning for the Animals: cleaning up the mess that Jody had made of the store, getting Drew to the emergency room to get his forehead sewn up where the wine bottle had hit him (they immediately passed around the painkillers he was prescribed, which help to take the edge off), then explaining the broken front window to the manager when he came in, and now this—

"You're the one with almost an MBA," Barry, the short balding one, said to Lash. "You should know what to do."

"They don't cover what to do with a dead hooker," Lash countered. "That's a whole different program. Political science, I think."

Despite the dulling they'd given themselves with the painkillers and a case of beer they'd shared in the parking lot at the Safeway, they were all feeling sad, and a little frightened.

"Gustavo is the porter," Clint said. "Shouldn't he do the cleanups?"

"Ahhhhh!" said Jeff, the tall ex-jock, as he thumped Clint on the head with a protruding knuckle. Feeling like the knuckle might not quite be enough, he snatched off Clint's horn-rimmed glasses and threw them to Troy Lee, who snapped them into four neat pieces and handed them back to Clint.

"This is all your fault," Lash said. "If you hadn't ratted Flood out to the cops, this wouldn't have happened."

"I just told them that Tommy was a vampire," Clint whined. "I didn't tell them he was here. I didn't tell them about your whore of Babylon."

"You didn't know her like we did," Barry added, his voice breaking a little. "She was special."

"Expensive," Drew said.

"*Sí*, expensive," added Gustavo.

"She probably could finally afford to go to Babylon," said Lash.

"Forgive them, for they know not what they do," Clint said.

Troy Lee bent and examined Blue, careful not to touch her. "It's hard to see bruising through the blue dye, but I guess she broke her neck. The blood must be Flood's. I don't see any marks on her."

"No bite marks, you mean," said Clint.

"Of course that's what I mean, nit wit. You know Flood's girlfriend did this, right?"

"How do you know?" Lash asked. "It could have been Flood."

"I don't think so," said Troy Lee. "Tommy was tied up here—see the orange crap all over the restraints. And these were unlocked, not broken."

"Maybe when Blue let him go he killed her."

Troy Lee picked something off of Blue's face, as delicately as if he were taking her ghost. "Except for this."

He held a long red hair up where Lash could see it. "No reason for her to be here, if Flood was loose."

"Dude, you're like one of those *CSI* guys," Drew said.

"We should call those two homicide cops," Barry said, like he was the first who might have thought of it.

"And tell them to come help us with our dead hooker," Lash said.

"Well they know about the vampires," Barry said. "Maybe they'll help us."

"How 'bout we move her to your apartment, and then call them?"

"Well, what are we going to do with her?" Barry said, standing feet apart, hands behind his back, a brave Hobbit ready to face a dragon.

Troy Lee shrugged. "Wait until dark, then drop her in the Bay?"

"I can't bear to touch her," Barry said. "Not after the moments we shared."

"You little *putas*," Gustavo said, stepping up and beginning to roll up the bloodstained rug. He had a wife and five children, and although he had never disposed of a dead hooker before, he thought that it couldn't be any worse than changing the diaper on a gloopy infant.

The other Animals all looked at one another, embarrassed, until Gustavo growled at them and they jumped to move the heavy bed frame out of his way.

"I never really liked her that much, anyway," Barry said.

"She really did take advantage of us," Jeff said.

"I just went along with you guys so I didn't ruin the party," said Troy Lee. "I didn't enjoy even half of those blow jobs."

"Let's just put her in my closet until tonight, then a couple of us can sneak the bitch out to Hunter's Point and drop her off."

"On Christmas?" Drew asked.

"Can't believe she took all our money and now she's going to ruin Christmas," said Troy Lee.

"Our money!" said Lash. "That bitch!"

Nobody likes a dead whore.

. .

I do like a dead whore now and then," said the vampire Elijah Ben Sapir, derailing a perfectly good theme. He'd snapped the whore's neck right before she was completely drained so there would be a body. "But one doesn't want to be too obvious." He dragged the whore's body behind a Dumpster, and watched as the wounds on her neck healed over. He'd taken her in an alley near Tenth and Mission streets. He'd had the hood up on the oversized tracksuit he was wearing, so she'd been surprised when they'd ventured down the alley and he threw it back to reveal a very pale Semitic man.

"Look at-chew. Thought baby was a playa—" the whore had said, her last words. She'd only had a hundred dollars on her, which, along with the tracksuit and a pair of Nikes, were the complete resources the ancient vampire had at his disposal.

He'd come to the city in a yacht worth millions, filled with art worth millions more, and now he was reduced to making kills for petty cash. Of course he owned several homes around the world, and had stashes of cash put away in a dozen cities, but it would take some time to access it. And perhaps it wasn't so bad to have the wolf at the door, for a change. After all, he'd come to the City and taken a new fledgling in order to alleviate his boredom. (It's very hard to feel alive when you've been dead for eight hundred years.) And she had done that. He was not bored—and he felt very much alive.

He walked out of the alley and checked the sky. Dawn was threatening—he had perhaps twenty minutes until sunup. "Where does the time go?" He crossed the street and was buzzed into a hotel with a sign that read FOR RENT. BY HOUR, DAY, OR WEEK. He could smell the cigarettes, sweat, and heroin on the desk clerk, and he kept his head down so the hood covered his face.

"Do you have a room without a window?"

"Twenty-five bucks, like all the others," the clerk said. "You want sheets? Sheets are five more."

The vampire smiled. "No, I don't want to spoil myself."

He paid the clerk, took the key, and trudged up the steps. Yes, he felt very much alive. One really can't appreciate what one has until it's gone. And without a significant loss, how would one enjoy the process of revenge?

Our Dead Homeys

The vampires sat side by side on the bare futon frame, watching as a five-legged bug limped up the big front window of the loft.

Tommy thought that the rhythm of the bug's steps made for a danceable backbeat—thought he might be able to set music to it, if he knew how to write music. *Suite for Angst and Limping Bug,* he'd call it.

"Nice bug," Tommy said.

"Yeah," Jody said.

We should save it for Abby, Jody thought. She was feeling guilty about having bitten the girl—not so much because of the violation, because obviously the kid had been willing, but because she felt as if she really didn't have any choice. She had been injured and her predator nature told her to survive, whatever the cost, which is what bothered her. Was her humanity drifting away?

"The Animals are going to come for us now," Tommy said. He was feeling angry, betrayed by his old crew, but most of all he felt separate from them now. He felt separate from everyone. Tomorrow was Christmas and he didn't even want to call his parents because they were a different species now. What do you buy for an inferior species?

"It's just the Animals," Jody said. "We'll be safe."

"I'll bet that's what Elijah thought, too, and they got him."

"We should go get him," Jody said. She imagined Elijah Ben Sapir, standing in the full sun by the Ferry Building, tourists passing him, wondering why someone would put a statue there. Would the brass protect him?

Tommy checked his watch. "We'd never get there and back in time. I tried that yesterday."

"How could you do that to him, Tommy? He was one of us."

"One of us? He was going to kill us, if you remember. He kind of did kill us. I resent that. Besides, if you're covered in bronze, what does it matter if you're underwater? I was just trying to get him out of sight so we could think about our future without him being part of it."

"Right. Okay," Jody said. "Sorry." Future? She'd lived with a half-dozen guys, none had ever willingly talked about the future before. And she and Tommy had a supersized buttload of future ahead of them as long as someone didn't catch them sleeping. "Maybe we really should leave the City," she said. "No one would know about us in a new city."

"I was thinking we should get a Christmas tree," Tommy said.

Jody looked away from the bug. "That's a thought, or we could put some mistletoe up, put on Christmas carols, and stand outside waiting for Santa until the sun comes up and incinerates us. How's that sound?"

"Nobody appreciates your sarcasm, missy. I'm just trying to get a handle on normal. Three months ago I was stocking groceries in Indiana, looking at community college, driving around in my crappy car, wishing I had a girlfriend, and wishing that there was some potential for something to happen beyond getting a job with benefits and living the same life as my dad. Now I have a girlfriend, and superpowers, and a bunch of people want to kill me, and I don't know how to act. I don't know what to do next. And it's going to be that way forever. Forever! I'm going to be scared out of my mind forever! I can't deal with forever."

He'd been barking at her, but she resisted the urge to snap back. He was nineteen, not a hundred and fifty—he didn't even have the tools for being an adult, let alone being immortal. "I know," she said. "Tomorrow night, first thing, we'll hire a car, go get Elijah, and pick up a Christmas tree on the way back. How's that sound?"

"Hiring a car? That sounds exotic."

"It'll be like prom." Was she being too patronizing?

"You don't have to do that," he said. "I'm sorry I'm acting like a weenie."

"But you're my weenie," Jody said. "Take me to bed."

Still holding her hand, he stood, then pulled her up into his arms. "We'll be okay, right?"

She nodded and kissed him, feeling for just a second like a girl in love instead of a predator. She immediately felt a resurgence of shame over feeding on Abby.

The doorbell rang.

"Did you know we had a doorbell?"

"Nope."

You can't beat a dead whore in the morning," said Nick Cavuto cheerfully, because apparently, everyone loves a dead hooker, despite what certain writer types might think. They were standing in the alley off Mission Street.

Dorothy Chin—short, pretty, and whip-smart—snorted a laugh and checked the thermometer probe she'd stuck in the deceased's liver like a meat thermometer into a roast. "She hasn't been dead four hours, guys."

Rivera rubbed his temples and felt his bookstore slipping away, along with his marriage. He'd known the marriage had been going for a while, but he was feeling a little brokenhearted about the bookstore. He figured he knew, but he asked anyway. "Cause of death?"

"Toothy blow job," Cavuto said.

"Yes, Alphonse," said Dorothy with a tad too much sincerity, "I'd have to concur with Detective Cavuto, she died of a toothy blow job."

"It just pisses some guys off," Cavuto added, "a professional without skills."

"Guy just snapped her neck and took his money back," said Dorothy with a big grin.

"So a broken neck?" said Rivera, mentally waving goodbye to a whole set of first-edition Raymond Chandlers, ten-to-six workdays, golfing on Mondays.

Cavuto snorted this time. "Her head's turned around the wrong way, Rivera. What did you think it was?"

"Seriously," Dorothy Chin said, "I have to do the autopsy to be sure, but offhand that's the obvious cause. I'd also say she's probably lucky to go that way. She's HIV positive and it looks like the disease had developed into full-blown AIDS."

"How do you know that?"

"See these sarcomas on her feet."

Chin had removed one of the hooker's shoes—she pointed to open sores on the corpse's foot and ankle.

Rivera sighed. He didn't want to ask, but he asked anyway, "What about blood loss?"

Dorothy Chin had done the autopsies on two of the previous victims and cringed a little. It was a pattern. They'd all been terminally ill, they'd all died of a broken neck, and they'd all shown evidence of extreme blood loss, but no external wounds—not even a needle mark.

"Can't tell out here."

Cavuto had lost his cheery manner now. "So we spend Christmas day canvassing dirtbags to see if anyone saw anything?"

At the end of the alley, uniforms were still talking to the grimy homeless man who had called in the murder. He was trying to get them to spring for a bottle of whiskey—because it was Christmas. Rivera didn't want to go home, but he didn't want to spend a day trying to find out what he already knew. He checked his watch.

"What time was sunrise this morning?" he asked.

"Oh, wait," Cavuto said, patting down his pockets, "I'll check my almanac."

Dorothy Chin snorted again, then started giggling.

"Dr. Chin," Rivera said, tightening down now, "could you be more precise about the time of death?"

Chin picked up on Rivera's tone and went full professional. "Sure. There's an algorithm for the cooling time of a body. Get me the weather from last night, let me get her back to the morgue and weigh her, and I'll get you a time within ten minutes."

"What?" Cavuto said to Chin. "What?" This time to Rivera.

"Winter solstice, Nick," Rivera said. "Christmas was originally set at the winter solstice, the shortest day of the year. It's eleven-thirty now. I'm betting that four hours ago the sun was just coming up."

"Uh-huh," Cavuto said. "Prostitutes have shitty hours—is that what you're saying?"

Rivera raised an eyebrow. "Our guy didn't travel far after sunrise, is what I'm saying. He's going to be around here."

"I was afraid that's what you were saying," Cavuto said. "We're never going to get the bookstore open, are we?"

"Tell the uniforms to look anywhere it's dark: under Dumpsters, in crawl spaces, attics—anywhere."

"Getting warrants on Christmas day might be a problem."

"You won't need warrants if you get permission from the owners—we're not looking to bust anyone living here, we're looking for a murder suspect."

Cavuto pointed to the eight-story brick building that composed one wall of the alley. "This building has something like eight hundred ministorage units in it."

"Then you guys had better get started."

"Where're you going?"

"There was a missing person report on an old guy in North Beach a couple of days ago. I'm going to check it out."

"Because you don't want to go Dumpster diving for v—"

"Because," Rivera cut him off before he could say the V-word, "he had terminal cancer. His wife assumed he just wandered off and got lost. Now I'm not so sure. Call me if you find anything."

"Uh-huh." Cavuto turned to the three uniforms who were interviewing the bum. "Hey, guys, have I got a merry Christmas detail for you."

The Animals decided to hold a small memorial service for Blue in Chinatown. Troy Lee was already there, as was Lash, who wouldn't go home to his apartment until Blue's body was removed, and Barry, who was Jewish, would be coming there for dinner with his family, as was the tradition in his faith. Plus, the liquor stores in Chinatown were open on Christmas, and if you slipped some money under the counter, you could get firecrackers. The Animals were fairly sure that Blue would have wanted firecrackers at her funeral.

The Animals stood in a semicircle, beers in hand, on a playground off Grant Street. The deceased was being honored in absentia—in her place was a half-eaten pair of edible panties. From a distance, they looked like a bunch of wastrels mourning a Fruit Roll-Up.

"I'd like to start, if I may," said Drew. He wore a long overcoat and his hair was tied back with a black ribbon, revealing the target-shaped bruise on his forehead where Jody had hit him with the wine bottle. Out of his coat he pulled a bong the size of a tenor sax, and using a long lighter designed for lighting fireplaces, he sparked that magnificent mama-jama up and bubbled away like a scuba diver having an asthma attack. When he could hold no more, he raised the bong, poured some water on the ground, and croaked, "To Blue," which came out in a perfect smoke ring, the sight of which brought tears to everyone's eyes.

"To Blue," everyone repeated as they placed one hand on the bong and tipped a bit out of their beers.

"To Broo, my nigga," said Troy Lee's grandma, who had insisted upon joining the ceremony once she realized there would be firecrackers.

"She will be avenged," said Lash.

"And we'll get our fucking money back," said Jeff, the big jock.

"Amen," the Animals said.

They had decided on a nondenominational ceremony, as Barry was a Jew, Troy Lee was a Buddhist, Clint was an Evangelical, Drew was a Rastafarian, Gustavo was a Catholic, and Lash and Jeff were heathen stoners. Gustavo had been called in to work that day because someone had to be in the store as long as the front was only boarded up with plywood, so in deference to his beliefs, they had bought some incense and holders and placed a picket fence of smoldering joss sticks around the edible panty. The incense also worked within Troy and Grandma's Buddhist tradition, and Lash pointed out during the ceremony that although they have their differences otherwise, all gods like a good-smellin' ho.

"Amen!" said the Animals again.

"And they're handy for lightin' firecrackers off of," added Jeff as he bent over an incense stick and set a string cracking.

"Hallelujah!" said the Animals.

Each offered to share some kind of memory of Blue, but all of their stories quickly degenerated to orifices and squishiness, and no one wanted to go there in front of Troy's grandma, so instead they threw firecrackers at Clint while he read from the Twenty-third Psalm.

Before they cracked the second case of beer, it was decided that after dark, three of them—Lash, Troy Lee, and Barry—would take Blue from Lash's apartment, load her into the back of Barry's station wagon, and take her out in the middle of the Bay in Barry's Zodiac. (Barry was the diver of the bunch, and had all the cool aquatic stuff. They'd used his spearguns to help take down the old vampire.)

Lash braced himself as he opened the apartment door, but to his surprise, there was no smell. He led Barry and Troy into the bedroom, and together they wrestled the rolled-up rug out of the closet.

"It's not heavy enough," Barry said.

"Oh shit, oh shit, oh shit," Troy said, trying furiously to unroll the rug.

Finally Lash reached down, grabbed the edge of the rug, and whipped it up over his head. There was a thudding sound against the far wall, followed by the jingle of metal, like coins settling.

The three Animals stood and stared.

"What are those?" Asked Barry.

"Earrings," answered Troy. Indeed, there were seven earrings settling on the hardwood floor.

"Not those. Those!" Barry nodded toward two clear, cantaloupe-sized, gelatinous lozenges that quivered on the floor like stranded jellyfish.

Lash shivered. "I've seen them before. My brother used to work in a plant in Santa Barbara that made them."

"What the fuck are they?" Said Troy, squinting through a drunken haze.

"Those are breast implants," Lash said.

"What are those wormy things?" asked Barry. There were two translucent sluglike blobs of something stuck to the rug near the edge.

"Looks like window caulk," said Lash. He noticed that there was a fine blue powder near the edge of the rug. He ran his hand over it, pinched some on his fingers, and sniffed it. Nothing.

"Where'd she go?" asked Barry.

"No idea," said Lash.

It's a Wonderful Life

Gustavo Chavez had been born the seventh child of a brick maker in a small village in the state of Michoacan, Mexico. At eighteen he married a local girl, the daughter of a farmer, herself a seventh child, and at twenty, with his second child on the way, he crossed the border into the United States, where he lived with a cousin in Oakland, along with a score of other relatives, and worked grueling, twelve-hour days as a laborer, making enough to feed himself and send more money home to his family than he could possibly have made in his father's brickyard. He did this because it was the responsible and right thing to do, and because he had been raised a good Catholic man who, like his father, would provide for his family and no more than two or three mistresses. Each year, about a month before Christmas, he would sneak back across the border to celebrate Christmas with his family, meet any new children that might have been born, and

make love with his wife, Maria, until they were both so sore
it hurt to walk. In fact, the vision of Maria's inviting thighs
would often begin haunting him around Halloween and the
hapless night porter would find himself in a state of semi-
arousal as he swung his soapy mop, to and fro, across fifteen
thousand square feet of linoleum every night.

Tonight he was in the store alone, and he was feeling far
from aroused, for it was Christmas night, and he could not
go to mass or take Communion until he confessed. He was
feeling deeply ashamed. Christmas night and he hadn't
even called Maria—hadn't spoken to her for weeks, because
like the rest of the Animals, he had gone to Las Vegas, and
had given all his money to the blue whore.

He had called, of course, after they'd first taken the
vampire's art and sold it for so much money, but since then,
his life had been a fog of tequila and marijuana and the evil
attentions of the blue one. He, a good man, who cared for
his family, had never hit his wife, had only cheated with a
second cousin and never with a white woman, had been
undone by the curse of the blue devil's pussy. *La maldición
de la concha del diabla azul.*

This is the saddest, loneliest Christmas ever, thought Gustavo as he dragged his mop past the canvas doors leading
into the produce-department cooler. *I am like the poor ca-
brón in that book* The Pearl, *where by simply trying to take advantage of some good fortune, I have lost all that I care about.
Okay, I did get drunk for a week and my pearl was a blue whore
who fucked the chimichangas out of me, but still, pretty sad.* He

thought these things in Spanish, so they sounded infinitely more tragic and romantic.

Then there came a noise from the cooler, and he was startled for a second. He wrung out his mop, so as to be ready for anything. He didn't like being in the store by himself, but with the front windows broken out, someone had to be here, and because he was far from home, had nowhere else to go, and the union would see that he was paid double time, Gustavo had volunteered. Perhaps if he sent home a little extra, Maria might forget the hundred thousand dollars he'd promised.

There, something was moving behind the plastic doors of the cooler, which were waving slightly. The stout Mexican crossed himself and backed out of the produce department, swinging his mop now in quick swaths, leaving barely a hint of dampness on the linoleum. He was by the dairy case now, and a stack of yogurts fell over inside the glass doors, as if someone had shoved them out of the way to look through.

Gustavo dropped the mop and ran to the back of the store, saying a Hail Mary peppered with swearwords as he went, wondering if those were footsteps he heard behind him, or the echoes of his own footfalls resounding through the deserted store.

Out the front door and away, he chanted in his head. *Out the front door and away.* He nearly fell rounding the turn at the meat case, his shoes still wet from the mop water. He caught himself on one hand and came up like a sprinter, while reaching back on his belt for his keys as he went.

There were footfalls behind him—light, slapping—bare feet on linoleum, but fast, and close. He couldn't stop to unlock the door when he got there, he couldn't look back, he couldn't turn to look—a second of hesitation and he would be lost. He exhaled a long wail and ran right through a rack of candy and gum by the registers. He tumbled over the first register in an avalanche of candy bars and magazines, many of which displayed headlines like I MARRIED BIGFOOT, or SPACE ALIEN CULT TAKES OVER HOLLYWOOD, or VAMPIRES HUNT OUR STREETS, and other such nonsense.

Gustavo scrambled out of the pile and was crawling on his belly like a desert lizard scrambling to get across hot sand, when a heavy weight came down on his back, knocking the air out of him. He gasped, trying to get his breath, but something grabbed him by the hair and yanked his head backwards. He heard crackling noises in his ear, smelled something like rotten meat, and gagged. He saw the fluorescent lights, some canned hams, and a very happy cardboard elf making cookies as he was dragged down the aisle and through the doors into the dark back room of the deli like so much lunch meat.

Feliz navidad.

"Our first Christmas together," Jody said, kissing him on the cheek—giving his butt a little squeeze through his pj bottoms. "Did you get me something cute?"

"Hi, Mom," Tommy said into the phone. "It's Tommy."

"Tommy. Sweetheart. We've been calling all day. It just rang and rang. I thought you were going to come home for Christmas."

"Well, you know, Mom, I'm in management at the store now. Responsibilities."

"Are you working hard enough?"

"Oh yeah, Mom. I'm working ten—sixteen hours a day sometimes. Exhausted."

"Well good. And you have insurance?"

"The best, Mom. The best. I'm nearly bulletproof."

"Well, I suppose that's good. You're not still working that horrible night shift, are you?"

"Well, sort of. In the grocery business, that's where the money is."

"You need to get on the day shift. You're never going to meet a nice girl working those hours, son."

It was at this point, having heard Mother Flood's admonition, that Jody lifted her shirt and rubbed her bare breasts against him while batting her eyelashes coquettishly.

"But I have met a nice girl, Mom. Her name is Jody. She's studying to be a nun—er, teacher. She helps the poor."

It was then that Jody pantsed him, then ran into the bedroom giggling. He caught himself on the counter to keep from tumbling over.

"Whoa."

"What, son? What's the matter?"

"Nothing, nothing, Mom. I just had a little eggnog with the guys and started to feel it."

"You're not on the drugs, are you, honey?"

"No, no, no, nothing like that."

"Because your father has rehab benefits on you until you're twenty-one. We can have one of those interventions if you can find a cheap flight home. I know that Aunt Esther would love to see you, even if you are strung out on the crack."

"And I her, and I her, Mom. Look, I just called to say Merry Christmas, I'll let you—"

"Wait, honey, your father wants to say hi."

"—go."

"Hey, Skeeter. Frisco turned you into an ass bandit yet?"

"Hi, Dad. Merry Christmas."

"Glad you finally called. Your mother was worried sick about you."

"Well, you know, the grocery business."

"You working hard enough?"

"Trying. They're cutting back on our OT—union will only let us work sixty hours a week."

"Well, as long as you're trying. How's that old Volvo running?"

"Great. Like a top." The Volvo had burned to the wheels his first day in the City.

"Swiss sure can build some cars, can't they? Can't say much for those little red pocketknives they make, but sons-abitches can build a car."

"Swedes."

"Yeah, well, I love the little meatballs too. Look, kid,

your mother's got me deep-frying a turkey out in the driveway. It's starting to smoke a little. I probably oughta should go check on it. Took an hour to get the oil up to speed—it's only about ten degrees here today."

"Yeah, it's a little chilly here, too."

"Looks like it's starting to catch the carport on fire a little. Better go."

"Okay. Love you, Dad."

"Call your mother more often, she worries. Holy cats, there goes the Oldsmobile. Bye, son."

A half hour later they were sipping coffee laced with William's blood when the doorbell rang again. "This is getting irritating," Jody said.

"Call your mom," Tommy said. "I'll get it."

"We should get some sleeping pills—knock him out so he doesn't have to drink all that booze before we bleed him."

The doorbell rang again.

"We just need to get him a key." Tommy went to the console by the door and pushed the button. There was a buzz and the click of the lock at street level. The door opened—William coming in to settle on the stairs for the night. "I don't know how he sleeps on those steps."

"He doesn't sleep. He passes out," said the undead redhead. "Do you think if we gave him peppermint schnapps the coffee would have a minty holiday flavor?"

Tommy shrugged. He went to the door, threw it open, and called down. "William, you like peppermint schnapps?"

William raised a grimy eyebrow, looking suspicious. "You got something against scotch?"

"No, no, I don't want to mess up your discipline. I was just thinking of a more balanced diet. Food groups, you know."

"I had some soup and some beer today," William said.

"Okay then."

"Schnapps gives me mint farts. They scare the hell out of Chet."

Tommy turned to Jody and shook his head. "Sorry, no way, minty farts." Then to William again: "Okay then, William. I gotta get back to the little woman. You need anything? Food, blanket, toothbrush, a damp towelette to freshen up?"

"Nah, I'm good," William said. He held up a fifth of Johnny Walker Black.

"How's Chet doing?"

"Stressed. We just found out our friend Sammy got murdered in the hotel on Eleventh." Chet looked up the stairwell with sad kitty eyes, which he sort of always seemed to have since he'd been shaved.

"Sorry to hear that," Tommy said.

"Yeah, on Christmas, too," William said. "Hooker got killed across the street last night, same way. Neck was snapped. Sammy has been sick for a while, so he splurged on a room for the holiday. Fuckers killed him right there in bed. Just goes to show you."

Tommy had no idea what it meant to show you. "Sad," Tommy said. "So how come Chet's stressed but you're not?"

"Chet doesn't drink."

"Of course. Well then, Merry Christmas to you guys."

"You, too," said William, toasting with his bottle. "Any chance of a Christmas bonus, now that I'm a full-time employee?"

"What'd you have in mind?"

"I'd sure like a gander at Red's bare knockers."

Tommy turned to Jody, who was shaking her head, looking pretty determined.

"Sorry," Tommy said. "How about a new sweater for Chet?"

William scowled. "You just can't bargain with *The Man*." He took a drink from his bottle and turned away from Tommy as if he had something important to discuss with his huge shaved cat and couldn't be bothered with management.

"Okay then," Tommy said. He closed the door and returned to the counter. "I'm *The Man*," he said with a big grin.

"Your mom would be so proud," Jody said. "We need to go see about Elijah."

"Not until you call your mom. Besides, he's waited this long, it's not like he's going anywhere."

Jody got up and came around the breakfast bar and took Tommy's hand. "Sweetie, I need you to play what William just said back in your mind, really slowly."

"I know, I'm *The Man!*"

"No, the part about his friend being killed by a broken neck, and how he has been sick, and how someone else was killed the night before, also by broken neck. I'll bet she was sick, too. Sound like a pattern you've heard before?"

"Oh my God," Tommy said.

"Uh-huh," Jody said. She held his hand to her lips and kissed his knuckles. "I'll get my jacket while you fluff up your little brain for traveling, 'kay?"

"Oh my God, you'll do anything to get out of calling your mom."

Ladies and Gentlemen, Presenting the Disappointments

He was the best one-handed free-throw shooter in the Bay Area, and that Christmas night he had sunk sixty-four in a row in his driveway hoop, shooting the new leather Spaulding ball his dad had left under the tree for him. Sixty-seven in a row, without ever setting down or spilling his beer. His record was seventy-two, and he would have broken it, had he not been dragged off into the bushes to be slaughtered.

Jeff Murray was not the smartest of the Animals, nor the most well-born, but when it came to squandering potential, he was the hands-down winner. Jeff had been a star power forward through his sophomore, junior, and senior years in high school, and he had been offered a full-boat ride to Cal, Berkeley—there had even been talk of his going pro after a couple of years in college, but Jeff had decided to impress his prom date by showing her he had enough vertical leap to clear a moving car.

It was a minor misjudgment, and he would have cleared the car had he not drunk most of a case of beer before the attempt, and had the car's height not been eight inches enhanced by the light bar on the roof. The light bar just caught Jeff's left sneaker, and somersaulted him four times in the air before he landed upright in a James Brown split on the tarmac. He was pretty sure that his knee wasn't supposed to bend that way, and a team of doctors would later agree. He'd wear a brace forever and he'd never play competitive basketball again. Although he was a smokin' one-handed H.O.R.S.E. player, and he might have even been a champion if it weren't for that slaughtered-in-the-bushes thing.

He liked the new leather ball, and he knew he shouldn't be using it on the asphalt, and especially this late at night, when the sound of his dribbling might disturb his neighbors.

He lived in a garage apartment in Cow Hollow, and the fog was blowing in damp streams up his street, making the basketball sound lonely and ominous, so no one complained. It was Christmas—if all some poor bastard had was some hoops, then you'd have to be a special kind of heartless to call the cops on him. A car turned at the end of the street; blue halogens swept through the fog like sabers, then went out. Jeff squinted into the fog, but couldn't make out what kind of car it was, only that it had stopped a couple of doors down and it was a dark color.

He turned to take his record-breaking shot, but distracted, he put a little too much backspin on the ball and it jumped out of the hoop. He ran it down at the junipers by the garage, but was only able to tip it, so that it went into the bushes. He set his beer down on the driveway and went in after it, and—well, you know . . .

Francis Evelyn Stroud answered the phone on the second ring, as she always did, as it was proper to do. "Hello."

"Hi, Mom, It's Jody. Merry Christmas."

"And to you, darling. You're calling rather late."

"I know, Mom. I was going to call earlier, but had a thing." *I was a thing,* Jody thought.

"A thing? Of course. Did you get the package I sent?"

It would be expensive and completely inappropriate, a cashmere business suit, or something in a houndstooth or a herringbone, something worn only by matronly academics or matronly spies with stout poison-dart shoes. And Mother Stroud would have sent it to the old address. "Yes, I got it. It's lovely. I can't wait to wear it."

"I sent a leather-bound set of the complete works of Wallace Stegner," Mother Stroud said.

Fuck! Jody kicked at Tommy for making her call. He skipped out of range, waving a scolding finger at her.

Of course. Stegner, the Stanford paragon. Mother was one of the first coeds to graduate from Stanford and she never missed an opportunity to point out that Jody hadn't gone there. Jody's father had also gone to Stanford. She was born to Stanford, and yet she had disgraced them by going to

San Francisco State, and not finishing. "Yeah, those will be great, too. I guess they just haven't caught up with me yet."

"You've moved again?" Mrs. Stroud had lived in the same house in Carmel for thirty years. Carpet and draperies never survived more than two years, but she'd been in the same house.

"Yeah, we needed a little more space. Tommy's working at home now."

"We? Then you're still with that writer boy?"

Mom said "writer" like it was a fungus.

Jody scribbled on a Post-it at the counter: *Note: Break Tommy's arms off. Beat him with them.*

"Yes. I'm still with Tommy. He's been nominated for a Fulbright. So, did you have a nice Christmas?"

"It was fine. Your sister brought that man."

"Her *husband*, Bob, you mean?" Mother Stroud did not care for men since Jody's father had left her for a younger woman.

"Well, whatever his name is."

"It's Bob, Mom. He went to school with us. You've known him since he was nine."

"Well, I had a smoked turkey delivered, and a lovely foie-gras-and-wild-mushroom appetizer."

"You had Christmas catered?"

"Of course."

"Of course." Of course. Of course. It would never occur to her that by having Christmas dinner catered, she was making other people work on Christmas. "Well, I put my present in the mail, Mom. I'd better go. Tommy's being honored at a dinner tonight because of his massive intellect."

"On Christmas?"

Oh, what the fuck. "He's Jewish."

She could hear the intake of breath on the other end of the phone. *This is the light version, Mom, imagine how scandalized you be if I told you he was dead and that I killed him.*

"You didn't tell me that."

"Sure I did. You must be losing details. Gotta go, Mom. I gotta help Tommy get his penis piercing in before the dinner. Bye." She hung up.

Tommy had been dancing naked in front of her for most of the phone call. When she hung up he stopped. "Did I mention that I worry about your ethical equilibrium?"

"Said the guy who was just playing *buff the scrotum* with my red scarf while I was making the merry Christmas call to my mother?"

"Admit it. You're a little turned on."

Dr. Drew—Drew McComber, the Ohm-budsman, the resident pharmacist and medical adviser to the Animals, was afraid of the dark. The fear had crept up on him, like a hash brownie, and coldcocked him with an inescapable paranoia after four years on the night crew at the Marina Safeway. Thing was, he awoke in the evening, to the pervasive grow lights in his garage apartment in the Marina, then drove four blocks under the streetlights to the brightly lit Safeway, then got off work in the morning when the sun was well off the horizon, to return to his grow-lit apartment, to sleep with a satin mask in place. He encountered darkness so infrequently that it seemed like a menacing stranger when he did.

On Christmas night, round midnight, Drew sat among a jungle of five-foot-tall pot plants in his living room, wearing sunglasses and watching a movie on cable about the special relationship between the lady of an English manor and her chimney sweep. (Because of his work schedule, and the constant demand to stay wasted, Drew found it difficult to keep a girlfriend. Until the Animals found Blue, his sex life had been a largely solitary affair, and (sigh) apparently had become so once again.) Each time the chimney sweep's sooty hand smacked the powdered bottom of the lady of the manor, Drew grieved a little—that dusky handprint on alabaster flank falling like a shadow on his erotic soul. There was arousal, but no joy. Sad and lonely wood did tent his hemp-fiber cargo pants.

Then, as if scripted by *Erecto, the Generously Endowed Pizza Delivery God of Improbable Trysts,* there was a knock at Drew's door. Rather than answer the door directly, Drew adjusted himself and ambled through the ganja forest to a small video screen in his kitchenette—a video peephole. He'd installed it in the days before his doctor had given him the prescription that made him a quasilegal medical marijuana grower *(patient complains that reality harshes his mellow—prescribe 2 grams cannabis every three hours by inhalation, ingestion, or suppository).*

Sure enough, as if he had called in an order, the video screen revealed a pale but pretty blonde standing on his doorstep in a conservative blue cocktail dress and heels. She might have just come from a party or a dinner out—her hair was pinned up with tiny blue bows. She might have shown up to audition for the role of the lady of the manor.

Drew keyed the intercom. "Hi. Are you sure you have the right house?"

"I think so," said the girl. "I'm looking for Drew." She smiled into the camera. Perfect teeth.

"Jeez," Drew said, then realizing that he had said it aloud, he cleared his throat and said, "I'll be right there."

He smoothed his erection down, pushed his hair behind his ears, and in five long strides he was through the forest and at the front door. At the last second he remembered the sunglasses, pushed them up on his head, smiled broadly, and threw open the door, releasing a wide beam of ultraviolet light into the night fog.

The pretty blonde dropped her smile, then screamed as she burst into flames and leapt out of the light. Drew ran out into the dark to save her.

Being the Chronicles of Abby Normal: Pathetic Nosferatu Noobsicle

Well, except for the murder, Christmas was like a slow drag over broken glass—I now truly know the ennui of passing eternity in total boredom—eating and hurling tofurky all day, stuck with Ronnie and Mom until like six, when Jared came over. His father has a fresh family with little crumb-snatcher stepsisters, so they like forget about him as soon as the squealing and presents start in the morning. He spent the whole day rewatching *The Nightmare Before Christmas* disc in his room and smoking cloves. His room is totally sacrosanct since he told his 'rents that he couldn't guarantee that he wouldn't be masturbating to gay porn if anyone came in. (He's so lucky sometimes—I could stand on my head and flick the bean right there at the dinner table and my mom would be all, "Honey, Christmas is family time, we should be together" and make me finish in front of everyone.)

So, we like watched *The Nightmare Before Christmas* disc with Mom and Ronnie until they fell asleep on the couch— then Jared and I drew some really cool tribal tattoos on Ronnie's shaved head with Magic Marker, but only like in red and black, so they look real.

Then he was all, "We should go get some coffee— my aunt gave me a hundred-dollar Starbucks gift card for Christmas."

And I hate it when people brag about their Christmas presents, because it's completely shallow and materialistic. So, I was all, "Yeah, well, I'd love to, but I am now one of the chosen, so I have duties."

And he was all, "No way, you're Jewish?"

And I was all, "No, I am nosferatu."

And he was all, "You are not."

And I was all, "Remember that sexylicious guy from Walgreens. It was him. Well, actually it's the Countess who brought me into the sacred circle of sanguinity."

And he was all, "You didn't even call me?"

"I'm sorry, Jared, but you are of an inferior species now."

So he goes, "I know, I totally suck."

And I know he's going to go all tragico-emo on me. So I say, "Buy me a Mochaccino and I'll reveal to you our dark ways and stuff."

We leave a note saying that Jared has impregnated me and we're running off together to join a satanic cult, so my mother won't panic when she wakes up, because she's to- talitarian about leaving notes. Then we head to the SOMA.

But apparently, the entire fucking country shuts down on Christmas, slammed under the oppressive iron fist of the baby Jesus, so out of nine Starbucks we try, all are closed.

And Jared is all, "Take me to meet them. I want to be in the dark fold, too."

And I was all, "No way, loser, your hair is totally flat." Which it was. He only had the one spike in front, and his sculpting gel had like failed hours ago, so in his PVC raincoat, he kinda looked like a black lacquer coatrack like you see in Chinatown, but that wasn't why I couldn't take him to see the Countess and my Dark Lord. I just couldn't. I knew the Countess would freak out if she saw I was exploiting her exquisite gift to show off for a friend, so I was all, "It's very secret." But Jared started to pout and brood at the same time, which he can totally pull off because he practices, so I started to feel like a malodorous soupçon of mashed assholes, as Lautréamont so aptly put it. (*Shut up, Lily says it sounds more romantic in French.*)

So I let him come, but I told him he had to stay outside across the street. But when we came around the corner of the Dark Lord's block, there was a guy in a yellow tracksuit standing in the middle of the street. Just standing there, with his hood up and his head down, looking like he was going to stand there forever. And he turned really slow in our direction.

Jared was all, *"Wanksta rappa,"* in my ear, and he giggled that high-pitched little-girl giggle he does sometimes that's like violence catnip to other guys. (Which is why Jared has to carry a foot-long double-edged dagger in his boot, which he calls his Wolf-fang. Fortunately it doesn't give him any false confidence and he is still a total puss, but he likes the attention he gets when doormen take it away from him at clubs.)

Anyway, I think my vampyre senses were, like, on edge, because I could just tell that this wasn't your normal hip-hop guy standing in the middle of a deserted street in a three-hundred-dollar tracksuit at midnight on Christmas night, so I grabbed Jared's arm and pulled him back around the corner.

And I'm all, "Dude. Shields up. Creep. Stealth. Lowest profile."

So we peek around the corner, totally cloaked this time, and the tracksuit guy is like over by the door of the loft, and someone is coming out. It's the crusty old drunk guy with the huge shaved cat, and he has his unit out, like he's going to take a leak, which I could have gone another sixteen years without seeing. And Tracksuit grabs him like he's a rag doll and pulls his head back by the hair, and bites him on the neck. And when he does, I can see that it's not a hip-hop guy at all, but some crusty white vampyre, his fangs were like visible from space. So the huge cat guy is thrashing and screaming and spraying whiz all over the place and I can hear the huge cat hissing behind the door, and Jared grabs me by my messenger bag and starts pulling me away, down the street. So that's all I saw.

And Jared was all, "Whoa."

And I was all, "Yeah."

And as soon as we got a few blocks away, I pulled out my cell and called the Countess's cell, but it went right to voice mail. So now we're at a special midnight showing of *The Nightmare Before Christmas* at the Metreon, drinking a huge Diet Coke to calm our nerves while we wait for a return call from my vampyre coven. (Jared forgot his inhaler and has been gasping since we saw the attack. It's so embarrassing. People are like looking, and I've moved a couple of seats over so they won't think I'm giving him a hand job or something.) I am totally overcome with dread and foreboding, and the time passes like a seeping infection on a bad eyebrow piercing. So we wait. I wish we had some pot. More later.

Oh yeah, and Mom got me a green Care Bear for Christmas! I totally love it.

You're sure this is where you left it?" Jody was looking up and down the Embarcadero. There were no people out on the street—the performers and hustlers were long gone. She could hear the Bay Bridge humming in the distance, a foghorn started to low over in Alameda. A BART train burped out of a tunnel onto the street a block away, headed toward the ballpark, empty. A police cruiser turning out of Market Street strafed them with its headlights before heading past the Ferry Building toward Fisherman's Wharf. Tommy waved to the cops.

"Yeah. I was right here and my watch went off. He weighed a ton. It would have taken a bunch of guys to move him."

Jody saw something shining on the bricks near her feet and crouched down to touch the source. Metal filings of some sort. She licked her finger and came up with a coating of yellowish metallic particles on her fingertip. "Unless someone cut it up."

"Who would do that? Who would cut a statue up and steal the pieces?"

"Doesn't matter. Maybe thieves, maybe city workers. If someone cut that bronze shell, one of two things happened. If it was daytime, Elijah fried out here in the sun. If it was dark, he's free."

"It wasn't light, was it?"

Jody shook her head. "I'm guessing no." She saw a light pattern among the bricks a few steps away and crouched down again. There was a fine, grayish powder between the bricks. She pinched some between her fingers and shook her head. "For sure no."

"What? What is that?"

She brushed her finger off on her jeans and dug into her jacket pocket. "Tommy, remember I told you that you didn't drink the whore dry because she wouldn't have been there if you had?"

"Yeah."

"Well, that's because when a vampire drains someone— when *we* drain someone, they turn to a fine gray powder.

I can't explain why, but it looks like that. Feels like that."
She pointed to the mortar lines between the bricks.

Tommy knelt down and touched the powder, looked
up. "How do you know that?"

"You know how I know that?"

"You've killed people."

She shrugged. "Just a couple. And they were sick. Terminal. They were asking for it, sort of."

"So that's why you weren't upset about the hooker?"

She pulled her cell phone out of her jacket pocket, then
held it behind her back and twisted back and forth looking
at her feet, like a little girl being interrogated about how
Mommy's lamp got broken. "Are you mad?"

"I'm a little disappointed."

"Really? I'm really sorry. You would have done the same
thing if you'd been there."

"I'm just disappointed that you didn't feel that you could
trust me."

"You were having a hard time with your change. I didn't
want to bother you."

"But it wasn't sexual or anything, right?"

"Absolutely not. Purely nutritional." She didn't think it
necessary to tell him about kissing the old man. It would
just confuse things.

"Well, I guess it's okay, then. I guess if you had to."

He stood and she ran to him and kissed him. "I can't tell
you how glad I am to have that off my chest."

"Yeah, well . . ."

"Hang on." She held up a finger and hit the power button on her phone.

"Calling your mom to tell her she was right about your being a tramp?"

"I'm calling the kid."

"Abby?"

"Yeah. I need to tell her to stay away from our place. Elijah is going to start messing with us like before."

Jody watched as the little icons on her phone showed that it was searching for a signal. "But she said she wasn't coming by tonight. It's Christmas."

"I know she said that, but I think she may come by anyway."

"Why?"

"Well, she has a thing for me, I think. I bit her last night."

"You bit Abby?"

"Yeah. I told you, I was hurt. I needed—"

"God, you're such a blood slut."

"I knew you'd be mad."

"Well, it's Abby, for fuck's sake. I'm her dark lord."

"Look, a voice mail."

Elijah Ben Sapir cast the twitching, pee-spraying alcoholic across the street, where he bounced off the metal garage door of the foundry and back out to the curb, where his head knocked the side mirror off an illegally parked Mazda.

Then the vampire walked with exaggerated steps, his arms held out from his sides like a bad stage monster to try to keep the urine-sotted velour fabric of his tracksuit from contacting his skin. Although he had experienced all manner of filth and gore in his eight hundred years, and had, in fact, spent whole days hiding naked under loamy soil to escape the sun, he didn't remember being quite so put off as he was at being pissed on by his lunch. Perhaps it was that he only had one set of clothes now, and there was no luxurious yacht with a full wardrobe to retire to, or perhaps it was that he had spent the day between two urine-stained mattresses under an unconscious junkie while police searched the hotel around him. He'd just hit his limit, that's all.

He'd known the desk clerk would give him up to the police, so as soon as he had gone to his room, the vampire had hidden his tracksuit in the corner of the closet, gone to mist, then slipped under the door into the next room and in between the mattress and box springs of a semiconscious junkie. He'd gone back to solid just as sunrise put him out for the day.

At sundown, he was surprised at how elated he was to find the tracksuit still in the closet, after he fed off the junkie (just a sip) and snapped his neck. (Leaving more or less a greeting card to the homicide inspectors who had attacked him with the others at the yacht club.) Now his precious tracksuit was all covered in whiz and he was furious.

He stalked over to where he'd thrown the bum and snatched him up by the ankle. Elijah was not tall by modern standards, but he found that if he held the bum's ankle high above his head, he could shake him sufficiently to get the job done.

"You're not even her minion, are you?" Elijah banged the bum's head against the sidewalk to punctuate his question.

"Please," said the bum. "My huge cat—"

Thud, thud, thud on the sidewalk. A little shake. Change, a few bills, a lighter, and a bottle of Johnny Walker rained out of the bum's pockets.

"You're just her little moo cow, aren't you? I tasted her on you."

"There's a kid," said the moo cow. "A spooky little girl. She takes care of them."

"Them?"

Elijah flung the bum against the garage and proceeded to pick up the change and the bills on the sidewalk. The steel door next to the garage door opened and a burly bald man in overalls stepped out on the sidewalk, smacking a lead-tipped tire thumper on his palm. "You motherfuckers making enough noise out here?"

Elijah bared his fangs and hissed at the biker, then leapt to the wall over the garage door and clung there, facedown, above the biker's head.

The biker looked up at the vampire, down at the prostrate bum, then at the damaged Mazda. "Well, okay then," he said. "I can see you fellas still have some shit to work out." He slipped back into the foundry and slammed the door.

Elijah dropped to his feet and headed up the street, not

even bothering to stop to snap the moo cow's neck. How could he have been so stupid? He wasn't going to terrorize her by killing a food source. He needed to threaten her minion, just as he had with the boy. How could he have known that she'd actually betray him and choose the boy? Turn the boy? It wouldn't happen again.

Amid all the anger, the hunger, and the excitement at having a purpose, Elijah Ben Sapir felt a twinge of heart-ache. He had begun this adventure thinking himself the puppet master; now he was all entangled in the strings. Making mistakes.

No worry. He cocked his head and focused. Past the rasp-ing breath of the moo cow, the buildings settling, the Bay Bridge humming, and a thousand hearts beating in the lofts around him, he could hear the retreating steps of the little girl and her friend.

Being the Chronicles of Abby Normal: The Hunted

Apparently I am the Hunted, which, I want to note here, I am totally not qualified for. Here I sit, perched in the rafters (I think these things are rafters) of the Oakland Bay Bridge like a crippled night bird, waiting for doom to descend on me in the form of an ancient, undead thing, to wrench the very limbs from my delicate body. So that sucks.

Fortunately I have some sustenance until my Dark Lord and Lady rise from their diurnal slumber to kick some fucking ass. I know I should be eating bugs and spiders and stuff to facilitate my vampyrism, but as a vegetarian, I haven't developed the hunting skills, so I've started with some Gummi Bears I got at the theater. (Supposedly they are made out of beef pectin or extract of horse hooves or something, so I think they make a good transition to the nosferatu diet. And I like biting off their tiny heads.)

Here, high above the City—well, actually, we're about

ten feet above some homeless people who live under the bridge—I feel like the guardian of an ancient tomb, willing to face any attacker to protect my master and mistress, who are wrapped in tarps, lying on the next beam or rafter or whatever.

OMFG, there are fucking pigeons everywhere! Sorry, one just pooped on my notebook. Never mind. Move along. I'm over it. But ewwwww!

Jared has gone to his dad's house in the Noe Valley to get the lawn cart and minivan so we can transport my masters to safety. He left me his dagger, which I've only had to brandish once, against a woman who wanted to take the tarp from over my Dark Lord. Then I used it to scrape off my old nail polish, which was totally chipped and stuff from doing minion manual labor.

So, my masters like met up with us outside the Museum of Modern Art and they were all, "Are you okay? Did he hurt you?" And they were being all secretive around Jared, like he didn't know we were vampyres. And I was all, "Just chill, he's assistant minion." So they relaxed.

Then Flood pulls this bronze hand out of his bag and he's all, "Abby, do you know what this is?"

And I was all, "Why yes, Lord Flood," because I speak *obvious* as a second language. "It's a bronze hand, correct?"

So the Countess took the hand from him. "Abby, this is what's left of the shell of the vampyre who turned me."

So I'm all, "Begging your pardon and whatnot, Countess, but that's a statue hand."

And she's all, "That's what I'm saying." Which is not what the fuck she was saying at all.

So it turns out that the bronze statue that used to be in the loft was actually the vampyre who turned the Countess, and then the Countess turned the vampyre Flood, except he was just Flood then. So the old vampyre, whose name is Elijah, got all PMS and started fucking with the Countess by leaving dead bodies all over town with evidence pointing toward her, and threatening to kill her minion, who was Flood at the time, and it got completely out of hand, with some cops and the geeks from the Safeway blowing up Elijah's yacht and really pissing him off, and then the Countess pretending to save Elijah when in fact she was extracting his ancient vampyry secrets, and Flood bronzing them both, but letting the Countess out because she is the love of his life and whatnot. So Flood, who is not a mysterious and ancient creature of the night at all, but has been a vampyre like a week longer than I have, took the statue down to the waterfront to drop it in the Bay, so it wouldn't remind the Countess of her heart being torn asunder by the yearning for two lovers and stuff. But the sun came up and Flood left the statue on the Embarcadero, and when they went back it was gone, and it turns out that Elijah is loose and he was the crusty vampyre in the yellow tracksuit I saw shaking the huge cat guy and he is now stalking me to get back at the Countess for being a duplicitous ho.

So Jared was all, "Fuck. That's awesome."

And I was all, "You lied to me."

And the Countess was all, "Yeah, sunshine, that's why I'm telling you this now." Which was completely unnecessary sarcasm on her part.

And Jared was like, "This is the best Christmas ever."

And I was all, "Shut up, gay-bait. I've been betrayed."

And the Countess was all, "You'll get over it. We have to go see if William is okay."

And I see now that she was right, but I brooded as we went back to the loft, just to make a point, because I hate it when people take me for granted. When we got to the Countess's block, there was an ambulance there and cops all over the place, so Flood and the Countess hung back and sent me over to get the 411. I could see that the huge cat guy was on a stretcher and they were strapping oxygen on him.

And I was all, "Let me through, this man is my father."

And the EMTs were all, "No way."

And I was all, "Who called you, anyway?"

And they were like, "The guy in the building. A sculptor or something."

And then the cat guy was all, "Let her through."

So they let me through.

So I blew by the EMT to the huge cat guy, and I was all, "Are you okay?"

And he was like, "Well, my head hurts like hell, and I think my leg is broke."

And I was all, "Is there anything I can do?" Because I was under orders of the Countess to gain information and offer assistance.

And he was like, "If you could take care of Chet. He's in the stairwell. He'll be hungry."

And I was all, "You got it."

So then he like pulled the oxygen mask off and had me bend over so he could whisper, and I was all, "Yes, Dad," for the EMTs who were watching.

And he whispered like, "Before they take me away, could I see your tits."

So I kicked him in the ribs. And the EMTs went all byzerk and shit, and told me to get away, but they were totally overreacting, because I had on my red Converse All Stars, which will hardly even bruise you.

So they loaded him into the ambulance, and just as they were shutting the doors, he reached out his hand, like he was a drowning man reaching for the last spark of his mortality before the inky waves of death swept him away—so I flashed my boobs for him, just a quick lift of my bra and top at the same time, because I don't think we do enough to help the homeless, and I wanted him to die a happy man. And besides, they're small and I don't get that many requests.

So I got Chet out of the stairway of the old loft and was carrying him kid-style when I saw the two cops from before—the ones the Countess said helped blow up Elijah—so I went up to the Hispano-cop and I was all, "So, what's up, cop?"

And he was all, "You need to get home, and you have no business out at this hour, and we should take you to the station and call your parents and blah, blah, blah, threat,

threat, disapproval, and fascist dogma all up in your darkly delicious grille." (I'm paraphrasing. Although I do have a delicious grille as I had to wear braces for three years when I was a kid, and now my teeth are like my most acceptable feature. I hope my fangs come in straight.)

And the big gay cop was all, "What are you doing here?"

And I was all, "I live here, bone-smoker, what are you doing here? Aren't you guys homicide cops?"

And he was all, "Let's see some ID blah, blah, bluster, bluster, Oh My God I am so full of shit."

And I was like, "I guess you wouldn't have to deal with this shit if you had properly blowed up that old vampyre when you stole his art collection."

So all of a sudden the Hispano-cop and his big gay partner were all, "Whaaa—?"

And I'm like, "Just so we know where we stand. How long you bitches going to be here?"

And they were like, "Just a half hour or so longer, miss. We need to interview some witnesses and go clean out our boxers where we have just completely shit ourselves. Do you need a ride somewhere?" (Again paraphrasing.)

So I walked off, while they were still stunned, let Chet into the new loft down the street like it was mine, then ran around the block and reported to the Countess and Flood. Jared was just staring at them like he was hypnotized or something. I was like, "Hey, Boo," to remind him what a tard he was being and Jared snapped out. (Lily and Jared and I watched the *To Kill a Mockingbird* DVD like six times

together and our favorite part is when Scout sees Boo Rad-
ley behind the door and goes, "Hey, Boo." It's like thanking
the universe for sending you a benevolent retard to help
you out, which is how I often feel about Jared.) So I was
like, "Buy me a coffee." And the Countess and Flood look at
each other and shake their heads. No money.

So I was like, "You guys are so fucking lame. You have
piles of cash and you roll with no money. You are no longer
the Dark Lord and Lady of me." Which I totally didn't mean,
but I was stressed and starting to get a low-on-caffeine headache. But Jared goes, "Hey, Boo" at me, and he's holding a
ten-dollar bill. And I pretended to find a snag in my fishnets
so everyone would quit looking at me.

The Countess said she knew of a Chinese diner off
Fremont Street that was open all night on Christmas and
we could hang out there until the cops left. Jared and I had
cups of coffee and an order of fries, which FYI, taste a little
like shrimp in a Chinese diner. And Flood and the Countess are watching us, looking all sad. So I'm like, "What?
What? What?"

And the Countess is all, "Nothing."

Which I know is totally something, because I say it all
the time. And I watch her eyes follow Jared's cup as he sips
his coffee and I'm all, "Oh, fucksocks, Countess, cowboy the
fuck up, would you?" Then I slipped Jared's dagger out of his
boot, grabbed his hand, and poked him in the thumb.

I'd like to say right here that the screaming was totally
unnecessary. And whatever the Chinese guy was saying at

me from behind the counter was a total overreaction and how does he expect me to understand him when he's talking that fast AND in Chinese? Anyway, after I squeezed Jared's thumb into his cup, then a little into my own and gave it to Flood, everyone calmed down, even the Chinese guy after Jared paid him for two more coffees—and the meeting of the Immortal SOMA Drama Queens officially came to order.

It seemed like we waited forever, and the Countess and Flood wouldn't answer any of my questions about the *way of the nosferatu*. It was like they had no idea what they were doing. Like last year I took Advanced Foods class (which is like cooking for nerds) after lunch, and so I usually took a nap. Which was fine, because I'm not even thrilled about regular foods, so, you know, what do I need with like advanced digital HD wi-fi foods and whatnot—so I took the course pass-fail and slept. But then, at the end of the semester, my mom springs this trap on me, like—"Oh, Allison, I've bought ingredients and you can prepare dinner for Ronnie and me to show what you learned in your Advanced Foods class. It'll be fun."

You can pretty much bet that anytime Mom uses the phrase "it'll be fun," she is about to drive a stake in fun's heart so that it may never rise again. Which is what happened. Artichokes? Who eats something like that? I thought it was a weapon.

So anyway, after nine eternities in the diner, we went back to the loft, where the Countess said she had my Christmas present waiting. When we got to the block, the cops and EMTs were gone and it looked like the coast was clear, but when the Countess opened the security door to the loft, there, sitting on the steps, was the old vampyre, naked.

Well, the Countess and Flood jumped about eighteen feet in the air and I'm pretty sure I peed a little. Yes, I definitely peed. Jared just started an asthma attack, not the whole attack, just the first gasp. He just stopped breathing after that.

So Elijah is all, "I needed to do some laundry."

Let me say right here, if I haven't made it clear, that I have seen as many pale, naked old-man parts in the last twenty-four hours to bruise my delicate psyche for a lifetime, so don't be surprised if you someday find me wandering the moors at midnight, a crazed look in my eye, babbling about albino Tater Tots nesting in Brillo pads and being pursued by sagging man ass, because that shit can happen when you've been traumatized.

Then Flood threw himself against the door and screamed for us to run as he bravely held the door against our ancient vampyre ancestor's assaults. I was beginning to doubt Flood's ability to fulfill his duties as my Dark Lord until he stepped up and saved us—valiant vampyre hero that he is—because I was starting to think he was just a geek with a passing knowledge of poetry.

As we ran I could hear Elijah saying, "He peed on my tracksuit," as he threw himself against the door, or I guessed he did, because I didn't turn around until we were two blocks away.

The Countess was all, "I've got to go back for him." But before she even turned around, my Dark Lord came running around the corner.

And he was all, "Go, go, go!" waving at us.

And we were all, "Where? Where? Where?"

And then as the Countess threw her arms around Flood and started to squeeze the bejeezus out of him, and Jared was all, "Gasp, get a room, gasp," her watch started beeping. Then Flood's watch was beeping, too. And they were all, "Uh-oh."

So we had like ten minutes to find someplace dark to hide them, and no one had any money for a hotel, even if we had the time to check in and whatnot. So they ran toward a big construction site under the Bay Bridge. And I was thinking, *I do not want to bury my masters in the construction site. What if they got paved?* It would totally freak them out to get paved.

And the Countess was all, "How did you get away?"

And the vampyre Flood was all, "The dryer buzzer went off."

And she was all, "He let you live because his laundry was done?"

And Flood goes, "Lucky, huh?" Totally not out of breath, even with the running.

So when we got to the construction site, everything was either open or would be when everyone came to work. And the Countess looked up into the rafters or whatever of the bridge and goes, "There."

So there is where we went. I grabbed some tarps that were covering this generator thing by the construction site and Jared and I climbed up into the rafters with our vampyre sires and helped tuck them in just in time for them to go out.

But as it got lighter, and we saw all the homeless people around, Jared and I realized that our masters would not be safe here when all the homeless people who lived under the bridge noticed the tarps and our delicate youth or smelled my Gummi Bears and came after us. So Jared went to get the garden cart, some trash bags and duct tape, and hopefully his stepmom's minivan so we can move our masters to a safer realm.

Oh, check it, before the Countess passed into the inky sleep of the undead, I was like, "So what did you get me for Christmas?"

And she was all, "Ten thousand dollars."

And I was like, "I didn't get you guys anything."

And she was like, "That's okay. You are our most special favorite minion and it's all good."

Which is why I love her and will guard her to the death. Then she like kissed the vampyre Flood and passed out. I'm sure their love will span the ages, if Jared and I don't fuck up and fry them during transport.

OMG! I just remembered, we forgot to feed Chet!

The Half-Life of American Cheese

The Cheddar Princess of Fond du Lac was toasted. It wasn't just the bursting into flames that had crispied her up more than somewhat physically, it was that Drew's blood tasted like bong water, and she was still a little mentally baked from feeding on him. She'd made the mistake of trying to get the taste out of her mouth with some orange juice and had been rewarded with five minutes of the dry heaves.

She brushed at her arms and great black flakes of burned skin came away, revealing fresh, unscarred skin below. Drew's blood was healing her, but it appeared that the process was going to take time and, like life in general, was going to be messy.

Maybe a bath.

She padded naked into the bathroom, which was done all in slabs of granite and green glass, and ran her bath. While the tub filled, she picked the last few burned tatters of her dress

away from her skin and dropped them into the toilet. There
was a swath of gray dust across the black tile, the remains of
the original owner, and she was tracking him all over the
bathroom and bedroom suite, so she stopped to sweep him
into the corner with a towel. That had sort of been a surprise
(in what was turning out to be a long line of surprises) when
her first victim had disintegrated in her arms two nights ago,
just as she was getting the hang of blood drinking.

"Oops."

He had been so nice, too. Had picked her up in his Mercedes not two minutes after she'd stumbled out of Lash's
apartment building wearing nothing but a leather bustier
and thigh-high platform boots. It wasn't the first time she'd
been on the street with her ass hanging out—that wasn't
what had thrown her. It was waking up feeling like her tits
were on fire to see her body rejecting the giant silicone globes
she had spent so much money having implanted. Even as she
tried to push them back in with her hands, the implants
pushed through her skin, opening her up like they were
aliens hatching out of her. She screamed as they broke
through and rolled to the floor, then lay there, quivering on
the carpet. As she watched, her skin mended, her breasts
tightened and lifted, the pain had turned to a tingling, but
now she felt a squirming in her face—her lips specifically, and
she wiped her mouth and came away with two sluglike lines
of silicone that had been injected years ago. It was only then,
in looking at the grotesque globs of lip filler on her hand, that
Blue realized she wasn't blue at all. Her palms were baby

white. Her arms, her legs—she ran to the bathroom and looked in the mirror. An old familiar stranger looked back at her—the Cheddar Princess of Fond du Lac. She hadn't seen this person since high school; the milky-white skin, hair almost white blond, still in the severe cut of the blue call girl, but looking somewhat like a pageboy cut now. Even the tattoos she'd had done in her early days in Vegas were gone.

I'm alive, she thought. Then: *And I'm going to be alive forever.* Then: *And I'm going to need some fucking money.*

She ran to Lash's bedroom to where she'd left her makeup case. It was gone. Her money was gone!

She ran out of the apartment and down the steps like she might see a green trail of bills blowing in the wind in the direction her money had escaped, but once on the street, she headed for the only place she knew, toward the Marina Safeway. She got half a block before the Mercedes pulled up and the electric window rolled down.

"Hey, you need a ride? It's a little chilly out here for that outfit."

His name had been David, and he did something that had to do with moving money around. Whatever it was, it must have paid well. He was wearing a two-thousand-dollar suit and his penthouse apartment on Russian Hill looked out on Golden Gate Bridge and the massive dome at the Palace of Fine Arts.

He'd given her his coat to wear up in the elevator. It was in the elevator that the hunger had come upon her. Poor David. They hadn't even talked price before she'd had him bent over the green glass vanity in the bathroom, drinking his life away.

"Oops." The difference, she realized, between what had happened to her and what had happened to David had been the bloody kiss she'd taken from Tommy. But for a kiss, she, too, would be a pile of dust. *There should be a song like that,* she thought. At least she'd learned before she took her victims.

Now she swept the last of David into the corner, then scraped him up with a piece of cardboard from his shirt drawer and dumped him into the wastebasket. Then she slipped into the tub full of bubbles and began to scrub off her charred skin.

She wouldn't be able to stay long. David had been married or had a girlfriend. Blue had found a whole closet full of women's clothes—expensive clothes, and the woman would probably be back. Of course, this would make a great base of operations, maybe she could just wait for the wife to return and sweep her into the wastebasket with David.

Blue leaned back and closed her eyes, listened to the bubbles popping, the wires humming through the building, the traffic out on the streets, to fishing boats leaving the wharf—then a sudden intake of breath from the living room, then another, deeper gasp as the second one found life, then a long man-scream. The dead Animals she'd collected were coming back to life.

"Sit tight, boys," Blue said. "Mama's just going to get cleaned up and put on a new dress, then we'll go get you something to eat and pick up my money."

She ran a sponge over her arm and smiled. She really could be Snow White now. *One dwarf at a time,* she thought.

Elijah Ben Sapir had roamed the planet for eight hundred and seventeen years. In that time he had seen empires rise and fall, miracles and massacres, ages of ignorance and ages of enlightenment: the full spectrum of mankind's cruelty and kindness. He had seen all manner of freakishness, from the perversions of nature to the perversions of mind, twisted, beautiful, terrifying: he thought he had seen it all. But for all of his years, and all the acuity of perception enabled by his vampire senses, he had never seen a huge shaved cat in a red sweater, and sitting there in his newly washed yellow tracksuit, still warm from the dryer and smelling of soap and fabric softener, he smiled.

"Hey, kitty," the old vampire said.

The huge cat eyed him suspiciously from across the loft. The cat could sense that he was a predator, just as Elijah could sense that the cat had been prey to a vampire. Kitty treat.

"I'm not going to eat you, kitty. I've fed quite enough."

It was true. Elijah was feeling a little bloated from trying to keep the body count up. Perhaps he should just kill the next few, not feed. But no, the police wouldn't know it was a vampire then, and there'd be no joy in terrorizing the fledgling. He just wasn't ready to feed yet. There was someone in the stairwell right now, he could hear her breathing and smell patchouli and clove cigarette odor wafting under the door. *Soon enough*, he thought.

"Perhaps we'll find something for you to eat, hey, kitty?"

Elijah vaulted off the bar stool and began opening cupboards. In the third one he found pouches of Tender Vittles. He took a bowl from the cupboard that looked as if it had never been used, dumped in the meatish nuggets, and shook them around.

"Come, kitty."

Chet padded a few steps toward the kitchenette, then stopped. Elijah put the bowl down and stepped away. "I understand, kitty. I don't like to eat in front of witnesses either. But sometimes—"

The vampire heard a car pull up outside, a car that hadn't been tuned in a while. He cocked his head and listened as the doors opened and slammed. Four got out. He heard their steps on the concrete, a female voice, hissing at the other three. In an instant he was at the window looking down, and in spite of himself, he smiled again. There was no vivid life aura around the four down on the sidewalk. No healthy pink glow, no black shadow of death. The visitors below were not human.

Vampires. On one hand, an indication of an enormous problem—one that just might attract attention that he could ill afford—but on the other, exciting in a way that he hadn't felt in a hundred years.

"Four against one. Oh my, kitty, how ever will I prevail?"

The old vampire ran his tongue over his fangs. For all the rage, frustration, and discomfort he'd endured since choosing the redhead as his fledgling, he was, for the first time in decades, not bored. He was having the time of his very long life.

"Killing time, kitty," he said, slipping into a pair of Tommy's Nikes.

Jody awoke to the smell of clove cigarettes and the crunching of Cheese Newts. There was music screeching, too—a whiny guy singing about some girl named Ligeia, who apparently he missed a great deal because he was talking about dragging her worm-worn corpse from the earth and caressing her cheek on a cliff above the sea before throwing himself off, with her in his arms. The singer sounded a little down, and like he could have used a throat lozenge.

She opened her eyes and was initially blinded until she adjusted to the black light, then she yelped. Jared White Wolf was sitting on the bed about two feet away from her, shoving handfuls of crunchy Cheese Newts into his mouth. There was a brown rat on his shoulder.

"Hi." Newt crumbs sprayed and fluoresced on the black sheets and clothing.

"Hi," Jody said, turning her head to avoid the crumbs.

"This is my room. Do you like it?"

Jody looked around, for once not really that thrilled with her vampire night-vision abilities. There were disturbing stains glowing on the sheets, and almost everything else in the room was black with a patina of vibrant blacklightenhanced dust or lint—there was even lint on the rat.

"It's swell," she said. *Interesting,* she thought. She was no longer afraid of gang members and street criminals, and would even throw down with an eight-hundred-year-old vampire if need be, but rodents still sort of gave her the willies. The rat's eyes were glowing silver in the black light.

"This is Lucifer Two." Jared scooped the animal off his shoulder and held him out.

Despite an attempt at self-control, Jody climbed backwards halfway up the wall, shredding a Marilyn Manson poster with her nails in the process.

"Lucifer One went on to his dark reward when I tried to dye him black."

"Sad," Jody said.

"Yeah." Jared turned the rat and rubbed noses with him. "I was hoping we could turn him to nosferatu when you bring Abby and me into the fold."

"Yeah, sure, that'll happen. Why am I in your room, Jared?"

"It was the only place we could think to bring you. It wasn't safe under the bridge. Abby had to go, so I'm in charge."

"Good for you. Where's Tommy?"

"Under the bed."

She would have known that—would have heard him breathing if the music wasn't cranked up to coffin-splitting volume.

"Could you turn the music down a little, please?"

"'Kay," Jared said. He tucked Lucifer Two in his pocket and spidered across the bed, getting a little tangled in his black duster, then rolled to the floor and across the room in a commando-under-fire move until he got to the stereo, where he twisted the dial, putting the keening Emo singer out of his misery, or at least shutting him the fuck up.

"Where are we?" Tommy's voice from under the bed. "It smells like gym socks stuffed with ground-up hippies."

"We're in Jared's room," Jody said. She let a hand drop off the edge of the bed. Tommy took it and she pulled him out. He was still partially wrapped in duct tape and garbage bags.

"Was I a hostage again?"

"We had to cover you up to keep you from burning in the sun."

"Well, thanks."

Tommy looked at Jody, who shrugged.

"I was unwrapped when I woke up," she said.

"That's because Abby says you're the Alpha vamp. Do you guys want to play Xbox or watch a DVD? I have *The Crow Special Collector's Edition*."

"Gee," Jody said, "that would be great, Jared, but we'd better be going."

Tommy had already picked up the Xbox controller, but set it down with marked disapproval, as if he'd notice a little botulism there on the trigger button.

"Oh, you can't go until the 'rents go to bed." Jared giggled, high and girlish. "The door is right by where they watch TV."

"We'll go out a window," Jody said.

Jared giggled again, then snorted a little, then started to honk, then took a hit from the inhaler that hung around his neck before he went on. "There's no window. This basement is totally windowless. Like we've been walled up in here with our own grotesque despair. Isn't it sweet?"

"We could go to mist," Tommy said. "Go out under the door."

"That would be so cool," Jared said, "but my dad put rubber gaskets around the door to contain my disgusting Goth stench. That's what he calls it: my 'disgusting Goth stench.' Although I don't think I'm really Goth, more like death punk. He just doesn't like cloves. Or pot. Or patchouli. Or gay people."

"Philistine," Tommy said.

"Oh, would you guys like some Cheese Newts?" Jared picked the box up off the floor and held it out. "I can open a vein on them if you need me to." He waved the thumb Abby had stabbed to prepare their coffee the night before, now wrapped in a ragged ball of gauze and medical tape the size of a racquetball.

"I'm good," Tommy said.

Jody nodded in agreement; although she would love a cup of coffee, she didn't think she should ask the kid to stab himself quite so soon.

She checked her watch. "What time do your parents go to bed?"

"Oh, around ten. You'll have plenty of time to stalk the

night and whatnot. Would you like to wash up or some-thing? There's a bathroom down here. And a washing ma-chine. My room was the wine cellar, then my dad crashed his car and started twelve-stepping, so I got this sweet room for my own. Abby says it's dank and disgusting—and she says it like it's a bad thing! I think it's just her perky side manifesting. I love her, but she really can be perky sometimes—don't tell her I said so."

Jody shook her head, then nudged Tommy, who shook his head in agreement. "We won't tell." The kid was sort of giving her the creeps. She thought she might have lost that ability with blood drinking and the sleep of the undead and all, but nope, she was getting completely creeped out.

"Jared, when is Abby coming back?"

"Oh, she should be here any minute. She went to your loft to feed the cat."

"She went to our loft? The loft where Elijah was?"

"No, it's okay. She went during daylight so he couldn't hurt her."

"It's not daylight anymore," Jody said.

"How do you know?" Jared said "No windows, duh."

Tommy Stooge-smacked his forehead with enough force to render a mortal man unconscious. "Because we're awake, you fucking moron!"

"Oh yeah, ha," Jared said. The trilling giggle again. "That's bad, huh?"

They Know Not What They Do

When Rivera and Cavuto arrived at the Safeway, they found that the remaining Animals had crucified Clint on a stainless-steel chip rack and were shooting him with paintball guns. Lash unlocked the door to let them in. The Emperor and his men followed. Clint's screaming sent Bummer into a barking fit and the Emperor snatched him up and stuffed him headfirst into the pocket of his overcoat.

"That really necessary?" Rivera asked, pointing to the paint-splattered martyr.

"We think so," Lash said. "He ratted us out." Lash turned, sighted down the pass-through of register three, and fired a quick volley of electric-blue paintballs into the center of Clint's chest. "Did he call you again?"

Rivera threw a thumb over his shoulder at the Emperor.

The Emperor bowed. "You needed help, my son."

Lash nodded, considering that the Emperor might be

right, then reeled and fired three quick shots into Clint's groin. "Just the same, motherfucker!"

"Stop that!" Rivera said. He snatched the paintball gun out of Lash's hand.

"It's cool. He's wearing a cup."

"And he's saved," said Barry, who had been firing from register four.

"Well, he is now," Cavuto said. As he approached the paint-sodden Evangelical, he pulled a serrated-edge pocket knife from his back pocket and flicked it open. "And just so you know," Cavuto added when his back was to them, "if I turn and there's a single paintball gun pointed in this direction, I will be forced to mistake it for a real weapon and unleash lead Disneyland on your pathetic asses."

Barry and Troy Lee immediately dropped their weapons onto the counter.

"So, the Emperor tells us that you guys have been up to some shit. I thought we all agreed that we were going to keep it on the down-low until things calmed down."

Lash looked at his shoes. "We just had a little party in Vegas."

Rivera nodded. "And you kidnapped Tommy Flood?"

Lash glared over Rivera's shoulder at the Emperor. "That was a secret. Really we were saving him from the daylight."

"So the redhead did turn him?"

"Looked like it. He was unconscious at dawn. Just a little sunlight hit his leg when we were moving him and it started to smoke."

"So you geniuses did what?"

"Well, we tied him to a bed at my apartment and left."

"You left?"

"We had to work."

Cavuto had cut the zip ties that held Clint to the chip rack and helped him to the register, where he sat him down, careful not to get any paint on his sport coat.

"Forgive them, they know not what they do," Clint said, wincing as he touched his paint-spattered shoulder.

"Because they're fucking idiots," Cavuto said, handing him a roll of paper towels.

Rivera ignored the scene at the register. "So you just left him there. So I'll find him there now, right?"

"That was a couple of nights ago," Lash said.

"Go on." Rivera looked at his watch.

"Well, in the morning he was gone."

"And?"

"It's awkward." For variety, Lash looked at Barry's shoes.

"Yeah, tying up your friends and torturing them can be that way," Rivera said.

"We didn't torture him. That was her."

"Her?" Rivera raised an eyebrow.

"Blue. A hooker we rented in Vegas."

"Now we're talkin'," Cavuto said.

"She came back with us. She wanted us to kidnap Tommy or his girlfriend."

"Why did she want that? To get their share of the art money?"

"No, she had plenty of money. I think she wanted to be a vampire."

Rivera tried to hide his surprise. "And?"

"When we went back to the apartment in the morning, Tommy was gone and Blue was dead."

"We had nothing to do with it," Barry added.

"But we didn't think you'd believe it," Troy Lee said.

Rivera felt a tension headache starting to throb in his temples. He closed his eyes and rubbed his forehead. "So you found a dead woman in your apartment. And you didn't think that *then* might be a good time to call the police?"

"Well, you know, dead hooker in your house—embarrassing," Troy Lee said. "I think we've all been there. Can I get a high five—" Apparently, he couldn't, and was thus left hanging.

"That's the weird thing," Barry said. "When we went to move her body, it was gone. But the rug we wrapped her in was still there."

"Yeah, that's the weird thing," Cavuto said, nudging his partner in the arm.

"Heinous fuckery most foul," said the Emperor.

"Ya think?" said Cavuto.

Bummer growled from his pocket sanctuary.

"You guys are not helping," Rivera said. Then to Lash again: "You have a description of this hooker?"

Lash described Blue, glossing quickly over the fact that

she was blue, and spending entirely too much time describing her breasts.

"They were outstanding," Barry said. "I kept them."

Rivera turned to Troy Lee, who seemed the most rational of these insane bastards.

"Explain, please."

"We found silicone implants wrapped up in the rug where we had left Blue."

"Uh-huh," Rivera said. "Intact?"

"Huh?" Troy inquired.

"Were they all cut up?"

"You think someone cut them out of her and took the body?" Troy asked.

"No," Rivera said. "So now you've lost three of your buddies?"

"Yeah. Drew, Jeff, and Gustavo didn't show up tonight."

Rivera had Lash get the addresses of the missing Animals from the office and wrote them down in his notebook.

"And you don't think that they might just be out partying?"

"We called all the phones, checked their houses," Lash said. "The door was hanging open at Drew's, and Jeff had left half a beer in the driveway, which he would never do. Besides, Jeff and Drew might flake, but Gustavo wouldn't. We even went to his cousin's house in Oakland looking for him."

"And he did not *está en la biblioteca* either," said Barry, who, for some reason, believed that all Spanish-speaking people spent a lot of time in the library and had therefore checked there for the intrepid night porter.

"No more bodies that you might have forgotten to mention?"

"Nuh-uh," Lash said. "Our money was gone, though. But we'd given it all to Blue anyway."

"I didn't," Clint said. "Mutual funds, less ten percent for the church."

"You gave six hundred thousand dollars to a hooker?" Rivera almost slapped the kid. Almost.

"Well"—Lash looked at Barry and Troy Lee, then, trying to suppress a grin—"yeah."

Rivera shook his head. "Keep the door locked and don't report this to anyone else."

"That's it?" Lash said. "You aren't going to arrest us or anything?"

"For what?" Rivera flipped his notebook closed and tucked it into the inside pocket of his suit coat.

"Uh, I don't know."

"Me either," said Rivera. "Emperor, you stay inside tonight with these guys. Okay?"

"As you wish, Inspector." The Emperor scratched behind Lazarus's ears.

"That okay?" Rivera said to Lash.

Lash nodded. "Are we going to be safe?" he asked.

Rivera stopped, looked around at the Animals and the Emperor and his dogs. "Nope," he said. "Let's go, Nick." He turned and walked out the door.

The foghorn was lowing across the Bay as the detectives walked back to their car. Fort Mason, just across the street, was barely visible in the rolling cloud of gray mist.

"You think the old vampire is hunting the Animals?" Cavuto asked.

"Someone is," Rivera said. "But I'm not sure it's him."

"You think it might be the redhead and the kid?"

"Could be, but I don't think so. You know, even with the vampire, we always had an identifiable MO—broken neck and massive blood loss, on a victim who turned out to be terminally ill, right?"

"Yeah."

"So if he went after these kids, why no bodies?"

"So it's Flood and the redhead. And they hide their bodies."

"I think it could be worse than that."

"Like worse in a way that we'll never be able to open the bookstore and may in fact end up doing time for taking the vampire's art collection?"

"Like worse in that the hooker and the missing Animals aren't dead at all."

"How is that worse?" Then Cavuto realized how that was worse.

They climbed into the car and stared at the windshield for a while without saying anything.

Finally, after a full minute, Cavuto said, "We're fucked."

"Yep," Rivera said.

"The whole city is fucked."

"Yep."

Being the Chronicles of Abby Normal: Star-Crossed Lover and Tragic Femme Fatale

OMG! We are doomed by our forbidden love! We are like from different feuding families, from the wrong side of the tracks, he is like year of the Rabbit and I am a Leo, so we are even star-crossed, and it's a well-known fact that rabbits and lions have a strained relationship. OMFG! He's so hot! He rocks my stripy socks. If we had moors, I would so be off brooding upon one, my delicate jaw muscles clenched as I stared off into the mist, feeling my profound missingness for him. (I can't believe that San Francisco doesn't have a moor. Everywhere you go we have automated, coin-operated robotic bathrooms, or Frisbee golf courses, or some new stainless-steel epileptic razor-blade public-art thingy, you'd think the least they could do would be to install a decent moor—because there are a lot more people who like brooding than like Frisbee golf. I'm pretty sure moors can be used for other purposes, too, like hauntings and hiding bodies and family picnics and whatnot.) Thus I am forced to do my brooding at Tulley's Coffee on Market Street.

It took most of the day for us to move the Countess and the vampyre Flood to Jared's room. First we had to wrap them up in duct tape and garbage bags to protect them from the sun, then get them down the hill from the Bay Bridge in the garden cart, which was totally physically hard, and not like taking X and dancing or playing DDR all night, more like work. Then, when we were loading them into the minivan, these two cops come by.

And they're all, "So, what are you doing with your piercings and your magenta-on-black hair, and what can we do to further repress your creativity? Bluster-blah-blah."

And Jared was all, "Nothing." All wussy and guilty-sounding. He had the front end of the Countess at the time and he totally just dropped her headfirst on the floorboard of the van.

So I was like, "Fucktard! The Countess is going to rip your nads off when she awakens!" (And she might, too, although when we unwrapped her she seemed unbruised.)

And the cop was all, "Hold it right there, kid." With his hand on his gun like I was going to go all Columbine on his ass or something. So I knew it was time for some strategy.

So I stepped over to the cop, and I started whispering like I didn't want Jared to hear. And I'm all, "Officer, I'm really embarrassed to even be seen like this. I'm a Kappa

Kappa Delta pledge and we're doing this hazing thing. I wouldn't be caught dead dressed like this, but it's like the most popular and powerful sorority on campus."

And the cop is all, "What about the guy? He's not in your sorority."

And I was all, "Shhhhhh. God, you want to hurt her feelings? They made her shave her head like that and she's having a hard enough time with that and being totally flat-chested. Frankly, I don't think she's going to make it. Everyone knows that KKDs are pretty. Hello." I batted my eyelashes and sort of pushed my basically invisible boobs together with my arms, as I have often seen done in music videos.

And the cop was all, "Can I see your student ID?"

And I was like, FUCK, because I didn't know which college would be most likely to have a sorority, so I went with my Berkeley student ID, because Berkeley is a well-known bastion of hippie behavior and higher learning in which a sorority girl would probably have to blow like a hundred football players just to keep her GPA up. And cops like football.

So he was all, "Okay, but make sure there's plenty of airholes so your friends can breathe."

And I was all, "Sure thing. See ya later, cop."

So when we got the masters to Jared's house, his step-mom was all, "So, I see you have your little friend with you."

And Jared had to play chilly, so he was like, yeah, we

have a school project. And stepmonster was so proto-orgasmic that Jared was with a girl that she didn't even say much when we dragged the bodies through the den. Jared was all, "They're for social studies. We're doing replicas of Egyptian mummies."

Despite the complete embarrassment for me as a fellow woman, I'm grateful that when fathers pick their trophy wives, they don't check résumés or SAT scores, because you couldn't get away with that shit with a woman of normal intelligence. But Jared's stepmonster was all, "Oh, how nice for you. Would you like some juice?" Fortunately she wasn't around in sixth grade when Jared and I actually did our mummy project. We got in trouble for charging three hundred dollars' worth of Ace bandages on my mom's Visa, and my sister Ronnie has never fully recovered the feeling in her feet (and has an anxiety attack whenever she's in an enclosed space). But there was no gangrene or amputations like the doctors threatened, and we got a B, so I don't see what all the noise and counseling was about.

Anyway, after we unwrapped the Countess, I knew I had to go back and feed Chet, like I promised the disgusting huge cat guy, and since we had now shared a moment of intimacy, I felt obligated. So we shoved the vampyre Flood under Jared's bed, because Jared wanted to sit on the bed and play Xbox and it's a single bed. So, anyway, I caught the bus on Twenty-fourth Street, and got back to the SOMA with just enough time to feed Chet before the old naked vampyre awakened from his undead slumber. And I took

Jared's dagger with me in my biohazard messenger bag, because I thought I would dispatch Elijah by decapitation as, like, an extra-credit thing for the Countess.

Shut up. It wasn't like I went down in the basement in my nightgown to check on a blown fuse when the radio clearly had stated that there was a psycho killer on the loose and he was probably in the basement. I'm not stupid. I put on Jared's motocross boots and his leather jacket and spiked dog collar, and tied my hair back, so I was totally Thunderdome-ready. How hard could it be to feed the cat and cut the head off a sleeping old guy, anyway? It's not like they wake up. I mean, we bonked Flood's head on the steps going to Jared's room like eight times and he didn't even groan.

So I would have been all good and totally in line to be Princess of Darkness or at least Assistant Manager of Darkness, except when I was going up the steps I heard the dryer open. And I was all, *Uh-oh*. Since when is sundown like at five-o'clock? What am I, nine years old that I should have sunset at five o'clock? Sunset shouldn't be until like eight or nine o'clock, right? Right?

So, I'm like, WHOA. And I froze. And I stood there for like a half an hour, not moving at all, because I didn't buckle like the top buckles of Jared's motocross boots, to show my casual badassness, so it was like I was wearing fucking sleigh bells. (I know, I'm a tard.) So I couldn't move.

Then, after about a year, I hear this car pull up outside and the doors open, and I'm thinking—*Hello, Diversion, my old friend*. And I ran out the security door and right into this tall blond ho. And she's dressed all couture and shit, like it's fashion week at church or something, except she's with three of the guys from the Hummer limo, and she's pale as albino monkey cum. And I don't mean in a good way either. I mean in a sort of *"Hey, Myrtle Joe Cornfed, y'all let go your stepdaddy's penis and get over here and turn the channel to NAS-CAR"* kind of way. I mean, she had no mascara on at all!

Then she just picks me up by the arms and it hurt a lot, and I'm like kicking and thrashing and all, and she throws back her head and here come the fangs.

And I'm all, "No way. They'll just let any-fucking-body into the coven."

And she's all, "Not you. Unless you know where my money is."

And I'm all, "Step off, skank."

And she goes to bite me, and something yanks her back off her feet and I go flying.

Next thing, I'm looking up at the old vampyre in his yellow tracksuit, who is holding the blond ho by the hair, and the pale limo guys are like coming in on him. And Tracksuit is all, "Against the rules, pet. You can't go willy-nilly turning everyone you meet. It attracts the wrong kind of attention."

And wham, he smacks her face on the hood of her Mercedes, leaving a face print on the paint, I swear on the crusty hippie grave of my mother.

So I'm all, "Owned! Bee-yatch! Dog fucking owned you!" Doing a minor booty dance of ownage, perhaps, in retrospect, a bit prematurely. (I believe hip-hop to be the appropriate language for taunting, at least until I learn French.)

So they all turn on me. And I'm all, "awkward." So I started backing across the street. And crusty old vampyre bounces monkey cum's face off the hood of the Mercedes a couple of more times, then drops her and comes for me. The limo guys are all sort of standing by the car like they are waiting for instructions or something. Then one of them says, "Hey," and starts coming my way, too.

So I'm at the wall across the street, and I know I can't run, so I reach into my bag and pull Jared's dagger. And Tracksuit starts laughing—like really stoner laughing, pointing at my ensemble.

And I was all, "Shut up, fuckface, this knife and boots totally go with fishnets." Except for the Countess, I realize now that vampyres lose all fashion sense at death.

But then I hear this really loud thumper coming from down the alley, like club music you can feel in your breastbone, and this totally race-pimped yellow Honda comes screaming out of the alley. Who knew you could even get a car down that alley.

So the old vampyre has to jump back to avoid being run over and the limo guys jump back, and I was kind of hiding my head in my arms, but I hear, "Get in," and it's the cool Manga-haired Asian guy who I'd seen outside the loft before.

And I'm all, "What?" Because the music is really loud.

And he's all, "Get in."

And I'm all, "What?"

And by this time the old vampyre has jumped over the hood of the Honda and is about to grab me when there's this flash. Really more than a flash, because it stayed on. But there was this blinding light. And the music goes down and I hear, "Get in."

So I look into the light, and I'm like, "Grandma, is that you?"

Okay, I didn't say that. I'm totally fucking with you. I looked into the light and saw the Manga-haired guy, wearing sunglasses, and he's waving for me to get in his car. And then I see that the old vampyre is charred like Wile E. Coyote after a bad rocket shoes test. And so are the limo guys, and they're smoking and limping away from the Honda, which is shining like a star or something.

And Manga is all, "Now!"

And I'm all, "Shut up, you're not the boss of me." But I got in the Honda and we totally drifted around the corner, and when we're a block or two away Steve (that's his name, Steve) kills the ginormous floodlights in the backseat and I can sort of see again.

And he's all, "High-intensity ultraviolet."

And I'm, "You, too."

And he's like, "What are you talking about?"

I'm like, "I thought it was a compliment."

Then he smiled, like the cutest smile, although he was still driving *muy* intense and totally badass, and he goes,

"No, that light back there was high-intensity ultraviolet. It burns them."

And I was all, "I knew that."

And he was like, "You know that those three guys were vampyres, too, right?"

And I'm all, "Duh." But I didn't know. So I'm like, "How did *you* know?"

Then he takes off his shades and puts on these binocular robot-glasses things, like they wear in Siphon Assassin Six for Xbox, which I am against because it glorifies violence in the minds of adolescent boys and because it's totally impossible to get a decent head shot when your squad mates are bumping into you, which needs to be fixed in the next version if I'm going to be able to do the "gray spray" on the sentry tower glass.

So Steve is all, "Yeah, they're infrared. You can see heat with them, and there was no heat coming off anyone back there but you."

And I'm like, "Who the fuck are you?"

And he's like, "My name's Steve. I'm working on my biochem masters at S.F. State."

"Stop," I said. "Please do not further endorken youself to me. You have great hair and a car that is most fly, and you have just saved me with your mad ninja driving skills, so do not sully your heroic hottie image in my mind by further reciting your nerdy scholastic agenda. Don't tell me what you're studying, Steve, tell me what's in your soul. What haunts you?"

And he was like, "Dude, you need to cut back on the caffeine."

Which was fair, and I know that he was only saying it out of concern for my welfare and whatnot, because I think he knew even then that we were destined to be together, soul mates.

So while he drives, Steve tells me that he was doing some experiments on some bodies for his master's thingy, and he found that the cells of the victims were regenerating when you added blood to them, and he thinks he can turn them back to normal human cells by using some gene therapy or something. And he's been talking to the Countess and Lord Flood about turning them back, but the Countess is all, "No way, hot Manga-haired science guy."

So I was all, "Why would she want to give up immortality and superpowers and whatnot?"

And he was all, "I don't know."

And I was all, "We should discuss it over coffee."

And he was like, "I would love to do that, but I'm already late for work."

And I was like, "I thought you were a mad scientist."

And he was all, "I work at Stereo City."

And I was like, "Dude, you should get a job at Metreon selling the big-screens, because they have like the best test couches."

And he was like, "Okay." Just like that, "Okay."

So he wanted to give me a ride home, so I would be safe,

which is so sweet, but I needed double-soy Mochaccino to calm my nerves, so here I am at Tulley's, totally brooding.

But before I got out of the car, I was like, "Steve, do you have a girlfriend?"

And he was like, "No, I put a lot of time into my studies, and I sort of always have."

And I was like, "So would you be in the market for a Gaijin princess?"

And he was like, "That's Japanese. I'm Chinese."

And I'm like, "Don't change the subject, Kung Pao, what I want to know is if you're ready to spend some up-close and personal time with ninety pounds of barbarian woman-flesh! Sorry, I don't know how much that is in kilos."

I don't know what came over me. I was just fizzing over with adrenaline and passion and whatnot, I guess. I usually don't throw myself at guys, but he was so mysterious and smart and hot.

So he got this big grin and he was like, "My parents would freak out if they saw you."

And I was like, "You live at home?"

And he was all, "Well, uh, yeah, uh, kinda, uh—"

So I grabbed the pen out of his pocket and wrote my cell number on his arm while he stuttered, then when I put the pen back I kissed him sort of hard and totally passionately, which I could tell he liked a lot, so I pushed him away and slapped him so he wouldn't think I was a slut. But not very hard, so he wouldn't think I wasn't interested.

And I was all, "Call me."

And he was all, "I will."

So I was like, "Do not fuck with your hair."

And he was all, "Okay."

And I was all, "Be careful."

And he was all, "I will. You, too."

And I was all, "Oh, yeah, thanks for the rescue and whatnot."

And he was all, "Sure. Thanks for the kiss."

And so I am his shameless White Devil Juliet and he is my sweet Ninja Romeo (unless Ninjas are also Japanese, in which case I will have to look some shit up for metaphors because the only thing Chinese I can think of right now is Dim Sum, and I believe it's disrespectful to refer to your soul mate in terms of finger food).

Fucksocks! My cell. Jared. L8rz.

Well, That Was Fucked Up

Then, Lucifer Two attains the blood sword and takes Jared the White as his consort, and they hold dominion over all of the Kindred for ever and ever," said Jared White Wolf, concluding the hour-long plot synopsis of his unwritten epic vampire adventure novel. "So what do you think?"

"I really liked it, but I think you may need to work on the characters more," Tommy said, flexing his writer muscles a little. It helped him to not think about the thirst that was rising in him.

Jared looked to Jody, and raised a drawn-on eyebrow.

"I think we must get out of this basement right now," Jody said, "and if that means murdering your parents and little sisters, well, you don't make an omelet—"

"But what did you think of my novel?" Jared said.

"I think it's not a novel, it's a sexual fantasy about you and your rat."

"It is not. That's just the characters' names."

"Try Abby's cell again, Jared." Jody was gritting her teeth.

"Tell her to get back here," Tommy said. He was starting to get cramps from the blood thirst.

"Hold on, I get shit reception down here." Jared took his cell and his rat and headed out the door and up the steps.

When he was gone, Tommy turned to Jody. "I'm really feeling the hunger."

"Me, too."

"Should we maybe just, you know, sample Jared?"

"I don't think that's a good idea."

"Well," Tommy said. "William is in the hospital, and we don't know where Abby is, and I don't see as we have that many options."

"Tommy, let's just walk out of here. What's the worst that can happen? We shock Jared's parents? I get the feeling they may be desensitized."

"That's fine, but then where do we go tomorrow? A hotel? I guess, if we get the money, we can have Abby guard the door to keep the maid from coming in and frying us." Tommy brightened. "Hey, maybe Abby grabbed some money from the loft?"

"Abby might not even be alive," Jody said, more than just irritation in her voice now. "You know how Elijah was going to kill you to fuck with me? If he's been watching us, he has to know about Abby. She'll be next. We should have left here right away. I feel horrible for leaving her out there alone."

"She went right to him." Tommy cradled his head in hands. "I hate this, Jody. Why did you do this to me? It could have worked. I could have looked out for you and had a real life. Now I just live from feeding to feeding, putting people in danger. Everyone wants to kill us or take something from us. I'm from Indiana, they don't prepare us for this kind of thing in the Midwest."

Jody slid off the bed to the floor and sat next to him, put her arm around his shoulders. "It's not like that, Tommy. We're like gods. Sure, we have to hunt, but if you let go to the predator part of you, you'll lose that anxious feeling. You have to feel the power of it."

"Power? What power? I was ready to have the rat as a snack."

"Well, you can have the rat if you need him, because that little fucker is creepy."

Tommy pulled away from her. "Don't."

Jared came through the door then, pumping his inhaler. "Oh my God! Oh my God! She met the hottest guy who is a ninja, and they're like totally into each other. And those guys you told us about, that kidnapped you, a bunch of them are vampires now. And there's a tall woman vampire, too, who tried to bite Abs. And Abby totally took them all on and burned them up with some kind of portable sunlight. Oh my God, she's so awesome. I wish I had balls like her."

"Where is she now?" Jody asked.

"She's having a Mochaccino at Tulley's on Market. I loaned her like twenty dollars. Which she's going to pay me back out of her Christmas bonus you're giving her. Hey, do I get a Christmas bonus, because—"

"Call her and tell her to stay right where she is," Jody said. "We're on our way."

"We are?" Tommy said. *They could get out of here, find a—a donor!*

"No, not you," Jody said. "We are." She patted Jared on the shoulder, careful not to get her hand near the rat.

"We are?" Jared said.

"Yes, Jared, you have to come out to your parents. You have to confess that you've had a girl in your room all day. We'll walk up and you can just introduce me as your girl-friend."

"Okay. I guess. You might want to borrow some eyeliner and touch up your lipstick a little first, okay?"

"I will slap the gloom off of you, rat shagger," Jody said with a smile that was just a few degrees below being warm.

Over his very long life, Elijah Ben Sapir had been hunted, beaten, tortured, drowned, impaled, imprisoned, and even burned on two occasions—tolerance for those who live off the lifeblood of others being what it is—but in eight centuries, this was the first time he had been flash-fried by a tricked-out Honda. Despite the novelty of it, when novelty had just become his new joy, he figured that if he went another eight hundred years before it happened again, he'd be okay.

Creeping down a SOMA alley, snatching rats from behind Dumpsters and draining them to dust just so he could
heal himself enough to hunt a real victim, was serving as an
abject lesson as to why he and his kind were sworn to remain
concealed. It was bound to happen: the application of new
technology for the detection and destruction of vampires.
Hadn't he adopted technology to protect himself? His self-
piloting yacht with its sensors and sealed vault had served
him as well as any guarded castle. But he'd forgotten the
rule—not forgotten, really, but ignored it—deciding to indulge in hope, to the point of faith, that he would always
prevail. So some clever cow had figured out how to package
sunlight and unleash it upon his arrogant carcass. The cow
would never have found the solution had the vampire not
shown him the problem. Humbled was Elijah, and angry,
and hungry, and a little sad, because he had loved his yellow
tracksuit, and now it was but beads of blackened polyester
burned into his skin.

He picked at them as he listened for prey, tucked between a Dumpster and a white step-van full of bread racks.
Here came one now—fat enough to complete the healing,
Elijah could tell by the weight of his step. The back door of
the bakery opened and the rotund baker stepped out and
shook a cigarette out of his pack. His life aura was pink and
healthy, his heart thumped strong, and would for a long
time if Elijah did not suck it dry. Normally he only took the
sick and the weak, those who were short for the grave anyway, but this was a desperate time. He leapt on the big

man's back and rode him to the ground, catching his scream in one hand, using the other to hit pressure points in his neck that had the baker unconscious in two seconds.

Elijah drank, listening to his blackened skin crackle, slough, and heal, even as the baker still breathed. There would be no neck snap, no body to find this time. He dumped the dust from the baker's clothes and slipped into them. His white Nikes were the only survivors of his previous outfit, so he threw the baker's clogs into the Dumpster along with his wallet, pocketed the cash, and took off, dressed in white from head to foot.

The vampire smiled to himself, not with joy, but with the grim irony of the situation. People often speak of things coming to them in a flash of inspiration, but the cliché held new meaning for Elijah. The flash meant that the game was over, that his foray into human desire, even for revenge, had gone far enough, and now it was time for damage control. They all had to die. He wouldn't enjoy killing her. Not her.

After being burned up for the second time in two days, Blue was ready for a healing massacre—a bloodbath—but the Animals had stopped her, citing sissy ethical reasons like murder was, you know, wrong.

"You're burned up!" Blue said. "This is no time to develop a conscience. Where was your conscience when you were making me do you a dozen times a day, huh?"

"That's different," said Drew. "You were in on it."

"Yeah," added Jeff. "And we paid you."

"No one was hurt, *amiga,*" Gustavo added.

Blue broke off some charred crust coming over the seat of the Mercedes at Gustavo, who was in the passenger seat. Drew dragged her back into her seat by her hips. She crossed her arms and pouted, huffing out little flakes of ash in exasperation. They were supposed to be doing her bidding. They were supposed to be her seven—well, *three*—dwarves.

"You shut the fuck up, bean town. I was hurt. I *am* hurt. Look at me."

They didn't look at her. They were all burnt black from the waist up, in the front at least. Their shirts hung on them in charred shreds. The linen dress that Blue had been wearing had incinerated almost completely. She was wearing only her panties and a severely singed bra. Her face was still a bit lopsided from where Elijah had banged it on the car hood.

"We didn't do this, Blue," Drew said.

Blue smacked him repeatedly in the head a half-dozen times, knocking off most of one of his charred ears and all of the carbon strands that were what was left of his hair. The tip of her little finger broke off in the process, at which point she sat back and growled like a beaten dog.

"We need blood to heal," Blue said. "Lots of it."

"I know," Jeff said. The charred power forward was driving. "I'm takin' care of it."

"You just passed five perfectly good teenagers," Blue said. "Where the fuck are you going?"

"Somewhere where the donors can handle our action," Jeff said.

"Well, we're broke until you get my money back, so your donors better have some fucking cash."

"We can't exactly go into a bar in the financial district," Drew said. "Not looking like this."

"Oh, like they'd let you dirtbags in at your best." Blue found that being burnt up put her on edge more than normal. She'd tried taking a Valium left by the Mercedes guy, just like Drew and the other had downed handfuls of his painkillers, only to find their vampire systems rejected them with extreme violence.

"We're here," Jeff said, pulling the Mercedes into a wide public parking lot.

"You're fucking kidding me," Blue said. "The zoo?"

Tommy waited half an hour before he called Jody's cell, only to get a dropped signal, then voice mail. He called three more times in the next half hour, played two rounds of Gunning for Nuns Xtreme on Jared's Xbox, called Abby's cell only to get voice mail, then made his first sincere attempt at turning to mist. Jody had said it was a mental thing, you just had to see yourself as mist, force yourself to mist, "like flexing a muscle," she had said. "Once you've done it once, you just know how it feels and you can do it again. Like getting up on water skis."

It wasn't that he could get out of the basement undetected, it was what Jody had said about being in the mist state—that time sort of just glided, like you were in a dream. It was the only reason, she said, that she hadn't beaten him senseless for having her bronzed. When you were mist, it just wasn't all that bad. Maybe if he could turn to mist, he could pass the time without driving himself nuts with worry.

For all his mental flexing, all he got was a flatulent toot that sent him diving for the door and fanning the room out with it. He was truly a foul dead thing—fouler than he'd even guessed. He looked for paint peeling off the walls.

That was it. He was not a kid hiding in his friend's basement, he was a—what did Abby call it?—he was one of the anointed, a prince of the night. He was going to walk out of here, right past the family, and if he had to take them out, well, so be it. That would teach Jody for leaving him behind and turning her phone off. *How do you feel now, Red? Huh? Massacred, dismembered family? Huh? Glad you saved your anytime minutes* now?!

He tramped up the steps and into Jared's parents' family room.

"Hi," Jared's father said.

Tommy had expected a bit of a monster based on Jared's description of his father. Instead what he saw was a bit of an accountant. He was about forty-five, in pretty good shape, holding a little girl on his lap who was coloring a picture of a pony. Another little girl, who looked about the same age, was coloring on the floor at his feet.

"Hi," Tommy said.

"You must be the vampire Flood," Jared's dad said, with a bit of a knowing smile.

"Uh. Well. Kinda." It showed. He could no longer hide among the humans. It must be because it had been so long since he had fed.

"Sort of a weak ensemble, don't you think?" Jared's dad said.

"Weak," repeated the little girl without looking up from her pony.

"Huh?" Tommy inquired.

"For a vampire. Jeans, sneakers, and flannel?"

Tommy looked at his clothes. "Black jeans," he pointed out. Shouldn't this guy be cowering in fear, maybe begging Tommy not to put his little daughter in a sack for his vampire brides?

"Okay, I suppose times change. You know that Jared and his girlfriend went up to Tulley's on Market to meet Abby, right?"

"His girlfriend, Jody?"

"Right," said Dad. "Cute girl. Not as many piercings as I expected, but we're just happy she's a girl."

An attractive blond woman in her late twenties came into the room carrying a tray with carrot and celery sticks on it. "Oh, hi," she said, dazzling a smile at Tommy. "You must be the vampire Flood. Hi, I'm Emily. Would you like some crudités? You're welcome to stay for dinner. We're having mac and cheese, it was the girls' night to pick."

I should drink her blood and put her kids in a sack, Tommy thought. But his vicious predator nature was overcome by his Midwestern upbringing, so instead he said, "Thank you very much, Emily, but I really should be going if I'm going to catch up to Jared and Jody."

"Well, okay then," said the woman. "Girls, say good-bye to the vampire Flood."

"Good-bye, the vampire Flood," the girls sang in chorus.

"Uh, bye." Tommy bolted out of the room, then back in again. "Where's the door?"

Everyone pointed through the kitchen, whence Jared's stepmonster had just come.

He ran through the kitchen and out the door, then stood with his back against the minivan in the drive, trying to catch his breath. "That was fucked up," he gasped, then realized that he wasn't out of breath from exertion at all. He was having an anxiety attack. "That was really, really fucked up."

Wallflowers of the Night

It was a lot like trying to get your courage up to ask a girl to dance, except that in this case it wasn't so much the fear of rejection, or that you'd be awkward and embarrass yourself, although that was a consideration, but that whoever you picked was going to be reduced to dust, which was somewhat more significant than trampling her toes.

Tommy stood on Castro Street looking for his next victim. His *first* victim, really. He was tired of being the apprentice. If Jody was going to just leave him in the basement because he wasn't vampire enough for her, then maybe he'd have to become like her. Maybe he'd learn about this predator nature she talked about. Maybe, like that guy in the basement in *The Phantom of the Opera*, he would have to hear "The Music of the Night." He wasn't sure what had happened to the basement guy. He'd gone to see the movie with a girl from his high school, but had to leave halfway through to keep from taking his own life. It hadn't been a good date.

There were plenty of people out on the street, even at this hour, but none of them screamed victim. There were no women in low-cut dresses who had just turned an ankle. There were no girls in negligees running down the street, glancing back over their shoulders. There were, in fact, not many girls at all. Lots of guys. Lots.

He reckoned that it wasn't really necessary that he pick a woman. After all, he'd fed off of William and Chet, both of whom were male, but this was different. This was really becoming the hunter, and despite his hunger, there was no little bit of revenge in his decision to bite someone. So it had to be a girl. He had to get back at Jody for ditching him at Jared's. He had to show her that she wasn't the only vein in the circulatory system. Or whatever.

The few women he saw were so healthy, with big bright pink life auras around them, and weren't alone either. He had to get someone alone.

Frustrated, he backed down the alley and started pacing back and forth. After a short time he took a run at the wall, ran up ten feet or so, then turned and ran back across the alley and up the other wall about ten feet, then back, and up the wall fifteen feet—like a skateboarder working a half-pipe, he ran back and forth, feeling the strength and speed of what he was—feeling his confidence rise.

I am a superior being, he thought. *I am a friggin' god!*

Then his foot went through a window and he sank up

to his crotch into the building, then dangled over the alley upside down, three stories up, flailing.

Stupid place for a window, he thought. Then he saw her.

She was sort of tall, but dressed in a red evening gown, with athletic curves, and long red hair that had been lacquered into ringlets. She was perfect, and she was coming down the alley. It was like he'd ordered her from an old Hammer film to be the hapless victim. Sweet!

So he was hanging upside down by one leg. That could be a tactic. He felt his fangs extending and he drooled a little, which hit her on the shoulder.

She started a little, and that's when he made his move. He'd always loved the scene in *Dracula* where Jonathan Harker sees the Count climbing, facedown, down the castle walls and thinks, *Hey, something is up here.* Tommy had pleaded with Jody to try it, but she never would, so this was his chance. He pulled himself out of the window, hooked his fingers between the bricks, and began his climb.

And dropped thirty feet to the alley, landing flat on his back.

"Ouch."

Upon Tommy's impact, his intended victim had let out a very masculine scream, jumped three feet straight up, and came down sideways on her high heels. She knelt over him rubbing her ankle.

"Cheesy Christ on a cracker, darlin'. Where did you come from?" Southern, and deep.

"Slipped," Tommy said. "You're a man, huh?"

"Well, let's say that is a street which I have walked, to which I do not wish to return."

"You're very pretty," Tommy said.

"Sweet of you to say." He tossed his hair a bit. "You want I should call an ambulance?"

"No, no. Thanks. I'll be okay."

"What were you doing up there, anyway?"

Conveniently, Tommy was still staring straight up at the sky, framed by the buildings, and he could see that she thought he'd fallen from the roof. "Listening for 'the music of the night.'"

"Were you watching the DVD? I heard people tried to kill themselves rather than sit through it."

"Something like that."

"Honey, just push pause. Just push pause."

"I'll remember that. Thanks."

"You sure you don't want me to call someone?"

"No, no. I'll call someone as soon as I catch my breath." Tommy reached into his back pocket and pulled out a handful of broken plastic and wires that had once been his cell phone.

"Okay then, y'all take care." She stood, turned, and walked slowly out of the alley, trying not to limp.

"Hey, miss," Tommy called after him. "I'm not gay."

"'Course you aren't, darlin'."

"I rule the night!"

She waved without looking as she rounded the corner.

"Redheads," he growled.

He could feel his broken ribs knitting together. It wasn't pleasant. As soon as they were healed enough, it was back to Jared's house to eat the rat. Move up the food chain slowly, maybe.

An hour later the torn and tattered vampire Flood limped up the driveway to Jared's house. Abby and Jared were smoking in the driveway.

"Lord Flood," Abby said. "What are you doing here?"

"You look like someone opened a whole six-pack of whup-ass on you," Jared said.

"You shut up. How did your family know I was a vampire?"

"Well, certainly not from your wardrobe."

"Jared, I am all busted up, and I'm feeling hungry, and a little fragile. Now answer my question or I will go inside and murder your family, feed on their blood, step on your rat, and break your Xbox."

"Whoa, drama queen much?"

"Fine," Tommy said. He shrugged, which hurt, and headed for the kitchen door. "Find me a sack big enough for your two little sisters."

Jared jumped in front of him. "I told them we were playing Vampire the Masquerade and that your part was the Vampire Flood."

Abby nodded. "We used to play all the time before we actually became minions."

"It's like Dungeons and Dragons but way cooler," Jared said.

"Okay." Tommy nodded. Which hurt. There they were, two perfectly healthy donors from whom he could feed, who would be willing. And he *was* hurt, and he needed to feed in order to heal. Still, he couldn't ask. He was staring at Abby's neck, then looked away when she appeared to notice.

"Where's Jody?"

"She'll be here soon," Abby said. "She sent us back to find you. We called but your cell wasn't on."

"Where is she?"

"She went to the new loft. She said she'd bring some money and what was left of William's blood back for you. You can stay in a hotel. Jared and I can guard you."

"She went to the loft? Where Elijah is?"

"Oh, that's not a problem," Abby said. "My Samurai prince burned him up while rescuing me from the blond vampire ho and her grocery-store vamplets."

Tommy looked at Jared. " 'Splain please."

Just knock," Drew said. "They'll unlock it for you. You're almost naked." They stood by the front door of the Marina Safeway. Drew had healed a little from his burns, but was still bald and covered with a dusting of soot. Blue was completely healed, but wore only her charred underwear and the beige high heels that had looked so lovely with her linen dress.

Since the first time she took the stage in high heels and a bikini back in her first Fond du Lac beauty pageant, right through her career stripping and then bonking for dollars, she thought the whole idea of high heels and underwear patently absurd. Yet here she was, rich, powerful, and immortal—yet still standing around wearing high heels and underwear. This time, however, there was some rationale for the outfit beyond that it floated some horndog's hormonal boat. At the zoo, while the Animals had pursued their prey among animals, she had found two night watchmen, each isolated on his rounds, and took them down. Unfortunately, she hadn't taken their clothing because she didn't want to have to explain to the Animals why she was dressed like a night watchman, since they had suddenly decided to take the moral high ground on slaughter.

The Animals had not fared so well. Drew was the only one in better shape than when they'd first been burned. He'd gone for a llama, because he'd always thought they were cute. He was able to feed only a little, however, before he was bitten and spat upon, and decided to call it a night. Gustavo had gone for a zebra, under the mistaken assumption that his experience with horses as a boy in Mexico would somehow give him an edge in handling the African equine. Consequently, he had been summarily stomped, and now had several broken bones, including a nasty compound fracture of one leg, in addition to being burned up. Jeff, the basketball failure, was still embarrassed about having been taken down by a girl, and so picked a jungle cat as his victim, thinking that he would take on the strength and speed of his donor. His right arm was attached only by a few muscles and much of that shoulder was gone altogether. His skin was still crusty black from the waist up.

"Fuck knocking," said Blue. The big front window had only that day been replaced, but she was going to lead her charge right through it. "Get in, find them, and take them." She found she was falling back on her dominatrix experience a lot lately, which was not a skill in which she had complete confidence, having only recently been killed while performing it.

She took three quick steps up, snatched up the steel-reinforced trash can that Jody had used on the window only days ago, and flung it underhanded with all her strength. The can rocketed through the air, bounced off the new, double-impact-resistant Plexiglas window, and knocked Blue on her ass.

Blue climbed to her feet without making any eye contact with her undead posse, dusted off her bottom, then snapped her newly broken nose back into place.

"Well, knock then, fuckstick," she said to Drew. "Knock, knock, knock. We don't have all night."

Don't You Hate Running into Your Ex?

As soon as she unlocked the new loft's security door from the street, Jody smelled blood, burned flesh, and shampoo. A case of the willies that felt like an electric serpent slithered up her spine. She went up the stairs, light on the balls of her feet, ready. She heard every tick in the apartment, the refrigerator motor, floorboards shifting, the huge cat Chet snoring in the bedroom, and, of course, someone breathing.

The lights were off. He was sitting in a canvas sling-back chair, barefoot, in a pair of Tommy's jeans and a T-shirt, drying his hair with a towel. Jody stopped by the kitchen.

"Fledgling," said the vampire. "I'm always pleasantly surprised when I am reminded of how lovely you are. Surprises are rare at my age."

"Must have surprised the fuck out of you to have that Honda toast you, then, huh?" She felt herself tightening down, the electric jangle channeling itself into an awareness, an edge. It wasn't fear anymore, it was readiness.

"An unpleasant one, yes. I assume your little servant is safe for now."

"Well, you know, she was winded for a few minutes from kicking your ass, but she *is* just a little girl."

The vampire laughed, and Jody couldn't help but smile. She went to the windows at the front of the loft and opened them. "Smells like burned meat in here."

"She'll have to go, you know," said the vampire, still smiling.

"No, she won't," Jody turned on her heel. Faced him.

"Of course she will. All of them but you. I'm quite tired of being alone, little one. You can come away with me, just as we planned."

Jody was stunned at his density. "I was lying to you, Elijah. I never intended to go away with you. I was just pretending to find out how to be a vampire."

"What were you going to do the next night, then—if your pet hadn't bronzed us, I mean?"

"I thought I'd send you away."

"No you didn't."

"I thought I'd let the Animals kill you, like they were going to anyway."

"No you didn't."

"I don't know." The edge was slipping. "I don't know." Maybe she was going to go with him. She had felt so alone, so lost.

"Ah, so here we are again. Let's pretend like all this un-pleasantness hasn't happened, and it's the next night, and here we are, just the two of us. The only ones of our kind. What will you do, Jody?"

"But we aren't the only ones of our kind."

"We are the only ones you need worry about. You do know that you are the first new vampire in a hundred years?"

Jody tried not to show her surprise. "How lucky for me," she said.

"Oh, you're not the only one I've turned. I've turned many. You're the only one who could weather the change with her mind intact. The others had to be, well, decom-missioned."

"You killed them?"

"Yes. But not you. Help me clean up and then we'll leave, together."

"Clean up?"

"There are certain rules, love. Rules that I set down my-self, and the first of them is make no more vampires. Yet you've let loose a storm of fledglings, and they all have to be cleaned up, including your boy pet."

"*Make no more?* What about me? You made me."

"I didn't expect you to survive, love. I thought you would be an amusement, a break in monotony, an interlude, but you distinguished yourself."

"And now you want me to run off with you."

"We'll live like royalty. I have resources you couldn't imagine."

"You're wearing stolen jeans, sugar daddy."

"Well, yes, I will have to make my way to one of my caches."

"I have an idea," Jody said, and this was really the reason she had come here, by herself, knowing that he would be here. Or at least hoping. "How about I give you enough money to get you out of town and you do that, just like we promised Rivera and Cavuto? You leave me alone, you leave Tommy alone, you just leave."

Elijah stood now, tossed the towel on the chair, and moved to her so quickly that she could barely even see him move. "Art, music, literature," said Elijah. "Desire, passion, power—the best of man and the best of beast. Together. You would say no to that?"

He put his hand on her cheek and she let him.

"Love?" Jody said, looking into his eyes—they reflected like drops of mercury in her night vision.

"For fairy tales. We are the stuff from which nightmares are made. Make nightmares with me."

"Wow, nice offer. Can't imagine why you haven't had any takers for a hundred years." Jody grabbed his wrist. If he wouldn't leave, she could take him. She was a vampire, too.

The vampire had been smiling, but his smile changed aspect, going from pleased to predatory. "So be it, then."

His hand was at her neck in an instant, she didn't see

him move or have a chance to react. Suddenly she couldn't move her arms or legs, and there was an intense pain behind her ear and under her jaw. She screamed, releasing a sound she couldn't imagine coming out of a human, more like something you'd hear from a tortured cat. He clamped his other hand over her mouth.

"I didn't teach you everything in our one night together, love."

She watched helplessly as he tossed his head back and his fangs unsheathed.

Troy Lee squared off against Drew at the end of the dog-food aisle, two short fighting swords in hand.

"Bring it, stoner," Troy Lee said. He spun the swords. Drew fell into a crouch by the dishwashing liquids.

"I'm fast now," Drew said.

"Uh-huh," Troy said. He whipped the swords through the air in a deadly fanning motion. He'd been training since he was a child; he wasn't afraid, especially of Drew.

"Hey," came a woman's voice from right beside him. Troy Lee looked over, lightning quick, just in time to register what looked like a full moon coming at his face.

There was a loud clang and Troy was nearly flipped over backwards when the iron skillet hit him in the forehead. Blue let it drop to her side and grinned at Drew. "I've always wanted to do that."

"Housewares used to be my aisle," Drew said.

"Take him," said Blue. "Let him drink some of your blood before he dies." She headed toward a commotion in the can aisle. "Save some, boys. Mama's got a broken nose that needs to heal."

Jody felt her own fangs extend and her kneecaps quiver as Elijah fed on her, but otherwise she couldn't move. How could she have been so stupid? He was eight hundred years old—of course he hadn't taught her everything. Of course he was stronger than she was—she was stronger than Tommy, and she had only been a vampire a couple of months longer than he had.

If she could stay conscious, maybe when he stopped feeding she could make her move. Could he reduce her to dust like a human, or would he have to do something else? Stupid. Stupid. Stupid. Why didn't she know all of this? Why wasn't she acting on instinct? Where was the predator mind when you needed it?

Her vision started to tunnel down—she was losing conciousness. She could hear rapid footsteps outside, though. First below, then across the street, then below again. Elijah heard them, too, and he loosened his grip for an instant, but before she could twist away, his fingers dug into her neck and jaw again. Then a black blur flew through the window and she heard something thud on the floor over by the kitchen. There was another loud thud and Elijah released her and she fell to the floor. She tried to push herself up, but something was thrown over her and she heard a buzzing sound. She heard screaming and smelled burning flesh, glass breaking, then someone was lifting her, carrying her. She couldn't move or even fight anymore. She let go, let herself float away, but the last thing she heard was a girl's voice saying, "Did you feed Chet?"

The Emperor sat on the dock of the St. Francis Yacht Club, watching the fog wash over the breakwater. He'd gone against the advice of the homicide detectives and had left the grocery store. It was his city, and it was his place to take the battle to its attackers. He had cowered in fear long enough. His wickedly pointed sword lay on the dock at his side. The men, Bummer and Lazarus, were sleeping in a fuzzy pile at his back.

"Ah, gentle warriors, how do we engage in battle when our enemy moves with such elegant stealth? Perhaps we should return to the Safeway and help defend."

Bummer's left ear twitched, and he let out a muffled *ruff* in his sleep.

A thick bank of fog was moving down from the opening in the breakwater and it caught the Emperor's attention because it appeared to be moving across the wind from the west. Yes, it was indeed—the cold breeze was coming straight over the breakwater from the north. The fog bank bubbled thick as it moved, tendrils reached out and then were reabsorbed like the false feet of some crawling creature.

The Emperor climbed to his feet and roused the men, snatched Bummer up before the sleepy terrier could get his bearings, and headed toward the clubhouse with Lazarus at his heels. He crouched in a shadow by the entrance to the restrooms, holding the hounds as he watched.

The fog bank enveloped the end of the dock, paused, then dissipated as if a fan had been turned on it, and three tall figures stood on the dock, a man and two women. They wore long coats, cashmere, the Emperor thought, but he couldn't for the life of him remember why he might know that. They moved down the dock toward him as if they were floating. The Emperor could see their outlines in the moonlight—jawlines and cheekbones that looked as if they'd been chiseled, square shoulders, and narrow hips. They might have been brother and sisters, except one of the women was of African descent, the other looked like she might be Italian or Greek. The man was a head taller than the women and looked Nordic, perhaps German, with close-cropped white hair. All were as pale as bleached bone.

As they passed him the Emperor pulled the hounds closer and Bummer let out a threatening *ruff.*

They stopped. The man turned. "How long have you been here?" he asked.

"Forever, I think," said the Emperor.

The man smiled and nodded, then turned and was on his way. "I know how you feel," he said without looking back.

· ·

Gustavo and Jeff found Barry hiding in the shelves among the toilet-paper packages. When they got close, Barry burst out of the TP and made a run for the end of the aisle, pulling napkins, aluminum foil, garbage bags, and plastic silverware off the shelves as he went to slow his pursuers. Gustavo went down first, slipping on a package of plastic forks. Jeff high-stepped through the obstacles and was right on Barry's ass until he was almost to the end of the aisle and Lash stepped out holding one of Barry's spearguns.

"Down!" Lash barked, and Barry hit the tile on his chest and slid.

There was a pneumatic hiss and the heavy stainless spear thudded into Jeff's sternum and blew him back off his feet.

"Ow, goddammit," said the power forward, clutching at the spear and trying to pull it out of his chest.

Gustavo climbed to his feet, ran to Jeff, and started yanking on the spear.

Lash handed Barry a four-foot-long stick with a blunt metal tip on it and fitted another spear into the gun.

"That the last one?" Barry asked.

Lash nodded. "Where's Clint?"

Just then the tall blond woman appeared at the far end of the aisle, dragging an unconscious Clint by his collar. A wide bloodstain ran from her chin to her crotch and they could see her fangs even from this distance. "Bad boys.

Leaving your born-again lying on the floor where people can trip over him."

She dropped Clint on his face, and headed up the aisle toward them, in long, slow strides.

Lash bolted, Barry right behind him, through the canvas doors into the back room, and into the walk-in dairy cooler. It was like a long hallway with plastic milk boxes stacked on one side and the glass dairy cases on the other. They pushed stacks of heavy one-gallon milk boxes in front of the door, then leaned with their backs against the back of the cooler, watching the store through the clear cooler doors in the dairy case, over the cartons of yogurt and cottage cheese.

"What's that she's carrying?" Barry asked.

"A frying pan," Lash said.

"Oh," Barry said "Sorry I let her in. She was almost naked."

"How could you have known?"

"Well, when she claimed she had a nooky-gram for my birthday, I should have figured something was up."

"Your birthday's like in March, isn't it?"

"Yeah."

Lash slapped Barry hard once on his bare scalp, then re-aimed the speargun over the yogurts.

"I deserved that," Barry said.

"Think that spear hit Jeff's heart?"

"Had to. It's a foot through his sternum."

"He doesn't seem dead."

"Guess that means head shot." Barry shook his head. "You want me to try?"

"Nah, if I miss, you have the bang stick." Lash nodded at the long stick Barry was holding at port arms. Essentially it was a twelve-gauge shotgun shell on the end of a stick, used for killing sharks. You poked them with it and the shotgun shell fired into them at point-blank range.

"I'll bet she doesn't even know what it is."

"Get it right," Lash said. "Blow her fucking brains out."

They looked at each other as they heard the refrigeration compressors and fans wind down. Then the lights went out.

"We're fucked," Lash said.

"Yep," Barry agreed.

Being the Chronicles of Abby Normal: Dark and Mysterious Goddess of Forbidden Love

Don't judge me. I have looked death in the face and made him my bitch! I did what I did out of love, and I don't want to sound conceited, but OMG, we are heroes! And when I say we, I mean us.

Had I told you before, you would have called me "losah!," pronounced me perky and cute beyond redemption, but now that I am secure in my own nefarious love lair and whatnot, I can at last confess, that in my naive youth, my favorite literary character was not the tentacled horror Cthulu from Lovecraft as I previously stated in AP English 235, but, in fact, Pippi Longstocking. Before you condemn me for my Pippism, check it out:

Pippi drank a lot of coffee. (Because, like me, she was wise.)

Pippi had unnaturally red hair (as I, myself have had, upon occasion).

Pippi often wore long, stripy socks (as yours truly has been known to do).

Pippi had superhuman strength. (It could happen.)

Pippi kicked ass. (Not unlike your humble narrator.)

Pippi was a kid who lived without parents in her own house. (Go, girl!)

With a monkey. (Haven't you always wanted a monkey?)

What Longstockings did not have, was the coolest cyber-ninja-sex-magic boyfriend to ever save the world and whatnot. (Props to Pip, but girlfriend needed some yang to rock her yin.)

> Steve. My darling, my love,
> My heart is aflame
> But OMFG, Steve,
> I grieve,
> That your name
> Is so fucking lame.

I call him Foo Dog, because he guards the gate of my temple, if you know what I mean. I'm wearing the jacket he made me right now. I had it on when they came for me, but that's not the thing. The thing is, I didn't save myself, I saved love.

So, that night, after I told the Countess how my sweet Foo Dog saved me from the vampyre, the Countess said she was going to go back to the loft to get some money and feed Chet and get the last of William's blood for Lord Flood, for their love is truly eternal. And Jared and I were like, "We'll go, too," but the Countess sent us back to liberate the vampyre Flood from Jared's basement and his hideous family. So we were all, "Well, okay."

But when we got to Jared's house, Flood was totally gone. And then Steve—I mean Foo Dog—called me and he was all, "I'm getting off work early, I don't want to leave you out there unprotected."

So I told him where we were. Then Lord Flood comes walking out of the dark and he's all, "What? What? What?"

And I'm all, "The Countess went back to the loft."

And he's all, "She is in danger. We must away."

And I was like, "Chill thee thus, for my sweet love-ninja is on the way in his fly ride."

So Flood was like, " 'Kay."

I see now that my attraction to the vampyre Flood was nothing more than childish infatuation, never to be re- quited, because he had eyes only for the Countess.

So it was a little awkward when Steve showed up and I had to chill the Lord Flood and make him sit in the back- seat to show that my real affections were with Foo Dog, who was formerly known as Steve.

And when we got to the loft, the windows were open, but there were no lights on. And Flood had us drive a block past, then we got out and he walked back. Then he runs up and he's like, "Elijah's up there. He's got her."

And I'm all, "Then go get her."

And Steve is like, "No, I'll go get her." And he pulls this long coat out of the trunk.

It's all covered with warts or something, and I'm like, "Nice coat, but you know, vampyre . . ."

And Steve is like, "They're UV LEDs. Like the lights we burned the vampires with before."

And I'm like, "Sweet!"

So Steve starts to put the coat on and Flood stops him and goes, "He'll hear you coming up the stairs. I'll go."

And Steve is all, "You can't. It will burn you, too."

And Flood is all, "No it won't."

So they are like five minutes behind the car putting together this über-cool ensem of like an old gas mask, and a hoodie, and full-on gloves and everything, until Flood is totally covered, wearing the long coat with the glass warts all over it, looking like one of the cenobites from *Hellraiser*.

And Steve is like, "Don't hit the switch until you know she's covered." And he hands Flood like a black rubber tarp and a baseball bat, which totally sucked the cool right out of the ensem, but I guess was necessary.

Then, just when I'm about to ask how he's going to get in without being heard, we hear the Countess scream, and Flood runs across the street and about halfway up the side of the building, then turns and runs down it, then across the street, up the side of his building, and goes through the window feet fucking first.

And I'm like, "Whoa."

And Steve and Jared are like, "Whoa."

And a second later we hear a thumping, and purple light comes on in the loft windows and the old vampyre comes crashing through the windows on fucking fire, falling like a comet! And he lands on his feet in the middle of the street, hisses once and looks at us, and that's when Steve holds up one of his UV floodlights, and the vampyre fucking scrams down the alley across the street so fast that he was just a blur.

Next thing, Flood is coming out of the building carrying the Countess, who is wrapped in the black rubber tarp and is totally roofied like a limp rag. And Steve's all, "Get her in the car."

And I'm like, "Did you feed Chet?"

And Jared is like, "Hello, Abby, the other vampyres."

So I'm like, "Shut up. I know." So we all piled into Steve's car and we took Flood and the Countess to a hotel off up on Van Ness, which Steve paid for with his Visa, which was generous and mature of him.

It was one of those motels where you have your own entrance to the parking lot so they don't see you in the hallway, so Flood carried the Countess up to the room, and we carried some stuff that Steve had packed up in the trunk of his car.

It was so sad. Flood just stroked the Countess's cheek and tried to get her to wake up, but she wouldn't. And he was all, "Abby, she needs to feed. I wouldn't ask, but he's done something to her, she's hurt."

And I would have totally done it, but Steve pulled me back, and he picks up this playmate cooler that he had us bring up, and he pulls out these pouches of blood.

And he hands them to Flood and says, "I took them from the university hospital. They could kick me out of school for this."

And Flood is all, "Thanks." And he bites a hole in one of the pouches and squeezes it on the Countess's lips and that's when I started to cry.

There were like four pouches, and when he was going for the last one, Steve was like, "You need to drink that one."

And Flood was like, "No way, it's for her."

And Steve was like, "You know you do."

So Flood like nodded and drank the last one himself, and then he just sat there by her, stroking her hair.

Then Steve was like, "Tommy, you know I can reverse your vampirism. I'm pretty sure the process works."

And Flood just looked at him and nodded. It was so sad. And then the Countess started to moan, and she opened her eyes and she saw the vampyre Flood and she was all, "Hey, baby." Just like that. And I started crying again like a big wuss and Steve took Jared and me out to the car to give them some space.

And Steve was like, "I made this for you from my jacket." And he put this leather motorcycle jacket on me that was covered with those glass LED thingies. It was kinda heavy, because there were batteries built into the padding, but cool. And he was all, "This will keep you safe. The switch is in the snap on the left cuff. Just squeeze it and the lights will come on. They won't hurt you, but you should wear sunglasses to protect your retinas." Then he put a pair of totally cyber wraparound sunglasses on me and kissed me. And I kissed him back, hard, with major tongue, and finally he pulled away, as gentle as a butterfly. So then I slapped him, so he wouldn't think I was a slut. But so he wouldn't think I was being frigid, I sort of jumped on him and wrapped my legs around him and sort of accidentally rode him to the ground and was accidentally kind of dry-humping him on the pavement when the lights on my jacket came on and people looked out their hotel windows and whatnot, so Jared ended our special romantic moment by hitting my light switch and dragging me off.

And I was all, "You are *THE MAN*, Foo!"

And he was all, "Huh?" Because I hadn't told him yet that his new name was Foo Dog.

But then he said he actually had to get home and check in or his parents would freak out. And said to watch the masters until I got back, if I got a chance try to talk them into being converted. So we made out on the hood of the Honda for a while and he drove off into night's cold loneliness like the superhero that he is. (The effect was ruined, kind of, in that Jared caught a ride with him.)

So I went back upstairs and sat at the foot of the masters' bed, keeping guard and listening to them.

They were talking softly, but I could hear them.

The vampyre Flood was all, "Maybe we should give it a try."

And the Countess was all, "What, the cure? Tommy, it can't work. You've seen what I can do, you know what you can do. This isn't biology, this is magic."

"Maybe it's not. Maybe it's science we don't know yet."

"It doesn't matter. We don't even know if it works."

"We should try."

"Why would we try, Tommy? You've only been immortal for a couple of weeks. Do you want to give up the power, the—I don't know—the command over your world?"

"Well—yes."

"You do?"

"Yeah. I don't like it, Jody. I don't like being afraid all the time. I don't like being alone. I don't like being a killer."

"That woman was torturing you, Tommy. That's never going to happen again."

"That's wasn't the problem. I'd get over her. The problem was that I liked it. I *liked* it."

Then the Countess was quiet for a while, and I thought it might be dawn or something, but I peeked over the edge of the bed and she was just staring into his eyes. She looked over at me.

"Hey, girlie girl," the Countess said, and she smiled at me and it felt like a gift or something. It was like, real. Then she took her watch off and threw it to me at the end of the bed. "That has an automatic almanac in it—how about you set the alarm to go off about twenty minutes before sunset, so you don't get caught out again, okay?" And I was going to tell her about the jacket that Foo made for me, but I kind of couldn't talk, so I just nodded and put the watch on and slid back down to the floor.

Then I heard the Countess go, "You aren't alone. I'm here. We can go where no one knows us, no one is chasing us, and I'll always be here for you."

And he goes, "I know. I mean alone from everyone else. Separate. I want to be human, not some foul dead thing."

"I thought you wanted to be special."

"I do, but I want to be human special—because of something I did."

Then it was quiet for a while, and finally the Countess goes, "I love it, Tommy. I'm not afraid all the time like you; just the opposite. I didn't realize how afraid I used to be until I became like this. I like walking the street knowing that I'm the Alpha animal, hearing and seeing and smelling everything, being part of everything. I like it. I wanted to share that with you"

"It's okay. You couldn't have known."

"I don't want to be alone either. That's why I turned you. I love you."

Then the alarm went off on Lord Flood's watch, and he shut it off.

Then he's all, "We can't go back to the way it was, before, I mean? Where I look after you?"

"It's not the same world, Tommy. You know that now. We were in the same room in different worlds."

"Okay then. I love you, Jody."

"I love you, too," goes the Countess.

Then they didn't say anything for a long time, and when my new watch showed that the sun was up, I looked, and they were lying there, holding each other, and I could see the red stains on the pillow from their tears.

And I was like, "Oh, hell no!"

Being the Chronicles of Abby Normal: Not Unlike the Toaster, I Control the Darkness

So I slept a little that day, and talked to my sweet love-ninja, Foo, a couple of times on the phone, then he came over and we left Jared with some blood for Lord Flood and the Countess when they awoke, and motored to the loft. It took like an hour to clean up all the broken glass and ash and stuff from the night before. We had just finished cleaning and counting the money and making out and whatnot when the alarm went off on the Countess's watch.

And I was like, "Dude, I'm not ready."

And he was all, "Dude, you are more ready than anyone I've ever known."

And I was all, "OMG, I am so going to sex you to death if we live through this."

And then he was all bashful and pretended to be doing something technical so we were ready.

Then, like an hour after sundown, I heard them coming. I was at the kitchen counter when the security door
downstairs opened, and when I turned around they were
just, like there. Lord Flood called them the Animals, but
now they were kind of the *roadkill*. And I like touched the
snap on my UV jacket, just to make sure it was there.

So I was all, "Hey, vampyre scum."

And the formerly black and now gray one, who was like
their leader, was all up in my grille, like, "We need the
money, where is the money?"

And I was like, "Step off, undead-tard. There's no
money."

And he was like, "Don't fuck with us. Flood and the
redhead took like six hundred grand from my apartment."

And I was all, "Actually, its like five hundred and eighty-
three thousand eight hundred and fifty-eight."

And he was all, "Give it!"

And all seven of them were like gathering around me—
even the born-again one the Countess had thrashed—like
they were going to do the massive gang-suck on me, so I had
my finger on my light button all the time, in case I needed to
flash-fry the motherfuckers. But I stayed chilly and I was
like, "Are you high?"

And he was all, "No, I'm not high. No one is high."

And they all started whining and whatnot, all, "We
can't even take a bong hit. We can't drink a beer. Our systems won't take it. Being sober sucks. We are useless undead stoners."

So I was all, "Step back and behold, bi-atches."

And I'm all taking a bottle of Stoli out of the freezer, and mixing in a glass with some of the blood from the pouches, just like the ones we left for the Countess and Lord Flood, and they're all drooling when they see the blood, so I was thinking, *Don't make me fry you.*

But then I give the glass to the gray vamp, and he's all, "Sweet."

And the others are like, "Me, me, me."

So I'm like mixing Bloody Marys all around, and the greasy hippyish one is like, "Can we dunk pot cookies in this?"

And I'm like, "Of course, stoner vamp."

And they're all, "You are a goddess. And we are not worthy. And oh please, may we have some more?" Until they started to drop.

So like two minutes later there's like this big pile of passed-out vampyres in the kitchen, and I'm all, "Yo, Foo, I got your shit ready."

And Foo comes out of the bedroom, all cute, holding his UV floodlight like he's going to save me, then sees that they are all out cold and gives me a big kiss and is like, "You rock."

And I'm like, "You have no idea, my Manga-haired love toy."

And he was like, "The sedative in the blood, blah, blah, four hours, blah, blah, nerdspeak, geektalk—"

And I'm like, "Whateva, studmuffin. Handle it."

So it took like two hours for Foo to do all his medical stuff with the Animals, taking some blood and doing various medical nerdism stuff to it, then putting it back in, but finally he was done and I called Jared to tell him that we were on our way to get Lord Flood and the Countess.

So I like made the other call to make sure everything was all in order and whatnot, and Foo was all, "Are you sure this is what you want to do?"

And I was all, "Foo, theirs is the greatest love of all time. It's the only thing to do."

And he was all, "Okay, as long as you're sure. Because we can do them the same as we did the others."

And I was all, "No, that won't work. They have to be together. And you don't have to live at home anymore. We'll have a completely sweet love lair."

So we did it.

Blue watched from the alley across the street as the Animals came out the security door, empty-handed, and stumbled into the street. She knew she should have gone herself, but that whole getting-burned-up thing had taught her that perhaps it was better to delegate. That they didn't have her money was bad enough, but that they didn't have her money and heat was coming off of them was disastrous. "Those dumbfucks can't get anything right," she said to herself. "I'm going to have to kill them all over again."

"I don't think so," said a voice from behind her. She whipped around, leading with her long fingernails in a swipe that would have taken off half a man's face.

Elijah caught her hand. He'd found another tracksuit, this one powder blue. "It's time to let it go. The genie must go back in the bottle, I'm afraid."

"Let me go, I need to go get my money."

"No, my dear, you don't want to do that. The residents of that loft have recently developed a very unpleasant fashion sense."

"You're fucking with my income, paleface."

"You don't need to worry about that anymore."

"Meaning what?"

"It ends here. Come with me, my dear."

"You want me to come with you? I don't even know you."

"Yes, but we share a special relationship."

"Special? You beat my face into the hood of a Mercedes."

"Well, yes. Sorry. To the innocent my behavior can sometimes be distasteful."

"Yeah? *Innocent*. I've fucked thousands of guys."

"Yes, well, I've killed enough to fill a city."

Blue shrugged. "Okay, you win."

"Revenge is a dish best served cold anyway, don't you think?"

"Or not at all," said a male voice behind Elijah.

Elijah and Blue turned. Three of them stood there in

their long coats, looking like sculptures, looking eternal, like they could wait forever.

"Can just anyone sneak up on me now?" said Blue.

"Time to go, Elijah," said the African woman.

"None of you would be here if it weren't for me," Elijah said.

"Yes, and we would have been hunted down and killed a long time ago if we hadn't adhered to your rules."

"Ah, my rules," Elijah said, looking down now.

"How many left to clean?"

Elijah looked across the street to the loft windows, then at Blue. She raised an eyebrow, smiled a little.

"She's the only one left." He lied.

"Then finish it."

"I'd rather not," Elijah said.

The Emperor of San Francisco wept for his city. He had done what he could, called the police, alerted the newspapers, even tried to take to battle himself, but by the time he'd gathered the courage to return to the Marina Safeway, it had been finished, and he could do nothing more than speculate to the uniformed police officers how the window had been broken and why the store was empty. They'd tried to track down the night crew, but none of them seemed to be home. And his city was plagued by vampires.

Now the Emperor wept and consoled the troops, rubbing Bummer behind the ears and gently patting Lazarus on the ribs as he lay sleeping on the dock. The fog was coming slow off the Bay tonight, not windblown like it was so often here.

He heard footsteps before he saw them, then there were five of them. The fiend, the three in the long coats he had seen come in the night before, and a blond woman in a blue party dress. They walked past, and only the fiend turned and paused. The Emperor held Bummer tight, afraid that he would burst into one of his barking fits and all would be lost.

"Old man," said Elijah. "The City is yours again." Then he joined the others at the end of the dock.

The Emperor could see their motor yacht waiting outside the breakwater—it had to be two hundred feet long, far too big to enter the marina.

"Very well, then, shall we go?" said Elijah.

"Can I get a coat like that?" asked Blue, nodding toward the tall blond man.

The blond man said, "You'll get one when you learn the secret handshake and get your decoder ring."

Blue looked at Elijah. "Is he fuckin' with me?"

"Yes," said Elijah. He offered her his arm. She took it, and stepped down into the longboat.

The Emperor watched the vampires disappear into the fog.

Rivera had six uniforms in SWAT gear with a battering ram ready to take down the door, so he and Cavuto were more than somewhat surprised when it opened almost as soon as they knocked. A shirtless, sleepy-looking Chinese guy with spiky hair stood in the doorway.

"Yes, can I help you?"

Rivera held up the warrant. "I have a warrant to search this apartment."

" 'Kay," said the Chinese guy. "Abby, cops are here."

The skinny broken clown girl appeared at the top of the stairs in a kimono.

"Hey, cops," said Abby Normal.

"What are you doing here?" Rivera said.

"I live here, cop." She popped the *p*. Rivera hated that.

"Actually, it's my apartment," said the Chinese guy. "Do you need to see ID?"

"Yeah, that would be nice, kid," said Cavuto. He whipped the kid around and marched him up the stairs as the kid read the warrant.

"Do not bruise the Foo, cop," said the broken clown girl.

Rivera turned to the uniforms and shrugged apologetically. "Sorry, guys, I guess we got this one." They shuffled away.

"What are you guys looking for?" asked the Chinese kid. "Maybe we could speed this up."

"We're looking for Thomas Flood and Jody Stroud. He's the one on the lease for this apartment and the one down the street."

"Oh, yeah. I'm subletting," said the Chinese kid.

"Steven Wong," Cavuto read off the kid's license.

Rivera was feeling very, very bad about this. They had found one more body in the Mission with the blood-loss-and-broken-neck MO—the guy had been naked, supposedly someone had stolen his powder-blue tracksuit, so they logged it as robbery, but then, a week ago, the killings stopped. That didn't mean it was over. He'd made the mistake of thinking it was over with these two before. Rivera had finally gotten the Christian kid at the Safeway to file charges on the redhead for assault. After a long talk with the other stoners, they'd gotten the Flood kid on the arrest warrant for conspiracy. They'd also implied that somehow Flood and the redhead had gotten their share of the old vampire's money. Maybe they *had* left town. If they had, well, good, but he still had a slew of unsolved murders.

"You're subletting from Thomas Flood?"

"I never met him, actually," said Steve. "We arranged it through the rental agent."

"Yeah, so step off, cop," said the skinny girl.

Rivera looked around the apartment. There was no need to tear the place apart. Obviously everything in here was new. Mostly decorated in Pier 1 Imports cheap wicker motif and some punky Urban Outfitter flair, which he guessed was the input of the creepy little girl.

The bronze sculptures were out of character, though. A life-sized nude of a young woman, a large snapping turtle, and a life-sized bronze of a couple posed as if in Rodin's *The Kiss*.

"These must have been expensive," Rivera said.

"Not really. I know the artists," the Chinese kid said. "Some biker guys down the street."

"Foo's in biotech," said the broken clown girl. "He makes like stupid money, cop."

"Yeah, that's swell," said Rivera. He'd watched this neighborhood turn from a rust slum of repair shops and the odd ethnic restaurant to a gentrified hive of hipster professionals in remodeled lofts during the dot-com boom, and it had never turned back. The whole neighborhood was full of kids who spent the equivalent of Rivera's annual salary on a car they wouldn't drive a dozen times a year. This kid apparently was just another one.

"So you don't know these people?" Rivera said, pointing to the warrant.

Steven Wong shook his head. "Sorry, I've never met them. I send my rent directly to the rental agency. You might check with them."

"Okay then. Sorry to bother you."

"Okay then?" Cavuto said. "That's it?"

"They're not here, Nick. These two don't know where they are."

"But, that's not enough."

"Yeah? You want to spend some time talking to Allison here, see what you can find out?" Rivera nodded toward the broken clown girl.

Cavuto had tried to keep someone between himself and the skinny girl since they'd come upstairs, but now he looked at her full on and shuddered. "No, I guess that's it." He turned and lumbered down the steps.

"You need to check your girlfriend's ID," Rivera said to Steve. "You may not be old enough for her." Then he turned and left as well.

Chill, Foo," Abby said. "They're gone. They won't be back. Let's go shopping."

"Abby, are you sure about this? It seems cruel." He patted the life-sized sculpture of the couple embraced in a kiss.

"I heard the Countess say once that it was like being in a dream. They just sort of float, all peaceful and dreamy. The main thing is they're together."

"You're sure?"

"Theirs is the greatest love of all time. It would be wrong for them to be apart, Foo."

"Well, I think we should just change them back. Now that we know the process works."

"Someday."

"Now."

"The Countess doesn't want that."

"It's wrong."

"How can it be wrong? It's my idea, and I am their dedicated minion and whatnot. I control the dark." She ran and jumped into his arms.

"I guess you do," he said. "Okay, let's go shopping for stuff for our most fly apartment."

. .

William arrived back at the loft just after dark, feeling very much rested and well fed from his hospital stay, but craving a sip or two of the good stuff, and terribly worried about Chet. He let himself into the stairway with his key, but when he rang the bell, no one answered, so he sat down to wait for the redhead and that guy to bring his bottle.

He hadn't been there ten minutes before he heard the meowing at the door, and his heart leapt as he opened the outer door to find Chet, his red sweater still intact, purring outside.

"Come on, boy. I missed you, buddy."

William scooped up his kitty and carried him into the stairwell. As soon as the door closed, Chet, the huge shaved vampire cat, was upon him.

TURN THE PAGE FOR
YOU SUCK EXTRAS,
INCLUDING

THE EMPEROR AND
HIS DOGS

AN AUTHOR'S NOTE

You Suck is the third of my books in which the Emperor and his dogs appear, and over the years I've gotten hundreds of letters asking about them. "Are they real or did you make them up?" is the question asked most often, and the answer is, simply, "Yes, they were real and I did make them up."

The Emperor is based on a historical figure named Joshua Norton, an English businessman from the 1840s who came to California to make his fortune and, instead, ended up losing it, supposedly in a lawsuit over a rice futures contract. (Norton, seeing the huge population in San Francisco's Chinatown, was trying to corner the market on rice.) Whether he was mad before or the deal sent him over the edge, Norton ended up living on the streets of San Francisco and soon issued a proclamation declaring himself the Emperor of the United States and Protector of Mexico. That a homeless fellow might indulge in delusions of grandeur is not unusual; that an entire city would be complicit in the delusion is.

The tailors of San Francisco supplied Norton with top hats and grand tailcoats with gold braiding and epaulets.

Restaurants allowed the Emperor to eat for free, and printers not only printed and posted Norton's proclamations, they created currency with his image on it, which was accepted from him by local businesses. Papers covered Norton as if he were a legitimate politician, despite some of his more insane proclamations: that a bridge be built across the Golden Gate, that another be built across the bay to Oakland, and that a league of nations be formed to resolve disputes without war.

The people of the city treated Norton with great respect, and he them, as if they were indeed his subjects and he a benevolent ruler. There is a story that Emperor Norton even diverted a race riot in Chinatown when, after a crop failure in California's Central Valley, jobless men blamed the Chinese for their fate and stormed the neighborhood bent on burning it to the ground. Supposedly, Norton stopped them by putting himself between the workers and Chinese and reciting the Lord's Prayer.

When Emperor Norton died in 1880, more than 30,000 people marched in his funeral procession. But his legacy lives on in the work of Mark Twain, who based his character of the King in Huckleberry Finn on Emperor Norton, as well as in the work of Robert Louis Stevenson and Neil Gaiman, and in a number of Western movies and television programs.

Bummer and Lazarus are the real names of two stray dogs that lived in San Francisco contemporaneous to Emperor Norton, and while it's rumored that they were the

Emperor's dogs, such was not the case. They were similarly adopted by the city of San Francisco, fed and cared for, but remained strays living on the street, and when Bummer died in 1865, his obituary was written by Mark Twain and it appeared in the *Californian*. There is a plaque commemorating Bummer and Lazarus in the small park at the base of the Transamerica Pyramid.

JODY

A CAΠΕΦ
An Excerpt from *A Dirty Job*

"Outstanding . . . ingeniously unpredictable . . . and the dialogue follows a zany illogic worthy of the Marx Brothers."
—*Washington Post Book World*

A Dirty Job, Christopher Moore's ninth novel, centers around Charlie Asher, a pretty normal guy with a normal life. He and his wife—a bright and pretty woman who actually loves him for his normalcy—live in San Francisco, in an apartment over the thrift shop Charlie owns. They're even about to have their first child. Yes, Charlie's doing okay—until people start dropping dead around him, and everywhere he goes a dark presence whispers to him from under the streets. Charlie Asher, it seems, has been recruited for a new job . . .

But, as we readers know, Charlie Asher isn't the only one in San Francisco who's recently found himself on the other side of normal. Read on for an excerpt from *A Dirty Job* featuring C. Thomas Flood's favorite redhead.

That evening Charlie was watching the store, wondering why he had lied to his employees, when he saw a flash of red passing by the front window. A second later, a strikingly pale redhead came through the door. She was wearing a short, black cocktail dress and black fuck-me pumps. She strode up the aisle like she was auditioning for a music video. Her hair cascaded in long curls around her shoulders and down her back like a great auburn veil. Her eyes were emerald green, and when she saw him looking, she smiled, and stopped, some ten feet away.

Charlie felt an almost painful jolt that seemed to emanate from somewhere in the area of his groin, and after a second he recognized it as an autonomic lust response. He hadn't felt anything like that since Rachel had passed, and he felt vaguely ashamed.

She was examining him, looking him over like you would examine a used car. He was sure he must be blushing.

"Hi," Charlie said. "Can I help you?"

The redhead smiled again, just a little, and reached into a small black bag that he hadn't noticed she'd been carrying. "I found this," she said, holding up a silver cigarette case. Something Charlie didn't see very often anymore, even in the secondhand business. It was glowing, pulsating like the objects in the back room. "I was in the neighborhood and something made me think that this belonged here."

She moved to the counter opposite Charlie and set the cigarette case down in front of him.

Charlie could barely move. He stared at her, not even conscious that to avoid her eyes he was staring at her cleavage, and she appeared to be looking around his head and shoulders as if following the path of insects that were buzzing around him.

"Touch me," she said.

"Huh?" He looked up, saw she was serious. She held out her hand; her nails were manicured and painted the same deep red as her lipstick. He took her hand.

As soon as she touched him she pulled away. "You're warm."

"Thanks." In that moment he realized that she wasn't. Her fingers had been ice-cold.

"Then you're not one of us?"

He tried to think of what "us" might be? Irish? Low blood pressure? Nymphomaniac? Why did he even think that? "Us? What do you mean, 'us'?"

She backed away a step. "No. You don't just take the weak and the sick, do you? You take anyone."

"Take? What do you mean, 'take'?"

"You don't even know, do you?"

"Know what?" Charlie was getting very nervous. As a Beta Male, he found it difficult enough to function under the attention of a beautiful woman, but she was just plain spooky. "Wait. Can you see this thing glowing?" He held out the cigarette case.

"No glow. It just felt like it belonged here," she said. "What's your name?"

"Charlie Asher. This is Asher's."

"Well, Charlie, you seem like a nice guy, and I don't know exactly what you are, and it doesn't seem like you know. You don't, do you?"

"I've been going through some changes," Charlie said, wondering why he felt compelled to share this at all.

The redhead nodded, as if confirming something to herself. "Okay. I know what it's like to, uh, find yourself thrown into a situation where forces beyond your control are changing you into someone, something you don't have an owner's manual for. I understand what it is to not know. But someone, somewhere, does know. Someone can tell you what's going on."

"What are you talking about?" But he knew what she was talking about. What he didn't know was how she could possibly know.

"You make people die, don't you, Charlie?" She said it like she had worked up the courage to tell him that he had some spinach in his teeth. More of a service to him than an accusation.

"How do you—?" How did she—

"Because it's what I do. Not like you, but it's what I do. Find them, Charlie. Backtrack and find whoever was there when your world changed."

Charlie looked at her, then at the cigarette case, then at the redhead again, who was no longer smiling, but was stepping backward toward the door. Trying to stay in touch with normal, he focused on the cigarette case and said, "I suppose I can do an appraisal—"

He heard the bell over the door jingle, and when he looked up she was gone.

He didn't see her moving by the windows on either side of the door; she was just gone. He ran to the front of the store and out the door onto the sidewalk. The Mason Street cable car was just topping the hill up by California Street and he could hear the bell, there was a thin fog coming up from the Bay that threw colorful halos around the neon signs of the other businesses, but there was no striking red-head on the street. He went to the corner and looked down Vallejo, but again no redhead, just the Emperor, sitting against the building with his dogs.

"Good evening, Charlie."

"Your Majesty, did you see a redhead go by here just now?"

"Oh yes. Spoke to her. I'm not sure you have a chance there, Charlie, I believe she's spoken for. And she did warn me to stay away from you."

"Why? Did she say why?"

"She said that you were Death."

"I am?" Charlie said. "Am I?" His breath caught in his throat as the day played back in his head. "What if I am?"

"You know, son," the Emperor said, "I am not an expert in dealing with the fairer sex, but you might want to save that bit of information until the third date or so, after they've gotten to know you a little."

STRAP YOURSELVES IN, LADIES AND GENTLEMEN,

IT'S CHRISTOPHER MOORE TIME!

YOU SUCK: A Love Story
ISBN 978-0-06-059030-7 (paperback) • ISBN 978-0-06-122718-9 (unabridged CD)

C. Thomas Flood (better known as Tommy) has just awakened. He and the girl of his dreams, Jody, have just shared a physical intimacy unlike any Tommy has known before. He opens his eyes, sees Jody smiling down at him, opens his mouth, and says, "You bitch, you killed me. You suck!" For Jody is a vampire. And now Tommy's one, too. They're still a couple, but they've got some things to work through. Tommy has new powers to explore. Jody doesn't know how much she should teach him, and how much she should let him discover for himself.

A DIRTY JOB: A Novel
ISBN 978-0-06-059028-4 (paperback) • ISBN 978-0-06-087259-5 (unabridged CD)

Charlie Asher has survived in the gene pool by doggie-paddling in the shallow end. But Charlie's safe life is about to take a really weird detour when his daughter, Sophie, is born—minutes before his wife dies of a freak medical condition. As if being a widower and the single parent of a newborn aren't enough, soon people begin to drop dead around Charlie, and he discovers that his worst fears were molehills compared to the mountain of poo he's in.

FLUKE: Or, I Know Why the Winged Whale Sings
ISBN 978-0-06-056668-5 (paperback) • ISBN 978-0-06-123879-6 (unabridged CD)

Every winter, whale researchers Nate Quinn and Clay Demolocus, partners in the Maui Whale Research Foundation, ply the warm Pacific waters, trying to solve an age-old mystery: Just why do humpback whales sing? Then one day a whale moons Nate, lifting its tail to display a cryptic scrawled message: Bite Me. But no one else saw a thing—not Clay, not fetching research assistant Amy, not even spliff-puffing white-boy Rastaman Kona (née Preston Applebaum). The weirdness only gets weirder when Nate gets a call telling him a whale has made contact—by phone.

ISLAND OF THE SEQUINED LOVE NUN
ISBN 978-0-06-073544-9 (paperback)

A wonderfully crazed excursion into the demented heart of a tropical paradise—a world of cargo cults, cannibals, mad scientists, ninjas, and talking fruit bats. Our bumbling hero is Tucker Case, a hopeless geek trapped in a cool guy's body, who makes a living as a pilot for the Mary Jean Cosmetics Corporation. But when he demolishes his boss's pink plane, Tuck must make a run for his life.

LAMB: The Gospel According to Biff, Christ's Childhood Pal
ISBN 978-0-380-81381-0 (paperback) • ISBN 978-0-06-123878-9 (unabridged CD)

The birth of Jesus has been well-chronicled, as have his glorious teachings, acts, and divine sacrifice after his thirtieth birthday. But no one knows about the early life of the Son of God—"the missing years"—except Biff. Ever since the day he came upon six-year-old Joshua of Nazareth resurrecting lizards in the village square, Levi bar Alphaeus, a.k.a. "Biff," had the distinction of being the Messiah's best bud. That's why the angel Raziel has resurrected Biff from the dust of Jerusalem and brought him to America to write a new gospel, one that tells the real, untold story.

THE LUST LIZARD OF MELANCHOLY COVE
ISBN 978-0-06-073545-6 (paperback)

The town psychiatrist has decided to switch everybody in Pine Cove, California from their normal antidepressants to placebos, so naturally—well, to be accurate, artificially—business is booming at the local blues bar. Trouble is, those lonely slide-guitar notes have also attracted a colossal sea-beast with a thing for explosive oil tanker trucks. Suddenly, morose Pine Cove turns libidinous and is hit by a mysterious crime wave, and a beleaguered constable has to fight off his own gonzo appetites to find out what's wrong and what, if anything, to do about it.

PRACTICAL DEMONKEEPING
ISBN 978-0-06-073542-5 (paperback)

Moore's ingenious debut novel introduces the reader to one of the most memorably mismatched pairs in the annals of literature. The good-looking one is one-hundred-year-old ex-seminarian and "roads" scholar Travis O'Hearn. The green one is Catch, a demon with a nasty habit of eating most of the people he meets. Behind the fake Tudor façade of Pine Cove, California, Catch sees a four-star buffet. Travis, on the other hand, thinks he sees a way of ridding himself of his toothy traveling companion. The winos, neo-pagans, and deadbeat Lotharios of Pine Cove, meanwhile, have other ideas.

THE STUPIDEST ANGEL: A Heartwarming Tale of Christmas Terror
ISBN 978-0-06-084235-2 (hardcover) • ISBN 978-0-06-073874-7 (unabridged CD)

Ah, Christmas—the hap-hap-happiest season of all! Except for Pine Cove Constable Theo Crowe, who's looking for the local evil developer who disappeared after playing Santa at the Caribou Lodge Christmas party. Meanwhile the town braces for the annual onslaught of holiday tourists and the storm of the century. Oh, and did we mention the tall blonde stranger with supernatural strength—a clueless angel sent to Earth on a mysterious mission—who arrives looking for "a child"? Yikes! Pass the eggnog.

www.ChrisMoore.com